W9-AUR-084

# Five Nights at Freddy's
## at
## Freddy's

# THE
# TWISTED
# ONES

# Five Nights at Freddy's

## THE TWISTED ONES

by

**SCOTT CAWTHON**
**KIRA BREED-WRISLEY**

Scholastic Inc.
New York

Copyright © 2017 by Scott Cawthon. All rights reserved.

Photo of tv static: © Klikk/Dreamstime

All rights reserved. Published by Scholastic Inc., *Publishers since 1920.*
SCHOLASTIC and associated logos are trademarks and/or registered trademarks
of Scholastic Inc.

The publisher does not have any control over and does not assume any
responsibility for author or third-party websites or their content.

No part of this publication may be reproduced, stored in a retrieval system,
or transmitted in any form or by any means, electronic, mechanical,
photocopying, recording, or otherwise, without written permission of the
publisher. For information regarding permission, write to Scholastic Inc.,
Attention: Permissions Department, 557 Broadway, New York, NY 10012.

This book is a work of fiction. Names, characters, places, and incidents are
either the product of the author's imagination or are used fictitiously, and any
resemblance to actual persons, living or dead, business establishments, events,
or locales is entirely coincidental.

ISBN 978-1-338-22116-9

10 9 8 7 6 5 4 3 2 1          17 18 19 20 21

Printed in the U.S.A.    23

First edition, July 2017

Book design by Rick DeMonico

# CHAPTER ONE

**D**on't trust your eyes."

Dr. Treadwell walked back and forth across the platform at the front of the auditorium. Her steps were slow and even, almost hypnotic.

"Your eyes deceive you every day, filling in the blanks for you in a world of sensory overload." An image of dizzying geometric detail lit up the canvas screen behind her. "When I say 'sensory overload' I mean that quite literally. At every moment, your senses are receiving far more information than they can process all at once, and your mind is forced to choose which signals to pay attention to. It does that based on your experiences, and your expectation of what is normal. The things we are familiar with are the things we can—for the most part—ignore. We see this most easily with olfactory fatigue: your nose ceases to perceive a smell when you've been around it for a while. You may be quite thankful for this phenomenon, depending on the habits of your roommate."

The class tittered dutifully, then became quiet as the image of another multicolored design flashed onto the screen.

The professor gave a hint of a smile and continued.

"Your mind creates motion when there is none. It fills in colors and trajectories based on what you've seen before, and calculates what you *should* be seeing now." Another image flashed onto the overhead screen. "If your mind didn't do this, then simply walking outside and seeing a tree would consume all your mental energy, leaving no resources to do anything else. In order for you to function in the world, your mind fills in the spaces of that tree with its own leaves and branches." A hundred pencils scribbled all at once, filling the lecture hall with a sound like scurrying mice.

"It's why when you enter a house for the first time you experience a moment of dizziness. Your mind is taking in more than usual. It's drawing a floor plan, creating a palette of colors, and saving an inventory of images to draw on later, so you don't have to go through that exhausting intake every single time. The next time you enter that same house, you'll already know where you are."

*"Charlie!"* An urgent voice whispered her name, inches from her ear. Charlie kept writing. She was staring straight

ahead at the display at the front of the lecture hall. As Dr. Treadwell went on, she paced faster, occasionally flinging an arm toward the screen to illustrate her point. Her words seemed to be falling behind as her mind raced on ahead; Charlie had realized by the second day of classes that her professor sometimes broke off in the middle of one sentence, only to finish an entirely different one. It was like she skimmed the text in her head, reading out a few words here and there. Most of the students in her robotics class found it maddening, but Charlie liked it. It made the lesson kind of like doing a puzzle.

The screen flashed again, displaying an assortment of mechanical parts and a diagram of an eye. "This is what you must re-create." Dr. Treadwell stepped back from the image, turning to look at it with the class. "Basic artificial intelligence is all about sensory control. You won't be dealing with a mind that can filter these things out for itself. You must design programs that recognize basic shapes, while discarding unimportant information. You must do for your robot what your own mind does for you: create a simplified and organized assembly of information based on what's relevant. Let's start by looking at some examples of basic shape recognition."

"*Charlie,*" hissed the voice again, and she waved her pencil impatiently at the figure peering over her shoulder—her friend Arty—trying to shoo him away. The gesture cost her a moment, put her half a step behind the professor. She hurried to catch up, anxious not to miss a single line.

The paper in front of her was covered in formulas, notes in the margins, sketches, and diagrams. She wanted to get everything down all at once: not just the math, but all the things it made her think of. If she could tie the new facts to things she already knew, she'd retain it much more easily. She felt hungry for it, alert, watching for new tidbits of information like a dog under the dinner table.

A boy near the front raised his hand to ask a question, and Charlie felt a brief flare of impatience. Now the whole class would have to stop while Treadwell went back to explain a simple concept. Charlie let her mind wander, sketching absently in the margins of her notebook.

John would be here in—she glanced restlessly at her watch—an hour. *I told him maybe someday we'll see each other again. I guess it's someday.* He had called out of the blue: "I'm just going to be passing through," he said, and Charlie hadn't bothered to ask how he knew where she was. *Of course he would know.* There was no reason not to meet him, and she found herself alternately excited and filled with dread. Now, as she absently sketched rectangular forms along the bottom of her note paper, her stomach jumped, a little spasm of nerves. It felt like a lifetime since she last saw him. Sometimes, it felt like she'd seen him yesterday, as if the last year hadn't passed. But of course it had, and everything had changed for Charlie once again.

That May, the night of her eighteenth birthday, the dreams had begun. Charlie was long accustomed to nightmares, the worst moments of her past forced up like bile, into twisted versions of memories already too terrible to recall. She shoved these dreams into the back of her mind in the morning and sealed them away, knowing they would only breach it when night fell again.

These dreams were different. When she woke, she was physically exhausted: not just drained but sore, her muscles weak. Her hands were stiff and aching, like they'd been clenched into fists for hours. These new dreams didn't come every night, but when they did, they interrupted her regular nightmares and took them over. It didn't matter if she was running and screaming for her life, or wandering aimlessly through a dull mishmash of the various places she'd been all week. Suddenly, from nowhere, she would sense him: Sammy, her lost twin brother, was near.

She knew he was present the same way she knew that *she* was present, and whatever the dream was, it dropped away—people, places, light, and sound. Now she was searching for him in the darkness, calling his name. He never answered. She would drop to her hands and knees, feeling her way through the dark, letting his presence guide her until she came to a barrier. It was smooth and cold, metal. She couldn't see it, but she hit it hard with one fist and it echoed. "Sammy?" she would call, hitting harder. She stood, reaching up to see if she could scale the slick surface, but it stretched up far above her head. She beat her fists against the barricade until they hurt. She screamed her brother's name until her throat was raw, until she fell to the floor and leaned on the solid metal, pressing her cheek to its cool surface and hoping for a whisper from the other side. He was there; she knew it as surely as if he were a part of herself.

She knew in those dreams that he was present. Worse, when she was awake, she knew he was not there.

In August, Charlie and Aunt Jen had their first fight. They'd always been too distant to really argue. Charlie never felt the need to rebel, because Jen provided no real authority. And Jen never took anything Charlie did personally, never tried to stop her from doing anything, as long as she was safe. The day Charlie moved in with her at the age of seven, Aunt Jen had told her plainly that she was not a replacement for Charlie's parents. By now, Charlie was old enough to understand that Jen had meant it as a gesture of respect, a way to reassure Charlie that her father wouldn't be forgotten, that she would always be his child. But at the time it had seemed like an admonishment. *Don't expect parenting. Don't expect love.* And so Charlie hadn't. Jen had never failed to care for Charlie. Charlie had never wanted for food or clothing, and

Jen had taught her to cook, to take care of the house, to manage her money, and to fix her own car. *You have to be independent, Charlie. You have to know how to take care of yourself. You have to be stronger than*—she'd cut herself off, but Charlie knew how the sentence ended. *Than your father.*

Charlie shook her head, trying to jerk herself free of her own thoughts.

"What's wrong?" Arty said next to her.

"Nothing," she whispered. She ran her pencil again and again over the same lines: up, over, down, over, the graphite wearing thicker and thicker.

Charlie had told Jen that she was going back to Hurricane, and Jen's face turned stony, her skin paling.

"Why would you want to do that?" she asked with a dangerous calm in her voice. Charlie's heart beat faster. *Because that's where I lost him. Because I need him more than I need you.* The thought of returning had been nagging at her for months, growing stronger with each passing week. One morning she awoke and the choice was made, final, sitting in her mind with a solid weight.

"Jessica's going to college at St. George," she told her aunt. "She's starting the summer semester so I can stay with her while I'm there. I want to see the house again. There's still so much I don't understand; it just feels . . . important," she finished weakly, faltering as Jen's eyes—dark blue, like marble—fixed on her.

Jen didn't answer for a long moment then she said simply, "No."

*Why not?* Charlie might once have said. *You let me go before.* But after what happened last year, when she and Jessica and the others went back to Freddy's and discovered the horrifying truth behind the murders at her father's old pizzeria, things had changed between them. Charlie had changed. Now she met Jen's gaze, determined. "I'm going," she said, trying to keep her own voice steady.

Then everything exploded.

Charlie didn't know which of them started shouting first, but she screamed until her throat was fiery and sore, hurling at her aunt every pain she'd ever inflicted, every hurt she had failed to prevent. Jen shouted back that she only ever meant to care for Charlie, that she had always done her best, flinging reassuring words that somehow dripped with poison.

*"I'm leaving!"* Charlie screamed with finality. She started for the door, but Jen grabbed her arm, yanking her violently back. Charlie stumbled, almost falling before she caught herself on the kitchen table, and Jen let her hand drop with a shocked expression. There was silence, and then Charlie left.

She packed a bag, feeling as if she had somehow diverged from reality, into an impossible parallel world. Then she got in her car and drove away. She didn't tell anyone she was going. Her friends here were not close friends; there was no one she owed an explanation.

When Charlie got to Hurricane, she'd intended to go straight to her father's house, to stay there for the next few days until Jessica arrived on campus. But as she reached the city limits, something stopped her. *I can't*, she thought. *I can't ever go back.* She turned the car around, drove straight to St. George, and slept in her car for a week.

It was only after Charlie knocked, and Jessica opened the door with a startled expression that Charlie realized that she'd never actually mentioned her plans to Jessica, on whom they all depended. She told her everything, and Jessica, hesitantly, offered to let her stay. Charlie had slept on the floor the rest of the summer, and as the fall semester approached, Jessica didn't ask her to leave.

"It's nice to have someone who knows me here," she had said, and uncharacteristically, Charlie hugged her.

Charlie had never cared about high school. She never paid much attention in her classes, but As and Bs came easily for her. She had never really thought about liking or disliking her subjects, though sometimes one teacher or another would make her feel a spark of interest for a year.

Charlie hadn't thought much beyond the end of the summer, but as she idly flipped through Jessica's course catalog and saw advanced courses in robotics, something clicked into place. St. George was among the colleges she'd been accepted into earlier that year, though she hadn't really intended to go to any of them. Now, however, she went to the administrative office and pleaded her case until she was allowed to enroll, despite having missed the deadline by months. *There's still so much I don't understand.* Charlie wanted to learn, and the things she wanted to learn were very specific.

Of course there were things she had to learn before a robotics course would make any sense at all. Math had always been straightforward, functional, sort of like a game to Charlie; you did the thing you were supposed to do and got the answer. But it had never been a very interesting game. It was fun to learn something new, but then you had to keep doing it for weeks or months, bored out of your skull. That was high school. But in her first calculus class, something had happened. It was as if she'd been laying bricks for years, forced to work slowly, seeing nothing but her mortar and her trowel. Then suddenly someone pulled her back a few steps and said, "Here, look, you've been building this castle. Go play inside!"

"And that's all for today," Professor Treadwell said at last. Charlie looked down at her paper, realizing she'd never stopped moving her pencil. She had worn dark lines right through the page, and drawn on the desk. She rubbed the marks halfheartedly with her sleeve, then opened her binder to put away her notes. Arty poked his head over her shoulder, and she closed it hastily, but he had already gotten a good look.

"What is that, a secret code? Abstract art?"

"It's just math," Charlie said a little curtly, and put the notebook in her bag. Arty was cute in a goofy way. He had a pleasant face, dark eyes, and curly brown hair that seemed to have a life of its own. He was in three of her four classes and had been following her around since the beginning of the semester like a stray duckling. To her surprise, Charlie found that she didn't mind it.

As Charlie left the auditorium, Arty took up his now-accustomed place at her side.

"So, did you decide about the project?" he asked.

"Project?" Charlie vaguely remembered something about a project he wanted to do together. He gave a little nod, waiting for her to catch up.

"Remember? We have to design an experiment for chem? I thought we could work together. You know, with your brains and my looks . . ." He trailed off, grinning.

"Yeah, that sounds—I have to go meet someone," she interrupted herself.

"You never meet anyone," he said, surprised, blushing bright red as soon as the words were out of his mouth. "I didn't mean it that way. Not that it's any of my business, but, who is it?" He gave a broad smile.

"John," Charlie said without elaboration. Arty looked crestfallen for a moment but recovered quickly.

"Of course, yeah. John. Great guy," he said teasingly. He

raised his eyebrows, prompting for details, but she gave none. "I didn't know you were—that you had a—that's cool." Arty's face took on a look of careful neutrality. Charlie looked at him oddly. She hadn't meant to imply that she and John were a couple but she didn't know how to correct him. She couldn't explain who John was to her without telling Arty far more than she wanted him to know.

They walked in silence for a minute across the main quad, a small, grassy square surrounded by brick and concrete buildings.

"So, is John from your hometown?" Arty asked at last.

"My hometown is thirty minutes away. This place is basically just an extension of it," Charlie said. "But yeah, he's from Hurricane." Arty hesitated, then leaned in closer to her, glancing around as if someone might be listening.

"I always meant to ask you," he said.

Charlie looked at him wearily. *Don't ask about it.*

"I'm sure people ask you about it all the time, but come on—you can't blame me for being curious. That stuff about the murders, it's like an urban legend around here. I mean, not just around here. Everywhere. Freddy Fazbear's Pizza—"

"Stop." Charlie's face was suddenly immobile. She felt as if moving it, making any expression at all, would require an arcane skill she no longer possessed. Arty's face had changed, too. His easy smile drained away. He looked almost frightened. Charlie bit the inside of her lip, willing her mouth to move.

"I was just a kid when all that happened," she said quietly. Arty nodded, quick and skittish. Charlie made her face move into a smile. "I have to go meet Jessica," she lied. *I have to get away from you.* Arty nodded his head again like a bobblehead doll. She turned and walked away toward the dorm, not looking back.

Charlie blinked into the sunlight. Flashes of what happened last year at Freddy's were batting at her, snatches of memory plucking at her clothing with cold, iron fingers. *The hook above, poised to strike—no escape. A figure looming behind the stage; red matted fur barely concealing the metal bones of the murderous creature. Kneeling in pitch-dark on the cold tile floor of the bathroom, and then—that giant, hard plastic eye glaring through the crack, the hot miasma of lifeless breath on her face.* And the other, older memory: *the thought that made her ache in ways for which she had no words, sorrow filling her as if it had been wrought into her very bones. She and Sammy, her other self, her twin brother, were playing their quiet games in the familiar warmth of the costume closet. Then the figure appeared in the doorway, looking down on them. Then Sammy was gone, and the world ended for the first time.*

Charlie was standing outside her own dorm room, almost without knowing how she'd gotten there. Slowly, she pulled her keys from her pocket and let herself into the room. The lights were off; Jessica was still in class. Charlie shut the door behind her, checking the lock twice, and leaned back against it. She took a deep breath. *It's over now.* She straightened decisively and snapped on the overhead light, filling the room with a harsh illumination. The clock beside the bed told Charlie that she still had a little under an hour before John arrived—time to work on her project.

Charlie and Jessica had divided the room with a piece of masking tape after their first week living together. Jessica suggested it jokingly, said she'd seen it in a movie, but Charlie had grinned and helped her measure the room. She knew Jessica was desperate to keep Charlie's mess off her side. The result was a bedroom that looked like a "before and after" picture advertising either a cleaning service or a nuclear weapon, depending on whose side you looked at first.

On Charlie's desk there was a pillowcase, draped over two indistinct shapes. She went to her desk and removed it, folding it carefully and placing it on her chair. She looked at her project.

"Hello," she said softly.

Two mechanical faces were held upright on metal structures and attached to a length of board. Their features were indistinct, like old statues worn away by rain, or new clay not yet fully sculpted. They were made of a malleable plastic, and where the backs of their heads ought to be there were instead networks of casings, microchips, and wires.

Charlie bent down toward them, looking over every millimeter of her design, making sure everything was as she'd left it. She flipped a small black switch and little lights blinked; tiny cooling fans began to whir.

They didn't move right away, but there was a change. The vague features took on a sense of purpose. Their blind eyes didn't turn to Charlie: they looked only at each other.

"You," said the first. Its lips moved to shape the syllable, but never parted. They weren't made to open.

"I," the second replied, making the same soft, constrained movement.

"You are," said the first.

"Am I?" said the second.

Charlie watched, her hand pressed over her mouth. She held her breath, afraid of disturbing them. She waited, but they had apparently finished, and were now simply looking at each other. *They can't see*, Charlie reminded herself. She turned them off and pulled the board around so that she could peer into their backs. She reached inside and adjusted a wire.

A key slid into the lock of the door, and Charlie startled at the sound. She snatched the pillowcase and threw it over the faces as Jessica entered the room. Jessica paused in the doorway with a grin.

"What was that?" she asked.

"What?" Charlie said innocently.

"Come on, I know you were working on that thing you never let me see." She dropped her backpack on the floor, then flopped dramatically back on the bed. "Anyways, I'm exhausted!" she announced. Charlie laughed, and Jessica sat up. "Come talk to me," she said. "What's up with you and John?"

Charlie sat down on her own bed, across from Jessica. Despite their different lifestyles, she liked living with the other girl. Jessica was warm and bright, and while her ease as she went about the world still intimidated Charlie a little, now she felt like a part of it. Maybe being Jessica's friend meant absorbing some of her confidence.

"I haven't seen him yet. I have to leave in . . ." She peered over Jessica's shoulder at the clock. "Fifteen minutes."

"Are you excited?" Jessica asked.

Charlie shrugged. "I think so," she said.

Jessica laughed. "You're not sure?"

"I'm excited," Charlie admitted. "It's just been a long time."

"Not that long," Jessica pointed out. Then she looked thoughtful. "I guess it sort of has been, though. Everything is so different since the last time we saw him."

Charlie cleared her throat. "So you really want to see my project?" she asked, surprising herself.

"Yes!" Jessica declared, springing up from the bed. She followed Charlie to her desk. Charlie switched on the power then flung off the pillowcase like a magician. Jessica gasped and took an involuntary step back. "What is it?" she asked, her voice cautious. But before Charlie could answer, the first face spoke.

"Me," it said.

"You," the other replied, and they both fell silent again. Charlie looked at Jessica. Her friend had a pinched expression, like she was holding something tightly inside.

"I," the second face said.

Charlie hurried to switch them off. "Why do you have that look on your face?" she said.

Jessica took a deep breath and smiled at her. "I just haven't had lunch yet," she said, but something lingered in her eyes.

Jessica watched as Charlie replaced the pillowcase lovingly over the faces, as if she were tucking a child into bed. She looked uncomfortably around the room. Charlie's half was a disaster: clothes and books were strewn everywhere, but there were also the wires and computer parts, tools, screws, and pieces of plastic and metal Jessica didn't recognize, all jumbled up together. It wasn't just a mess; it was a chaotic tangle where you could lose anything. Or hide anything, she realized, with a pang of guilt at the thought. Jessica turned her attention back to Charlie.

"What are you programming them to do?" she asked, and Charlie smiled proudly.

"I'm not exactly programming them to do anything. I'm helping them learn on their own."

"Right, of course. Obviously," Jessica said slowly. As she did, something caught her eye: a pair of shiny plastic eyes and long floppy ears were peering out from a pile of dirty laundry.

"Hey, I never noticed you brought Theodore, your little robo-rabbit!" she exclaimed, pleased to have remembered the name of Charlie's childhood toy. Before Charlie could respond, she picked the stuffed animal up by his ears—and came away with only his head.

Jessica let out a shriek and dropped it, clapping a hand over her mouth.

"I'm sorry!" Charlie said, hastily grabbing the rabbit's head off the floor. "I took him apart to study; I'm using some of his parts in my project." She gestured at the thing on her desk.

"Oh," Jessica said, trying to hide her dismay. She glanced around the room and suddenly realized that the rabbit's parts were everywhere. His cotton-ball tail was on Charlie's pillow, and a leg hung off the lamp above her desk. His torso lay in the corner, almost out of sight, ripped open savagely. Jessica looked at her friend's round, cheerful face, and frizzy shoulder-length brown hair. Jessica closed her eyes for a long moment.

*Oh, Charlie, what's wrong with you?*

"Jessica?" Charlie said. The girl's eyes were closed, her expression pained. "Jessica?" This time she opened her eyes and gave Charlie a sudden, bright smile, turning on cheer like a faucet. It was disconcerting, but Charlie had gotten used to it.

Jessica blinked hard, like she was resetting her brain. "So, are you nervous about seeing John?" she asked. Charlie thought for a moment.

"No. I mean, why should I be? It's just John, right?" Charlie tried to laugh, but gave up. "Jessica, I don't know what to talk about!" she burst out suddenly.

"What do you mean?"

"I don't know what to talk about *with him*!" Charlie said. "If we don't have something to talk about, then we'll start talking about . . . what happened last year. And I just can't."

"Right." Jessica looked thoughtful. "Maybe he won't bring it up," she offered.

Charlie sighed, glancing back at her covered experiment with longing. "Of course he will. It's all we have in common." She sat down heavily on her bed and slumped over.

"Charlie, you don't have to talk about anything you don't want to talk about," Jessica said gently. "You can always just cancel on him. But I don't think John's going to put you on the spot. He cares about you. I doubt what happened in Hurricane is what's on his mind."

"What does *that* mean?"

"I just mean . . ." Jessica gingerly pushed aside a pile of laundry and sat next to Charlie, placing a hand on her knee.

"I just mean that maybe it's time that you *both* move past that. And I think John is trying to."

Charlie looked away and stared fixedly at Theodore's head, facedown on the floor. *You mean, get over it? How do I even begin?*

Jessica's voice softened. "This can't be your whole life anymore."

"I know." Charlie sighed. She decided to change the subject. "How was your class, anyway?" Charlie wiped her eyes, hoping Jessica would take the hint.

"Awesome." Jessica stood and stretched, bending over to touch her toes and incidentally giving Charlie a chance to compose herself. When Jessica stood again, she was smiling brilliantly, back in character. "Did you know that corpses can be preserved in peat bogs like mummies?"

Charlie wrinkled her nose. "I do now. So is that what you're gonna do when you graduate? Crawl around in peat bogs looking for bodies?"

Jessica shrugged. "Maybe."

"I'll get you a hazmat suit for your graduation gift," Charlie joked. She looked at her watch. "Time to go! Wish me luck." She brushed her hair back with her hands, peering into the mirror that hung on the back of the door. "I feel like a mess."

"You look great." Jessica gave her an encouraging nod.

"I've been doing sit-ups," Charlie said awkwardly.

"Huh?"

"Forget it." Charlie grabbed her backpack and headed for the door.

"Go knock his socks off!" Jessica called as Charlie left.

"I don't know what that means!" Charlie replied, letting the door swing closed before she'd finished speaking.

Charlie spotted him as she approached the main entrance to the campus. John was leaning on the wall, reading a book. His brown hair was as messy as ever, and he was wearing a blue T-shirt and jeans, dressed more casually than the last time she'd seen him.

"John!" she called, her reluctance falling away as soon as she saw him. He put away his book, grinning widely, and hurried to her.

"Hey, Charlie," he said. They stood there awkwardly, then Charlie extended her arms to hug him. He held her tightly for a moment then abruptly released her.

"You got taller," she said accusingly, and he laughed.

"I did," he admitted. He gave her a searching look. "You look exactly the same, though," he said with a puzzled smile.

"I cut my hair!" Charlie said in mock-outrage. She ran her fingers through it, demonstrating.

"Oh yeah!" he said. "I like it. I just mean, you're the same girl I remember."

"I've been doing sit-ups," Charlie said with a rising panic.

"Huh?" John gave her a confused look.

"Never mind. Are you hungry?" Charlie asked. "I have about an hour before my next class. We could get a burger. There's a dining hall not far from here."

"Yeah, that would be great," John said. Charlie pointed across the quad.

"That way, come on."

"So what are you doing here?" Charlie asked as they sat down with their trays. "Sorry," she added. "Did that sound rude?"

"Not rude at all, although I would have also accepted, 'John, to what circumstance do I owe the pleasure of this delightful reunion?'"

"Yeah, that sounds like me," Charlie said drily. "But seriously, what are you doing here?"

"Got a job."

"In St. George?" she asked. "Why?"

"In Hurricane, actually," he said, his voice self-consciously casual.

"Aren't you in school somewhere?" Charlie asked.

John blushed, looking down at his plate for a moment. "I was going to, but . . . it's a lot of money to read books when a library card is free, you know? My cousin got me a job in construction, and I'm working on my writing when I can. I figured even if I'm gonna be an artist, I don't have to be a starving one." He took an illustrative bite of his hamburger, and Charlie grinned.

"So why here?" she insisted, and he held up a finger as he finished chewing.

"The storm," he said. Charlie nodded. The storm had hit Hurricane before Charlie came to St. George, and people talked about it in capital letters: The Storm. It wasn't the worst the area had ever seen, but it was close. A tornado had risen up from nowhere and ripped through whole towns, razing one house to the ground with sinister precision, while leaving the one next to it untouched. There hadn't been much damage in St. George, but Hurricane had seen real destruction.

"How bad is it?" Charlie asked, keeping her tone light.

"You haven't been?" John said incredulously, and it was Charlie's turn to look awkwardly away. She shook her head. "It's bad in places," he said. "Mostly on the outskirts of town. Charlie . . . I assumed you'd been." He bit his lip.

"What?" Something about his expression was worrying her.

"Your dad's house, it was one of the ones that got hit," he said.

"Oh." Something leaden was growing in Charlie's chest. "I didn't know."

"You really didn't even go back to check?"

"I didn't think of it," Charlie said. *That's not true.* She'd thought a thousand times of going back to her father's house. But it had never occurred to her that the house might have been hit in the storm. In her mind, it was impregnable, unchanging. It would always be there, just as her father had left it. She closed her eyes and pictured it. The front steps sagged in disrepair, but the house itself stood like a fortress, protecting what was inside. "Is it—gone?" Charlie asked, the words faint.

"No," John said quickly. "No, it's still there, just damaged. I don't know how much; I just drove by. I didn't think I should go there without you."

Charlie nodded, only half listening. She felt far away. She could see John, hear him, but there was a layer of something between them, between her and everything else, everything but the house itself.

"I would have thought—didn't your aunt tell you what happened?" John asked.

"I have to get to class," Charlie said. "It's that way." She gestured vaguely.

"Charlie, have *you* been okay?" She didn't look at him, and he placed his hand over hers. She still couldn't look up. She didn't want him to see her face.

"Okay," she repeated, then slipped her hand out from under his and shrugged her shoulders up and down, like she was trying to get something off her back. "I had my birthday," she offered, and she finally leveled her gaze to meet his.

"I'm sorry I missed it," John said.

"No, no, that's not . . ." She tipped her head from side to side, as if she could level out her thoughts, too. "Do you remember how I had a twin?"

"What?" John sounded puzzled. "Of course I do. I'm sorry, Charlie, is that what you meant about your birthday?" She nodded, making tiny motions. John held out his hand again, and she took it. She could feel his pulse through his thumb.

"Ever since we left Hurricane . . . You know how twins are supposed to be connected, have some kind of special bond?"

"Sure," he said.

"Ever since we left—ever since I found out he was real—I've felt like he was there with me. I know he's not. He's dead, but for that whole year, I didn't feel alone anymore."

"Charlie." John's hand tightened on hers. "You know you're not alone."

"No, I mean *really* not alone. Like I have another self: someone who's a part of me and is always with me. I've had these feelings before, but they came and went, and I didn't pay much attention to them. I didn't know they meant something. Then when I learned the truth, and those memories started coming back to me—John, I felt *whole* in a way I don't even know how to describe." Her eyes began to fill with tears and she pulled her hand back to brush them away.

"Hey," he said softly. "It's okay. That's great, Charlie. I'm glad you have that."

"No. No, that's the thing. I don't!" She met his eyes, desperate for him to understand what she was so awkwardly trying to say. "He's disappeared. That sense of completeness is gone."

"What?"

"It happened on my birthday. I woke up and I just felt—" She sighed, searching. There wasn't a word for it.

"Alone?" John said.

"Incomplete." She took a deep breath, pulling herself back together. "But the thing is, it's not just loss. It's—it's like he's trapped somewhere. I have these dreams where I can *feel* him on the other side of something, like he's so close to me, but he's stuck somewhere. Like he's in a box, or I'm in a box. I can't tell."

John stared at her, momentarily speechless. Before he could figure out what to say, Charlie stood abruptly. "I need to leave."

"Are you sure? You haven't even eaten," he said.

"I'm sorry—" She broke off. "John, it's so good to see you." She hesitated then turned to walk away, possibly for good. She knew she'd disappointed him.

"Charlie, would you like to go out with me tonight?" John's voice sounded stiff, but his eyes were warm.

"Sure, that would be great," she said, giving a half smile. "Don't you have to get back to work tomorrow, though?"

"It's only half an hour away," John said. He cleared his throat. "But I meant, do you want to *go out* with me?"

"I just said yeah," Charlie repeated, slightly irritated.

John sighed. "I mean on a date, Charlie."

"Oh." Charlie stared at him for a moment. "Right." *You don't have to do anything you don't want to do.* Jessica's voice echoed in her head. And yet . . . she realized she was smiling.

"Um, yes. Yes, a date. Okay, yeah. There's a movie theater in town?" she hazarded, vaguely recalling that movies were something people did on dates.

John nodded vigorously, apparently as lost at sea as she was, now that the question had been asked. "Can we have dinner first? There's that Thai place down the street. I can meet you there around eight?"

"Yeah, sounds good. 'Bye!" Charlie grabbed her backpack and hurried out the dining room door, realizing as she stepped into the sunshine that she'd left him to clean up their table alone. *Sorry.*

As Charlie headed across the quad to her next class, her step grew more purposeful. This was a basic computer science class. Writing code wasn't as exciting as what Dr. Treadwell taught, but Charlie still liked it. It was absorbing, detailed work. A single error could ruin everything. *Everything?* She thought of her impending date. The idea that a single error could ruin everything suddenly carried an awful weight.

Charlie hurried up the steps to the building and stopped short as a man blocked her path.

It was Clay Burke.

"Hey, Charlie." He smiled, but his eyes were grave. Charlie hadn't seen Hurricane's chief of police—her friend Carlton's father—since the night they'd escaped Freddy's together. Looking now at his weathered face, she felt a rush of fear.

"Mr. Burke, er, Clay. What are you doing here?"

"Charlie, do you have a second?" he asked. Her heart sped up.

"Is Carlton okay?" she asked urgently.

"Yes, he's fine," Burke assured her. "Walk with me. Don't worry about being late. I'll give you a note for class. At least, I *think* an officer of the law has authority do that." He winked, but Charlie didn't smile. Something was wrong.

Charlie followed him back down the stairs. When they were a dozen feet from the building, Burke stopped and met her gaze, as if he were looking for something.

"Charlie, we've found a body," he said. "I want you to take a look at it."

"You want *me* to look at it?"

"I need you to see it."

*Me.* She said the only thing she could.

"Why? Does it have to do with Freddy's?"

"I don't want to tell you anything until you've seen it," Burke said. He started walking again, and Charlie hurried to keep up with his long stride. She followed him to the parking lot just outside the main gate, and got into his car without a word. Charlie settled into her seat, a strange dread stirring within her. Clay Burke glanced at her and she gave a sharp, quick nod. He pulled the car out onto the road, and they headed back to Hurricane.

# CHAPTER TWO

So, how are you enjoying your classes?" Clay Burke asked in a jovial tone.

Charlie gave him a sardonic look. "Well, this is the first murder of the semester. So things have been going fine."

Burke didn't answer, apparently aware that further attempts to lighten the mood would fail. Charlie looked out the window. She thought often of going back to her father's house, but each time the memory of the place rose up she slammed it back down with almost physical force, cramming it into the tiny corners of her mind to gather dust. Now something was stirring in the dusty corners, and she feared she might not be able to keep it away much longer.

"Chief Burke—Clay," Charlie said. "How's Carlton been?"

He smiled. "Carlton's doing great. I tried to convince him to stay close for college, but he and Betty were adamant. Now he's out east, studying acting."

"Acting?" Charlie laughed, surprising herself.

"Well, he was always a prankster," Clay said. "I figured acting was the next logical step."

Charlie smiled. "Did he ever . . ." She looked out the window again. "Did you and he ever talk about what happened?" she asked with her face turned away. She could see Clay's reflection faintly in the window, distorted by the glass.

"Carlton talks to his mother more than he talks to me," he said plainly. Charlie waited for him to go on, but he remained silent. Though she and Jessica lived together, from the beginning they had an unspoken pact never to talk about Freddy's, except in the barest terms. She didn't know if Jessica was sometimes consumed by the memories, as she was. Maybe Jessica had nightmares, too.

But Charlie and Clay had no such pact. She took in shallow, quick breaths, waiting to hear how far he would go.

"I think Carlton had dreams about it," Clay said finally. "Sometimes in the morning he would come downstairs looking like he hadn't slept in a week, but he never told me what was going on."

"What about you? Do you think about it?" She was overstepping but Clay didn't seem ruffled.

"I try not to," he said gravely. "You know, Charlie, when

terrible things happen you can do one of two things: you can leave them behind or you can let them consume you."

Charlie set her jaw. "I'm not my father," she said.

Clay looked immediately contrite. "I know, I didn't mean that," he said. "I just meant you have to look forward." He flashed a nervous grin. "Of course, my wife would say there's a third thing: you can process the terrible things and come to terms with them. She's probably right."

"Probably," Charlie said distractedly.

"And what about you? How are you doing, Charlie?" Clay asked. It was the question she had practically solicited, but she didn't know how to answer it.

"I have dreams about it, I guess," she muttered.

"You guess?" he asked in a careful tone. "What kind of dreams?"

Charlie looked out the window again. There was a weight pressing on her chest. *What kind of dreams?*

Nightmares, but not of Freddy's. *A shadow in the doorway of the costume closet where we play. Sammy doesn't see; he's playing with his truck. But I look up. The shadow has eyes. Then everything is moving—hangers rattle and costumes sway. A toy truck drops hard on the floor.*

*I'm left alone. The air is growing thin, I'm running out. It's getting hard to breathe and I'll die like this, alone, in the dark. I pound against the closet wall, calling for help. I know he's there. Sammy is on the other side, but he doesn't answer my cries as I begin to gasp, choking for air. It is too dark to see, but even so I know my vision is going black, and in my chest my heart is slowing, each pump swelling me with pain as I struggle to call his name one more time—*

"Charlie?" Clay had pulled over and stopped the car without her noticing. Now he was looking at her with his piercing detective's gaze. She looked at him for a moment before she could remember how to answer, and she made herself smile.

"I've mostly been focused on school," she said.

Clay smiled at her but it didn't touch his eyes. He looked worried. *He's wishing he hadn't brought me*, she thought.

He opened his door but didn't get out of the car. The sun had begun to set as they drove, and now it was verging on dark. The turn signal was still on, flashing yellow onto the dirt road. Charlie watched it for a moment, hypnotized. She felt as if she might never move again, just sit here watching the endless, measured blinking of the light. Clay switched the signal off, and Charlie blinked, as if a spell had been broken. She straightened her spine and unbuckled her seat belt.

"Charlie," Clay said, not looking directly at her. "I'm sorry to ask this of you, but you're the only person who can tell me if this is what I think it is."

"Okay," she replied, suddenly alert. Clay sighed and got out of the car. Charlie followed close behind him. There was a barbed wire fence all along the road, and there were cows in the field beyond it. They stood around, chewing and staring in the vacant way of cows. Clay lifted the top wire for

Charlie and she climbed gingerly through. *When's the last time I got a tetanus shot?* she wondered as a barb caught briefly on her T-shirt.

She didn't have to ask where the body was. There was a floodlight and a makeshift fence of caution tape strung between posts that jutted from the soil in a scattered formation. Charlie stood where she was as Burke climbed through the fence after her, and they both surveyed the area.

The field was flat, and the grass was short and patchy, worn down daily by dozens of hooves. A single tree stood some distance from where the crime scene was marked. Charlie thought it was an oak. Its branches were long and ancient, heavy with leaves. There was something wrong with the air; along with the smell of cow dung and mud wafted the sharp, metallic scent of blood.

For some reason, Charlie looked at the cows again. They weren't as calm as she'd assumed. They shifted back and forth on their feet, clustering in groups. None of them came anywhere near the floodlight. As if sensing her scrutiny, one of them lowed a mournful cry. Charlie heard Clay's sharp intake of breath.

"Maybe we should ask *them* what happened," Charlie said. In the stillness, her voice carried. Clay started toward the floodlight. Charlie followed closely, not wanting to fall too far behind. It wasn't just the cows; a weight of something *wrong* hung over the place. There was no sound, only the shocked quiet that follows a terrible violence.

Clay stopped beside the marked-out spot and ushered Charlie forward, still saying nothing. Charlie looked.

It was a man, stretched in a ghastly posture on his back, his limbs contorted impossibly. In the glaring, unnatural light, the scene looked staged; he might have been an enormous doll. His whole body was drenched red with blood. His clothes were torn, almost shredded, and through the holes Charlie thought she could see ripped-up skin, some bone, and other things she couldn't identify.

"What do you make of it?" Clay said softly, as if he were afraid of disturbing her.

"I need to get closer," she said. Clay climbed over the yellow tape, and Charlie followed. She knelt in the mud beside the man's head, the knees of her jeans soaking with mud. He was middle-aged, white, his hair short and gray. His eyes, thankfully, were closed. The rest of his face slack in a way that could almost have looked like sleep, but did not. She leaned forward to peer at the man's neck and blanched, but didn't look away.

"Charlie, are you all right?" Clay asked, and she held up a hand.

"I'm fine." She knew those wounds; she'd seen the scars they left. On each side of the dead man's neck was a deep, curved gash. This was what had killed him. It would have been instantaneous. *Or maybe not.* Suddenly she pictured Dave, the guard at Freddy's, the murderer. She had watched him die. She'd triggered the spring locks and seen his startled eyes as the locks drove into his neck. She'd watched his body jolt and seize as the costume he wore shot jagged metal through his vital organs. Charlie stared at this stranger's wounds. She reached down and ran her finger along the edge of the cut on the man's neck. *What were you doing?*

"Charlie!" Clay said in alarm, and Charlie drew back her hand.

"Sorry," she said self-consciously, wiping her bloody fingers on her jeans. "Clay, it was one of them. His neck, he died like . . ." She stopped talking. Clay had been there; his son had almost died the same way. But if this was happening again, he had to know what he was dealing with.

"You remember how Dave died, right?" she asked.

Clay nodded. "Hard thing to forget." He shook his head, patiently waiting for her to get to the point.

"These suits, like the rabbit suit that Dave was wearing, they can be worn like costumes. Or they can move around on their own, as fully functional robots."

"Sure, you just put the suit on a robot," Clay said.

"Not exactly . . . The robots are always inside the suits; they're made of interlocking parts that are held back against the inner lining of the costumes by spring locks. When you want an animatronic, you just trip the locks, and the robotic parts unfold inside, filling the suit."

"But if there's someone inside the suit when the locks are tripped . . . ," Clay said, catching on.

"Right. Thousands of sharp metal parts shoot through your whole body. Like, well—that," she finished, gesturing at the man on the ground.

"How hard is it to accidentally trigger the spring locks?" Clay asked.

"It depends on the costume. If it's well cared for, pretty hard. If it's old, or poorly designed—it could happen. And if it's not an accident . . ."

"Is that what happened here?"

Charlie hesitated. Dave's image came to her again, this time alive, when he bared his torso to show them the scars he bore. Dave had once survived being crushed like this, though the second time had killed him. Somehow he had survived the lethal unfolding of a costume, a thing that should have been impossible. But it had left its marks. She cleared her throat and started again. "I need to see his chest," she said. "Can you get his shirt off?"

Clay nodded and took a pair of plastic gloves from his pocket. He tossed them to Charlie but they fell to the ground unnoticed. "If I'd known you were going to stick your fingers in the corpse, I'd have given these to you earlier," he said drily. He put on a pair of his own and produced a knife from somewhere on his belt. The man was wearing a T-shirt. Clay dropped to his knees, took hold of the bottom, and began to saw through the cloth. The sound of wet, tearing fabric cut through the silent field like a cry of pain. At last he was done, and he pulled back the shirt. Dried blood clung to the fabric, and as Clay pulled it back the body pulled with it, giving a brief, false sense of life. Charlie bent over, picturing Dave's scars. She compared the pattern to the wounds she saw here. *This is what happened to Dave.* Each piercing of the man's flesh seemed like a killing blow; any one of them might have punctured something vital, or simply been deep enough to drain him of blood in minutes. What was left of him was grotesque.

"It was one of them," Charlie said, looking up at Clay for the first time since they reached the body. "He must have been wearing one of the costumes. It's the only way he could end up like this. But . . ." Charlie paused and scanned the field again. "Where's the suit?"

"What would someone be doing wearing one of those things out here?" Clay said.

"Maybe he wasn't wearing it willingly," Charlie answered.

Clay leaned forward and reached for the man's open shirt, pulling it closed as best he could. Together they got up and headed back to the car.

As Clay drove her back to campus, Charlie stared out the window into the darkness.

"Clay, what happened to Freddy's?" she asked. "I hear it was torn down." She scratched her fingernail on the car seat nervously. "Is that true?"

"Yes. Well, they started to," Clay said slowly. "We went through the whole place, clearing everything out. It was a funny thing; we couldn't find the body of that guard, Dave." He paused and looked directly at Charlie, as though expecting her to answer for something.

Charlie felt the warmth drain from her face. *He's dead. I saw him die.* She closed her eyes for a moment and forced herself to focus.

"That place was like a maze, though." Clay turned his eyes casually back to the road. "His body probably got stuffed into some crevice no one will find for years."

"Yeah, probably buried in the rubble." She looked down, trying to put the thought out of her head for the moment. "What about the costumes, the robots?" Clay hesitated. *You must have known I would ask*, Charlie thought with some annoyance.

"Everything we took out of Freddy's was thrown away or burned. Technically I should have treated it like what it was: a break in the missing kids case, over a decade old. Everything would have been bagged up and gone over. But no one would have believed what happened there, what we saw. So I took some liberties." He glanced at Charlie, the suspicious look gone from his face, and she nodded for him to continue. Clay took a deep breath. "I treated it only as the murder of my officer; you remember Officer Dunn. We recovered his body, closed the case, and I ordered the building to be demolished."

"What about . . ." Charlie paused, trying not to let her frustration show. "What about Freddy, and Bonnie, and Chica, and Foxy?" *What about the children, the children who were killed and hidden inside each one of them?*

"They were all there," Clay said gravely. "They were lifeless, Charlie. I don't know what else to tell you." Charlie didn't respond.

"As far as the demolition crew was concerned, all they'd found were old costumes, broken robots, and two dozen folding tables. And I didn't correct them," he said with hesitation in his voice. "You know how these things go. Whether building up or tearing down, it takes time. From what I hear, the storm hit and suddenly everyone was needed elsewhere; the demolition was put on hold."

"So it's all still standing there?" Charlie asked, and Clay gave her a warning look.

"Some parts are standing, but for all intents and purposes, it's gone. And don't even think about going back there. There's no reason to and you'll get yourself killed. Like I said, everything that mattered is gone anyway."

"I don't want to go back there," Charlie said softly.

When they reached the campus, Clay let her out where

he'd found her. She'd only taken a few steps from the car, however, when he called to her from the car window. "I feel like I need to tell you one more thing," he said. "We found blood at the scene, in the main dining room where Dave . . ." He looked around cautiously. There was something unseemly, talking about gruesome things on the sheltered grounds of the campus. "It wasn't real blood, Charlie."

"What are you talking about?" Charlie took a step back toward the car.

"It was, like, costume blood, or movie blood. It was pretty convincing, though. We didn't realize it was fake until the crime lab looked at it under a microscope."

"Why are you telling me this?" Charlie asked, although she knew the answer. The terrible possibility was pounding in her mind like a headache.

"He survived once," Clay said plainly.

"Well, he didn't survive the second time." Charlie turned to walk away.

"I'm sorry you have to be involved in this," Clay called.

Charlie didn't answer. She looked down at the pavement and clenched her teeth. Clay raised the window without another word and drove away.

# CHAPTER THREE

harlie checked her watch: she was on time to meet John, even early. She passed under a streetlight and looked down at herself, checking her clothes. *Oh no.* The knees of her jeans were wet with mud, and there was a dark stain where she had wiped her fingers clean of the dead man's blood. *I can't show up covered in blood. He's seen me like this too many times already.* She sighed and turned around.

Thankfully, Jessica was gone when she got back to the room. Charlie didn't want to talk about what had just happened. Clay hadn't explicitly told her to keep it a secret, but she was fairly sure she shouldn't broadcast her private visit to a crime scene. Charlie cast a glance at the faces under their pillowcase cover, but didn't go to them. She wanted to show her project to John, but, like Jessica, he might not understand.

She opened a dresser drawer and stared down at the contents without registering them. In her mind, she saw the body again, its limbs splayed out as if it had been thrown down where it lay. She covered her face with her hands, taking deep breaths. She had seen the scars, but she'd never seen the wounds of the spring locks fresh. Now Dave's eyes came to her, the look of shock just before he fell. Charlie could feel the locks in her hands, feel them resist, then give way and snap. *That's what happened. That's what I did.* She swallowed, and slid her hands down to her throat.

Charlie shook her head like a dog shaking off a wet coat. She looked at the open drawer again, concentrating. *I need to change. What is all this?* The drawer was filled with brightly colored shirts, all unfamiliar. Charlie startled, a dim panic seizing her. *What is all this?* She picked up a T-shirt and dropped it again, then forced herself to take a deep breath. *Jessica. They're Jessica's.* She'd opened the wrong drawer.

*Get it together, Charlie*, she told herself sternly, and somehow it sounded like Aunt Jen's voice in her head. Despite everything that lay between her and her aunt, just imagining her cold, authoritative voice made Charlie a little calmer. She nodded to herself, then grabbed what she needed: a clean T-shirt and jeans. She dressed hurriedly, then left to meet

John, her stomach fluttering, half-excited, half-sick. *A date*, she thought. *What if it doesn't go well? Worse, what if it does?*

As she neared the Thai restaurant, she saw that John was already there. He was waiting outside, but he didn't look impatient. He didn't spot her right away, and Charlie slowed her pace for a moment, watching him. He seemed at ease, gazing into the middle distance with a vague, pleasant expression. He had an air of confidence he hadn't possessed a year ago. It wasn't that he'd been unsure of himself then, but now he looked . . . adult. Maybe it was because he'd gone straight to work after high school. *Maybe it was what happened last year at Freddy's,* Charlie thought with an unexpected sense of envy. Although she'd moved out on her own, to a new home and a new college, she felt as if the experience had left her more a child, not less. Not a cared-for or protected child, but one who was vulnerable and unmoored. A child who had looked under the bed and seen the monsters.

John noticed her and waved. Charlie waved back and smiled, the expression unforced. Date or not, it was good to see him.

"How was your last class?" he said by way of greeting, and Charlie shrugged.

"I don't know. It was class. How was the rest of work?"

He grinned. "It was work. Are you hungry?"

"Yes," Charlie said decisively. They headed inside and were motioned to a table.

"Have you been here before?" John asked, and Charlie shook her head.

"I don't get out much," she said. "I don't even come out to town that often. The college is sort of its own little world, you know?"

"I can imagine," John said cheerfully. Now that the secret was out that he wasn't in school, he'd apparently shed his earlier discomfort. "Isn't it a little bit . . . ?" he searched for words. "Doesn't it feel a little isolated?"

"Not really," Charlie said. "If it's a prison, it's not one of the worst."

"I didn't mean to compare it to a prison!" John said. "So, come on, what are you studying?"

Charlie hesitated. There was no reason not to tell John, but it seemed too soon, too risky to announce that she was eagerly following in her father's footsteps. She didn't want to tell him she was studying robotics until she had some idea of how he would respond. Just like with her project.

"Most colleges make you do a set of classes your first year: English, math, everything like that," she said, hoping it would sound like a response. Suddenly Charlie didn't want to talk about school; she wasn't sure she could keep up a conversation about *anything*, really. She looked at John, and for a moment imagined the spring-lock wounds in his neck. Her eyes widened and she bit the inside of her cheek, trying to ground herself.

"Tell me about your job," she said, and saw her own hesitation mirrored on his face.

"I mean, I like the work," he said. "More than I thought I would, actually. There's something about doing physical labor that kind of frees my mind. It's like meditation. It's hard, though, really hard. Construction workers always make it look so easy, but it turns out it takes a while to build up that kind of muscle." He stretched his arms comically over his head, and Charlie laughed, but couldn't help noticing that he was clearly well on his way to that kind of muscle. John leaned to his left and gave his armpit a quick sniff, then made a look of mock-embarrassment. Charlie looked down at her menu and giggled.

"Do you already know what you want?" she said. Then the waitress appeared out of nowhere, as if she'd been listening nearby.

John ordered, and Charlie froze. She'd said it just to say something, but she didn't know what to get. Suddenly she noticed all the prices. Everything on the menu was impossibly expensive. She hadn't even thought about money when she accepted John's invitation, but now her mind jumped to her wallet, and her nearly empty bank account.

Misreading her expression, John leaped in. "If you've never had Thai food, Pad Thai is good," he suggested. "I should have asked," he said awkwardly. "If I'm buying a lady dinner, I should make sure she likes the food!" He looked embarrassed, but Charlie was flooded with relief. *Buying a lady dinner.*

"No, I'm sure I'll like it," she said. "Pad Thai, thanks," she told the waitress, then gave John a mock-glare. "Who are you calling a lady?" she said playfully, and he laughed.

"What's wrong with that?"

"It just sounds weird, you calling me a lady," Charlie said. "So anyway, what do you all day besides meditate?"

"Well, the days are long, and like I said, I'm still writing, so there's that. It's strange being in Hurricane again, though. I didn't mean to put down roots."

"Put down roots?"

"Like, join a bowling team or something. Ties to the community, things like that."

Charlie nodded. She of all people understood the need to remain apart. "Why did you take the job here, then?" she asked. "I know they needed people because of the storm, but you didn't *have* to come, right? People are still building things in other places."

"That's true," he admitted. "To be honest, it was more about getting away from where I was."

"Sounds familiar," Charlie muttered, too softly for him to hear.

The waitress returned with their food. Charlie took a quick bite of rice noodles and immediately burned her mouth. She grabbed her water glass and drank. "Yikes, that's hot!" she said. "So what were you getting away from?" She asked the question casually, as if the answer would be simple. *Do you have nightmares, too?* She held back the words, waiting for him to speak.

John hesitated. "A . . . girl, actually," he said. He paused, searching for a reaction. Charlie stopped chewing; that wasn't at all the answer she'd been expecting. She swallowed, nodding with self-conscious enthusiasm. After an excruciating silence, John went on.

"We started dating the summer after . . . after Freddy's. I told her I wasn't looking for anything serious, she said she wasn't, either. Then suddenly it was six months later, and we were serious. I had just started working. I'd moved out on my own, and had this grown-up relationship. It was a shock, but a good one, I guess." He stopped, not sure whether he should continue. Charlie wasn't sure she wanted to give him permission.

"So, tell me about her," she said calmly, avoiding eye contact.

"She was—is, I mean. I'm not dating her, but it's not like she's dead. Her name is Rebecca. She's pretty, I guess. Smart. She's a year older than me, a college student studying English; has a dog. So yeah, she was all right."

"What happened?"

"I don't know," he said.

"Really," Charlie said drily, and he smiled.

"No. I felt . . . on guard around her. Like there were things I couldn't tell her, things she'd just *never* understand. It wasn't because of her. She was great. But she knew I was holding something back; she just didn't know what it was."

"I wonder what it could have been?" Charlie asked quietly. The question was rhetorical; they both knew the answer.

John smiled. "Well, anyway, she broke up with me, and I was devastated, blah, blah, blah. Actually, I don't think I was that devastated." John looked down, focusing on his food but not touching it.

"Have *you* ever tried to tell anyone about Freddy's?" John glanced back up and pointed his fork at Charlie. She shook her head. "It wasn't just what happened," he went on. "I can't imagine telling that story and having her believe me, but it wasn't only that. I wanted her to know the facts of it, but more, I wanted to tell her what it did to me. How it changed me."

"It changed all of us," Charlie said.

"Yeah, and not just last year. From the beginning. I didn't realize it until after we'd all gone back, how much that place had just . . . *followed* me." He glanced at Charlie. "Sorry, it must be even weirder for you."

Charlie shrugged uncomfortably. "Maybe. I think it's just different."

Her hand was resting on the table beside her water glass, and now John reached out to touch it. She stiffened, and he drew back.

"Sorry," he said. "I'm sorry."

"It's not you," Charlie said quickly. *His dead face, the dead skin of his throat.* She had barely noticed it at the time, overwhelmed by the whole experience, but now the feeling of the dead man's neck came back to her. It was as if she were touching him right now. She could feel his skin, slack and cold, and slick with blood; she could feel the blood on her fingers. She rubbed her hands together. They were clean— she knew they were clean—but still she could feel the blood. *You're being dramatic.*

"I'll be right back," she said, and got up before John could respond. She made her way around the tables to the bathrooms at the back of the restaurant. It was a three-stall bathroom; thankfully it was empty. Charlie went straight to the sink and turned the hot water on full-blast. She pumped soap onto her hands and scrubbed them for a long time. She closed her eyes and focused on the feeling of hot water and soap, and slowly the memory of blood faded. As she dried her hands she looked at herself in the mirror: her reflection looked wrong somehow, off, as if it wasn't herself she saw, but a copy. Someone else dressed as her. *Get it together, Charlie*, she thought, trying to hear the words in Aunt Jen's voice, as she had before. She closed her eyes. *Get it together.* When she opened them again she was back in the mirror. Her reflection was her own.

Charlie smoothed her hair, and went back out to the table, where John was waiting for her with a concerned expression.

"Is everything okay?" he asked nervously. "Did I do something?"

Charlie shook her head. "No, of course not. It's been a long day, that's all." *There's an understatement.* She glanced at her watch. "Do we still have time for a movie?" she asked. "It's almost eight thirty."

"Yeah, we should go," John said. "Are you done?"

"Yeah, it was really good, thank you." She smiled at him. "The 'lady' liked it." John smiled back, visibly relaxing. He went to the counter to pay, and Charlie went outside, waiting for him on the sidewalk. Dark had fallen, and there was a chill in the air. Charlie wished briefly that she'd thought to bring a sweatshirt. John joined her after a moment.

"Ready?"

"Yeah," Charlie said. "Where is it?"

He looked at her for a moment and shook his head. "The movie was your idea, remember?" He laughed.

"Like I said, I don't get out much." Charlie looked down at her feet.

"The theater's only a few blocks away."

They walked in silence for a while.

"I found out what happened to Freddy's," she said without thinking, and John looked at her, surprised.

"Really? What happened?"

"They were tearing it down, then the storm came and everyone got called away. Now it's just standing there, half collapsed. All the stuff is gone, though," she added, seeing the question in John's eyes. "I don't know what they did with . . . them." It was a lie; Charlie couldn't tell him what had really happened without telling him how she knew. All those questions led back to the same place: the dead man in the field. *Who were you?*

"What about your father's house?" John asked. "Did you ask your aunt Jen about it? What's she going to do with it?"

"I don't know," Charlie said. "I haven't talked to her since August." She fell silent, not looking at John as they walked.

They reached their destination, a shabby, one-screen movie theater named the Grand Palace. Its name was either ironic or wishful thinking. Emblazoned on the marquee was their current showing: *Zombies vs. Zombies!*

"I think it's about zombies," John joked as they went inside.

The movie had already started. Someone onscreen was screaming, as what were apparently zombies came at her from all sides. She was surrounded. The creatures crouched like wild dogs, ready to spring and devour her. They moved to attack—and a man grabbed her arm, pulling her to safety.

"Charlie." John touched her arm, whispering. "Over there." He gestured to the back row. The place was half-full, but the back row was empty, and they made their way furtively to the middle. They sat, and Charlie turned her attention to the screen. *Thank goodness*, she thought. *Maybe we can finally relax.*

She settled back in her seat, letting the images on the screen blur past her. Shrieks, gunfire, and thrumming music filled the silence between them. From the corner of her eye she saw John glance at her nervously. Charlie focused her attention on the movie. The main characters, a man and woman with the generic, angular good looks of the big screen, were shooting automatic weapons into a crowd of zombies. As the first ranks were killed—not killed, stopped; though severed in half by the guns, they still twitched on the ground—the ones behind climbed over their fallen cohorts. The camera switched back to the man and woman, who jumped a fence and took off running. Behind them the zombies kept coming, struggling forward, oblivious to the undead bodies they waded through. The music was urgent, the baseline pounding like an artificial heartbeat, and Charlie relaxed against the seat, letting herself be absorbed into it all.

*What was he doing there?* The image of the dead man returned to her. Something about the wounds bothered her, but she hadn't been able to put her finger on it. *I recognized those wounds. They all matched what I remembered, but* something *was different. What was it?*

She sensed movement next to her, and saw John trying to stretch an arm toward her. *Really?* she thought.

"Do you have enough room?" she asked him, and scooted away without waiting for a response. He looked embarrassed, but she glanced away, planting her elbow on the other armrest and staring fixedly at the screen.

*Enough room, that's it.* She closed her eyes, concentrating on the image in her head. *The wounds were slightly larger and more spaced out. The suit he was wearing was bigger than the suits from Freddy's. The man was probably five foot ten or five foot eleven, which means the suits must have been at least seven feet tall.*

Onscreen, there was quiet again, but it was short lived. Charlie watched, mesmerized, as the dirt spilled away of its own volition, moving like magic as the zombie rose. *It wouldn't be like that*, Charlie thought definitively. *It's not that easy to get out of a grave.* By now the zombie onscreen was halfway out, crawling to the surface and looking around with its glassy, mindless eyes. *You can't get out that fast.* Charlie blinked and shook her head, trying to stay focused.

*Zombies. Lifeless things. The closet was full of costumes, lifeless yet ever-watching, with plastic eyes and dead, hanging limbs. Somehow their corpselike stares had never bothered her, or Sammy. They liked to touch the fur, sometimes put it in their mouths and giggle at the funny way it felt. Some was old and matted; some new and soft. The closet was their place, just for the two of them. Sometimes they babbled together in words that had meaning only to them; sometimes they played side by side, lost in separate worlds of make-believe. But they were always together. Sammy was playing with a truck when the shadow came. He ran it back and forth on the floor, not noticing that their ribbon of light had been cut off. Charlie turned and saw the shadow, so still he could be an illusion, just another costume out of place. Then the sudden movement, the chaos of fabric and eyes. The truck clanked as it fell to the floor, and then: loneliness. A dark so complete that she began to believe she'd never seen at all. The memories of sight had only been a dream, a trick of the utter blackness. She tried to call his name—she could feel him nearby—but all around her were solid walls. "Can you hear me? Sammy? Let me out! Sammy!" But he was gone, and he was never there again.*

"Charlie, are you okay?"

"What?" Charlie looked at John. She realized she'd pulled her feet up on the chair and was hugging her knees to her chest. She sat back, setting her shoes back on the floor. John gave her a concerned look. "I'm fine," she whispered, and gestured to the screen.

John put a hand on her forearm. "Are you sure you're okay?" he asked.

Charlie stared straight ahead. Now there were people running, the zombies lurching after them. "This doesn't make sense," Charlie muttered, mostly to herself.

"What?" John leaned toward her.

Charlie didn't move, but she repeated herself. "It doesn't make sense. Zombies don't make sense; if they're dead, the central nervous system is shot, and they can't do any of this. If there's a functioning central nervous system, which has somehow decayed to the point that movement and thought are possible, but severely hindered, fine. If it makes them violent, fine. But why would they want to eat brains? It doesn't make sense."

*That man wouldn't have been able to walk on his own in a suit so oversized. He didn't walk into that field; the suit did. The animatronic was carrying him inside. It walked into that field of its own accord.*

"Maybe it's symbolic," John suggested, eager to engage, however odd the conversation. "You know, like the idea that you eat your enemy's heart to gain their power? Maybe the zombie eats its enemy's brain to gain its . . . central nervous system?" He glanced at Charlie, but she was only half listening.

"Okay," she said. She'd been irritated by the movie, now she was irritated by the conversation she herself had introduced. "I'll be right back," she told John, and got up without waiting for him to respond. She made her way out of the row, through the lobby, and out the door. On the sidewalk, she took a deep breath and felt an intense relief at the wash of fresh air. *Dreams about being trapped are common,* she reminded herself. She'd looked it up when they began. They were only slightly less common than dreams of showing up to class naked, plummeting from a great height, or having your teeth all suddenly fall out. *But this didn't feel like a dream.*

Charlie jostled her thoughts back to the present, where even the crime scene of a gruesome murder seemed like a safer place to keep them.

*There must be tracks. He didn't walk there himself. There must be some clue of what carried him into that field, and where it came from.*

Charlie shivered. She went back inside the building. *John's going to think I'm nuts.* She arrived at the swinging theater doors and stopped—she couldn't do it. She had to know. There was a young man at the concession stand, and she asked him if the place had a pay phone. He pointed silently to his right, and Charlie went, fishing in her pocket for a quarter, and for Chief Burke's card.

She dialed carefully, pausing between numbers to check the card again, as if the writing might have changed since she looked. Clay Burke answered on the third ring.

"Burke."

"Clay? It's Charlie."

"Charlie? What's wrong?" He was instantly alert; Charlie could picture him leaping to his feet, ready to run.

"Nothing, I'm fine," she assured him. "Everything is okay, I just wanted to see if you've found anything else."

"Not so far," he told her.

"Oh." Burke let the silence stretch between them, and Charlie finally broke it. "Is there anything else you can tell me? I know it's confidential, but you've brought me in this far. Please, if there's anything else you know. Anything else you found, anything you know about the man—the victim."

"No," Clay said slowly. "I mean, I'll let you know when we find something."

"Okay," Charlie said. "Thanks."

"I'll be in touch."

"Okay." Charlie hung up the phone before he could say good-bye. "I don't believe you," she said to the phone on the wall.

Back in the theater, her eyes took a moment to adjust as she inched along the back row toward her seat, careful not to make noise. John looked up at her with a smile as she sat down, but didn't say anything. Charlie smiled back with a grim determination, and settled back in her seat, then scooted over until her shoulder was pressed against his. From behind her head, she heard him make a surprised noise, then he shifted, putting his arm around her shoulders. He gripped her tightly for a moment, halfway to a hug, and Charlie leaned in a little, unsure how else to reciprocate.

*What if someone put him in the costume, like some kind of wind-up deathtrap? Stuck him inside that thing, then sent it walking until the spring locks went off. But who would know how to do that? Why would someone do that?*

"Did I miss anything?" Charlie asked, though she hadn't paid any attention to the first half of the movie anyway. It was daytime onscreen, and it looked like there were more people, holed up in some sort of bunker. Charlie couldn't remember which of them had been the original characters. She wriggled in her seat; John's arm around her had relaxed, but now the arm of the seat was digging into her side. He started to move away, but she settled herself again.

"No, it's okay," she whispered, and his arm circled her again. "Just get on with it," Charlie said, flustered. John startled.

"Sorry, I didn't want to be too aggressive."

"No, not you." Charlie gestured toward the screen. "They should just build a minefield around the bunker and wait for them to all blow up. The end."

"I think that's actually what they do in the sequel, but we'll have to wait to watch it for ourselves." He winked.

"There's another one?" She sighed.

When the credits started to roll, they gathered their things and headed to the exits with the rest of the small crowd, not speaking until they got outside. On the sidewalk, they stopped.

"This has been nice," John said, sounding—somehow— like he meant it, and Charlie laughed, then groaned, covering her face with both hands.

"This has been *awful*. This has been the worst date ever. I'm so sorry. Thanks for lying, though."

John gave an uncertain smile. "It was nice to see you," he said with cautious levity.

"It's just—can we go somewhere to talk?"

John nodded, and Charlie started back toward campus with him following behind.

The quad was usually empty late at night, or at least mostly empty. There was always someone walking across, some student finishing up late night work in a lab, some couple ensconced in a dark corner. Tonight was no different, and it was easy enough to find their own dark corner to talk. Charlie sat down under a tree, and John copied her, then waited for her to talk as she stared at the gap between two buildings, where you could almost see the woods.

Finally, he prompted her. "So what's up?"

"Right." She met his eyes. "Clay came to see me today." John's eyes widened, but he didn't say anything. "He took me to see a body," Charlie went on. "He had died inside one of the mascot costumes."

John was frowning; she could almost see his thoughts, working through what this meant, and why it involved Charlie.

"That's not all: Clay told me that they found blood in the main dining room at Freddy's. Fake blood."

John's head jerked up. "You think Dave's alive?"

Charlie shrugged. "Clay didn't come out and say it. But all those scars—he had survived the spring locks of a mascot costume before. He must have known how to escape the building."

"It didn't look to me like he escaped," John said doubtfully.

"He could have faked it; it would certainly explain the blood."

"So what then? Dave is alive and stuffing people into spring-lock suits and killing them?"

"If I could just go back to the restaurant one more time, to make sure that—" Charlie stopped, suddenly aware of growing anger in John's face.

"To make sure that *what*?" he asked sternly.

"Nothing. Clay has it under control. Everything is best left with the police." She clenched her jaw, gazing out over the horizon.

*Jessica will go with me.*

"Right," John said with a surprised look. "Right, you're right."

Charlie nodded with forced enthusiasm.

"Clay has men for this sort of thing," she continued with a furrowed brow. "I'm sure they're on top of it."

John took Charlie's shoulders lightly. "I'm sure it's not

what you think it is, anyway," he said in a hearty, reassuring tone. "There's a lot of crime in this world that doesn't involve self-imploding furry robot suits." He laughed and Charlie forced a smile.

"Come on." John extended a hand and Charlie took it. "I'll walk you to your dorm."

"I appreciate the gesture," she said. "But Jessica's there, and we'd have to go through the whole reunion, you know?"

John laughed. "Okay, I'll save you from Jessica and her relentless camaraderie."

Charlie grinned. "My hero. Where are you staying, anyway?"

"That little motel you stayed at last year, actually," John said. "I'll see you tomorrow maybe?"

Charlie nodded and watched him go, then started on her own way home. Excruciating though the date had been, the last half hour felt like a homecoming. It was her and John again; they were familiar again. "All we needed was a good old-fashioned murder," she said aloud, and a woman walking her dog gave Charlie an odd look as she passed in the opposite direction. "I was at a movie, *Zombies vs. Zombies!*" Charlie called halfheartedly after her retreating back. "You should go check it out! They don't put mines around the bunker; spoiler alert."

Charlie had half hoped Jessica would be asleep, but the

lights were on when she reached their room. She flung open the door before Charlie had her key out of her pocket, her face flushed.

"So?" Jessica demanded.

"So what?" Charlie asked, grinning in spite of herself. "Hey, before you start into this, I need to ask you something."

"So you know what!" Jessica cried, ignoring her question. "Tell me about John. How did it go?"

Charlie felt the corner of her mouth twitch. "Oh, you know," she said casually. "Listen, I need you to go somewhere with me in the morning."

"Charlieee! You have to tell me!" Jessica moaned exaggeratedly, and flopped back on her bed. Then she sprang back up into a sitting position. "Come here and tell me!" Charlie sat, drawing her legs up under her.

"It was weird," she admitted. "I didn't know what to say. Dates just seem so . . . uncomfortable. But about what I was saying—"

"But it's John. Shouldn't that outweigh the 'date' part?"

"Well, it didn't," Charlie said. She looked at the floor. She could tell her face was red, and suddenly she wished she hadn't told Jessica anything at all.

Jessica put her hands on Charlie's shoulders and looked at her seriously. "You are amazing, and if John isn't just falling all over himself for you, that's his problem."

Charlie giggled. "I think he kind of is. It's *part* of the problem. But there is something else if you would just listen for a second."

"Oh, there's more?" Jessica laughed. "Charlie! You need to save *something* for the second date, you know."

"What? No, no. *NO!* I need you to go somewhere with me in the morning."

"Charlie I have a lot going on right now; I have exams coming up, and . . ."

"I need you . . ." Charlie clenched her jaw for a moment. "I need you to help me pick out new clothes for my next date," she said carefully, then waited to see if Jessica would believe a word of it.

"Charlie are you kidding me? We'll go first thing in the morning!" She jumped up and gave Charlie a giant hug. "We'll have a girls' day out! It will be amazing!" Jessica flopped back to her bed. "Sleep for now, though."

"It won't bother you if I work on my project for a while, will it?"

"Not at all." Jessica waved limply, then went still.


Charlie turned on her work lamp: a single, bright beam that was focused enough to not illuminate the whole room. She uncovered the faces; they were at rest, their features smooth as if in sleep, but she didn't turn them on yet. The switches that made them move and talk were only one part of the whole. There was another component: the part that made them listen was always on. Everything that she and Jessica said, every word spoken in the room, outside the window, or even in the hall, they heard. Each new word went into their databases, not only as a single word, but in all its configurations as they emerged. Each new piece of information was stuck to the piece of information most like it; everything new was built on something old. They were always learning.

Charlie turned on the component that allowed them to speak. Their features rippled softly, as if they were stretching themselves.

*I know*, said the first, more quickly than usual.

*So what?* said the second.

*Know what?*

*You know so what?*

*Know what?*

*Now what?*

*What now?*

*Know how?*

*Why now?*

Charlie switched them off, staring as the fans slowed to a stop. *That didn't make sense.* She looked at her watch. It was about three hours too late for bed. She changed quickly and climbed under the sheets, leaving the faces uncovered. There was something unnerving about their exchange. It was faster than it had ever been, and it was nonsensical, but there was something about it that rang familiar—it struck her.

"Were you playing a game?" she asked. They couldn't answer, and just stared blankly into each other's eyes.

# CHAPTER FOUR

She removed the pillowcase gently, taking care not to let it catch on anything. Beneath their shroud, the faces, blank and sightless, were placid; they looked like they could wait, ever listening, for eternity. Charlie switched them on, and bent over to watch as they began to move their plastic mouths without sound, practicing.

Where? *said the first.*

Here, *said the second.*

Where? *said the first again. Charlie drew back. Something was wrong with the voice; it sounded strained.*

Here, *repeated the second.*

Where? *said the first with a rising intonation, like it was growing upset.*

That's not supposed to happen! *Charlie thought, alarmed. They shouldn't be able to modulate their voices.*

*Where?* *the first wailed, and Charlie stepped back. She leaned down slowly to peer under the desk, as though she might find an entanglement of wires that would explain the strange behavior. As she stared, puzzled, a baby began to cry. She stood at once, knocking her head painfully on the edge of the desk. The two faces looked suddenly more human, and more childlike. One was crying, the other watching with an astonished look on its face. "It's okay," said the calmer face. "Don't leave me!" The other wailed as it turned to look at Charlie.*

*"I'm not going to leave you!" Charlie cried. "Everything will be okay!" The sound of crying swelled, higher and louder than human voices should be, and Charlie covered her ears, looking desperately around for someone to help. Her bedroom had darkened, and heavy things hung from the ceiling. Matted fur brushed her face, and her heart jolted:* the children are not safe. *She turned back, but an acre of fabric and fur had somehow fallen between her and the wailing babies.*

*"I'll find you!" She shoved her way through, tripping on limbs that dragged on the ground. The costumes swung wildly, like trees in a storm, and a little distance away, something fell to the floor with a hard clunk. At last, she reached her desk, but they were gone. The howling went on and on, so loud Charlie couldn't hear herself think, even as she realized that the screaming was her own.*

Charlie sat up with a loud, raw gasp, as if she had actually been screaming.

"Charlie?" It was John's voice. Charlie looked around with one bleary eye to see a head peering through the bed-room door.

"Give me a minute!" Charlie called as she sat up straight. "Get out!" she cried, and John's head shrank back; the door closed. She felt shaky, her muscles weak. She'd been holding them tense in her sleep. She changed quickly into clean clothes and tried to brush her slightly tangled hair into something more manageable, then opened the door.

John poked his head in again, taking a cautious look around.

"Okay, come in. It's not booby-trapped, though maybe it should be," Charlie joked. "How did you get in here?"

"Well, it was open, and I . . ." John trailed off as he took in the room around him, momentarily distracted by the mess. "I thought maybe we could go to breakfast? I have to work across town in about forty minutes, but I have some time."

"Oh, what a nice thought, but I . . . ," she said. "Sorry for the mess. It's my project, I sort of get wrapped up in it and forget to—clean." She glanced at her desk. The pillowcase was in place as it should be, the vague outlines of the faces just visible beneath it. *It was just a dream.*

John shrugged. "Yeah? What's the project?"

"Um, language. Sort of." She looked around the room curiously. Where had Jessica wandered off to? Charlie knew John would be suspicious of her sudden, unprecedented interest in clothes shopping, and was hoping to avoid explanations. "Natural language programming," she went on. "I'm taking . . . computer programming classes." At the last moment, something stopped her from saying the word *robotics*. John nodded. He was still eyeing the mess, and Charlie couldn't tell what had caught his attention. She plunged back into her explanation. "So, I'm working on teaching language—spoken language—to computers." She walked briskly to the door and peered out into the hall.

"Don't computers already know language?" John called.

"Well, yeah," Charlie said as she returned to the room. She looked at John. His face had changed, stripped down to something more adult. But she could still see him as he'd been the year before, captivated as he watched her old mechanical toys. *I can tell him.*

But then a look of alarm crossed John's face. He surged forward to her bed, stopping a few inches from it. He pointed.

"Is that Theodore's head?" he asked carefully.

"Yeah," Charlie said. She walked to the windows and peeped through the blinds, trying to spot Jessica's car.

"So you *have* been to the house?"

"No. Well, yeah. I went back once," she confessed. "To get him." She looked back at John guiltily.

He shook his head. "Charlie, you don't have to explain yourself," he said. "It's your house." He grabbed the chair from her desk and sat down. "Why did you take him apart?"

She studied his face worriedly, wondering if he was already asking himself the next, obvious question: *What if it runs in the family?*

"I wanted to see how he worked," Charlie said. She spoke carefully, feeling like she had to appear as rational as possible. "I would have taken Stanley and Ella, too, but, you know."

"They're bolted to the floor?"

"Pretty much, yeah. So I took Theodore; I'm actually using some of his components in my project." Charlie looked down at the disembodied bunny's head, into its blank glass eyes. *Took him apart. Using his component parts. That sounds rational.*

She had gotten Theodore from her father's house just before school began. Jessica hadn't been home. It was early evening, not quite dark, and Charlie had smuggled Theodore inside her backpack. She took him out, set him on the bed, and pressed the button to make him talk. As before, there was nothing but a strangled sound: "—ou—lie," the scrambled, decayed traces of her father's voice. Charlie had felt a pang of anger at herself for even trying.

"You sound pretty awful," she said harshly to Theodore, who just looked up at her blankly, immune to the reprimand. Charlie rifled through her bag of tools and parts, which hadn't yet taken over her side of the room. She found her utility knife, then went grimly to her bed where the bunny waited.

"I'll put you back together when I'm done." *Right.*

She looked up at John now, saw the doubt on his face. Or maybe it was concern, just like Jessica. "Sorry, I know everything's a mess," she said, hearing the edge in her own voice. "Maybe I'm a mess, too," she added quietly. She set the bunny's head down on her pillow, and the part of his leg beside it. "So, do you still want to see my project?" she asked.

"Yes." He smiled reassuringly and followed her to her desk. Charlie hesitated, looking down at the pillowcase. *Just a dream.*

"So," she said nervously. Charlie carefully switched everything on before unveiling the faces. Lights began to blink and fans began to whir. She glanced at John again, and took off the cloth.

The faces moved in little patterns, as if stretching out after waking, though there was little they could stretch. Charlie swallowed nervously.

*You, me,* said the first one, and Charlie heard John make a surprised sound behind her.

*Me,* said the second. Charlie held her breath, but they fell silent.

"Sorry, they usually say more," Charlie said. She grabbed a small object from the table and held it up: it was an oddly shaped piece of clear plastic with wiring inside. John frowned for a moment.

"Is that a hearing aid?" he asked, and Charlie nodded enthusiastically.

"It used to be. It's something I'm experimenting with: they listen all the time, they pick up everything that's said around them, but they're just collecting data, not interacting with it. They can only interact with each other." She paused, waiting for a sign that John understood. He nodded, and she went on. "I'm still working out the kinks, but this thing should make the person wearing it . . . visible to them. Not literally visible, I mean—they can't see—but they'll recognize the person wearing the device as one of them." She looked expectantly at John.

"Why . . . What does that mean?" he asked, seeming to search for words. Charlie closed her hand on the earpiece, frustrated. *He doesn't understand.*

"I made them. I want to interact with them," she said. His expression grew thoughtful, and she looked away, suddenly regretting having shown him the object. "Anyway, it's not really finished." She edged to the door and glanced out.

"It's really cool," John called after her. When Charlie returned from the hallway, he gave her an odd look. "Is everything okay?"

"Yes. You should go, though. You'll be late for work." Charlie approached the faces. She looked down thoughtfully at her creations, then sighed and reached for the pillowcase to cover them. As she did, the second face moved.

It jerked back on its stand and pivoted, locking its blind eyes on Charlie's. She stared back. It was like looking at a statue; the eyes were only raised bumps in the molded plastic. But Charlie swallowed hard, feeling herself rooted to the spot. She studied the blank gaze until John put a hand on her shoulder. She jumped, startling him as well, then looked down at the earpiece in her hand. "Oh, right," Charlie mumbled, and pressed the tiny power button on the side of it. She placed the earpiece carefully on top of the mess in her desk drawer, then closed the drawer. The face was still for a moment, then it slowly turned back to its place. It settled there, locked in a mirrored stare with its double, as if it had never moved at all. Charlie covered them and switched them off, leaving them with only enough power to listen.

At last she looked up at John. "Sorry!" she said.

"Does that mean *no* to breakfast?"

"I have plans this morning," Charlie said. "Me and Jessica. You know, girl stuff."

"Really?" John said quietly. "Girl stuff? You?"

"Yes! Girl stuff!" Jessica squealed as she entered the room excitedly. "Shopping; I finally convinced Charlie it's worth trying on her clothes before she buys them. We might even move past jeans and boots! Are you ready?"

"Ready!" Charlie smiled, and John squinted at her.

Jessica began escorting him gently out the door. "Right," John said. "I'll see you later then, Charlie?" Charlie didn't respond, but Jessica gave a bright smile as she closed the door behind him.

"So." Jessica clasped her hands. "Where do you want to start today?"

When they got to the parking lot of the abandoned mall, it was early afternoon.

"Charlie, this isn't what I had in mind," Jessica cried as they got out of the car. Charlie started for the entrance, but Jessica didn't follow. When Charlie turned, she was leaning against the car with her arms crossed.

"What are we doing here?" Jessica asked, her eyebrows raised.

"We have to look inside," Charlie said. "People's lives might depend on it. I just want to see if there is anything left of Freddy's, then we can go."

"Whose lives depend on it? And why now, suddenly?" Jessica asked.

Charlie looked at her shoes. "I just want to see," she said. She felt like a petulant child, but she couldn't bring herself to tell Jessica the whole story.

"Is this because John is here?" Jessica asked suddenly, and Charlie looked up, surprised.

"What? No."

Jessica sighed and uncrossed her arms. "It's okay, Charlie. I get it. You haven't seen him since all of this happened, and then he shows up again—of course it brings everything back."

Charlie nodded, gratefully latching on to this rationale. It was easier than hiding the truth from her. "I doubt there's much left, anyway," she said. "I just want to walk through and remind myself that—"

"That it's really over?" Jessica finished. She smiled, and Charlie's heart sank.

*It's really, really not over.* She forced a smile. "Something like that."

Charlie walked quickly through the mall, but Jessica lagged behind. The place felt entirely different. Sunlight poured in through massive gaps in the unfinished walls and ceiling. Shafts of light sifted between smaller cracks and splashed against stacks of concrete slabs. Charlie could see moths—maybe butterflies—hovering at the windows, and as they passed through the empty halls on their way to Freddy's, she could hear birds chirping. The deathly quiet she remembered, the overpowering sense of dread, was gone. Yet, Charlie thought as she glanced at the half-constructed storefronts, it still felt haunted, maybe even more than before. It was a different kind of haunting, not frightening. But Charlie had the sense that something was present, like stepping onto hallowed ground.

"Hello," Charlie said softly, not sure whom she was addressing.

"Do you hear something?" Jessica slowed her pace.

"No. It feels smaller." Charlie gestured at the open mouths

of the never-opened department stores, and the end of the hall ahead of them. "It seemed so intimidating last time."

"It actually seems kind of peaceful." Jessica spun in place, enjoying the air from outside, which was flowing freely through the empty spaces.

Jessica followed Charlie through the doorway and they stopped dead, blinded by bright sunlight. Freddy's had been torn apart. Some of the walls still stood—the far end looked almost intact—but in front of her was a field of debris. Old bricks and broken tiles were strewn in the dirt.

The two of them stood now on a slab of concrete that lay baking in the sun. The passage inward, along with the entire side wall of the restaurant, was gone. The walls and ceiling were just a line of rubble against the trees. The concrete walkway was still there, worn dark by years of dank and leaking pipes.

"So much for Freddy's," Jessica said in a hushed voice, and Charlie nodded.

They made their way through the debris. Charlie could make out where the main dining room had been, but everything was gone. The tables and chairs, the checkered cloths, and the party hats had all been removed. The merry-go-round had been ripped out, leaving nothing but a hole in the floor and some stray wires. The stage itself had been assaulted, though not removed. They must have been in the middle of that when the job was stopped. Boards were torn up across the main stage area, and the left-hand set of stairs was gone. What was left of the wall behind the stage broke off at the top, like jagged mountains along the sky.

"Are you okay?" Jessica looked to Charlie.

"Yeah. It's not what I expected, but I'm okay." She thought for a moment. "I want to see what's still here." Charlie gestured to the stage, and they crossed what was left of the dining area. The floorboards cracked, the linoleum torn. Jessica peered under a pile of rock where arcade machines had been. The consoles that had stood like dusty gravestones were gone, but they could see the outlines of each one. Square patches remained where they'd been torn from their posts. Stray wires huddled in small piles in the corners. Charlie turned her attention back to the main stage. She climbed up to where the animatronic animals had once performed.

"Careful!" Jessica cried. Charlie nodded an absent acknowledgment. She stood to one side, remembering the layout. *This is where Freddy stood.* The boards were torn up in front of her and in two more places—the destruction here was where they had taken out the pivoting plates that bolted the mascots to the stage. *Not that they stayed bolted very long,* Charlie thought wryly. She could see it now if she closed her eyes. *The animals were going through their programmed motions, faster and faster, until it was clear they were out of control. Moving wildly, as if they were afraid. They were rocking on their stands, and then the awful sound of cracking wood as Bonnie lifted his bolted foot and tore himself free of the stage.*

Charlie shook her head, trying to rid herself of the image. She made her way to the back of the stage. The lights were all gone, but a skeleton of exposed beams crisscrossed the open sky where the lights had been.

"Jessica!" she called. "Where are you?"

"Down here!"

She followed the sound of the girl's voice. Jessica was crouched in the place where the control room had been, peering into the gap under the stage.

"Nothing?" Charlie asked, not sure what answer she was hoping for.

"It's been gutted," Jessica said. "No monitors, nothing." Charlie climbed down beside her, and they peered in together.

"This is where we were trapped last time," Jessica said quietly. "Me and John; there was something at the door, and the lock caught. I thought we would be stuck in that little room and . . ." She looked at Charlie, who simply nodded. The horrors of that night were unique to each of them. The moments that beset them in their sleep, or assailed their thoughts without warning in the middle of the day, were private.

"Come on," Charlie said abruptly, heading again toward the mound of rubble where more games had been. Charlie crouched under a large slab that leaned to the side and acted as a doorway to what was left of the place.

"This seems dangerous." Jessica tiptoed over the loose rock.

The floor was still covered in carpet in most places, and Charlie could see the deep grooves where the arcade machine had been. *She hurled herself at the console, and somehow, it was enough. It wobbled on its base, then fell, knocking Foxy to the ground and pinning him there. She ran, but he was too quick: he caught her by the leg and ripped his hook right through her; she screamed, staring down at the snapping, twisted metal jaws, and the burning, silver eyes.* She heard a noise, almost a whimper, and realized it was her. She clapped her hands over her mouth.

"I thought we were all going to die," Jessica whispered.

"Me too," Charlie said. They looked at each other for a moment, an eerie stillness settling over the sunlit wreckage.

"Hey, this place is probably going to fall on us soon, so . . ." Jessica broke the silence, gesturing to the leaning slabs of concrete surrounding them. Charlie crawled back out the way they'd come and stood up. Her knees were crawling with pins and needles. She rubbed them, then stomped the ground.

"I want to check the costume room, see if anything is left," Charlie said without expression.

"You mean to see if any*body* is left?" Jessica shook her head.

"I have to know." Charlie gave her jeans a final brush and started off toward it.

The room stuck out of the rubble, alone and intact. It was the place where the costumes had been kept, and where Carlton had briefly been held prisoner. Charlie cautiously poked her head inside, studying the physical details around her: the chipped paint on the wall, the carpet that someone had begun to tear up but left unfinished. *Don't think about last time. Don't think about what happened here.* She let her eyes adjust a moment longer, then went inside.

The room was empty. They did a cursory search, but everything had been removed—there was nothing left but walls, floor, and ceiling.

"Clay did say they had gotten rid of everything," Charlie said.

Jessica gave her a sharp look. "Clay? When?"

"He said he was going to, I mean," Charlie said hastily, covering the slip. "Last year."

They took a final look around. As they were leaving, Charlie spotted a glint of light from something in the corner. It was the plastic eyeball of some unknown animatronic mascot. Charlie was about to go to it, but stopped herself. "There's nothing here," she said.

Not waiting for Jessica, she headed back through the debris, looking down at her feet as she stepped over bricks and stones and shattered glass.

"Hey, wait," Jessica called after her hastily. "Pirate's Cove. Charlie! Look!" Charlie stopped. She watched Jessica as she climbed over a steel beam and stepped carefully over the remains of a fallen wall. In front of her, a curtain lay strewn across what had appeared to be a pile of rubble. Charlie followed her, and when she caught up she could see that the curtain concealed a gap in the ruins. The tops of a few glittering chairs peeked out from the stones. A row of broken stage lights lay across the top of the curtain, as though holding it in place.

"It looks pretty good, compared to the rest of the place," Jessica said. Charlie didn't answer. There was a dirty poster lying flat on the ground, depicting a cartoonish Foxy delivering pizzas to happy children.

"Jessica, look." Charlie pointed to the ground.

"Those look like claw marks," Jessica said after a moment. There were long scratches and scrapes running the length of the floor, and dark marks that looked like traces of blood. "It's like someone was being dragged." Jessica stood and followed the scratches. They led behind the curtain, away from the area where Pirate's Cove once stood.

"The stage," Jessica said.

When they moved the curtain aside, they found the stage had a small hatch at the back. "Storage," Charlie murmured. She pulled on it, but the hatch wouldn't open.

"There has to be a latch somewhere," Jessica said. She cleared away dirt and broken wood from the base of the stage, uncovering a deadbolt that went into the floor.

She pulled it up, releasing the door, which swung open like something was pushing against it.

A face lurched out of the darkness, two gaping eyes swinging forward. Jessica screamed and fell backward. Charlie recoiled. The masked face hung lifelessly from a rotted fur costume. An entire mascot suit was inside, crammed into a space much too small for it. Charlie stopped, her whole body numb with shock as she stared at the thing with a dread almost as old as she was. "The yellow rabbit," she whispered.

"It's Dave," Jessica gasped. Charlie took a deep breath, forcing herself back into the present.

"Come on, help me," she said She stepped forward and grabbed at the fabric, pulling on whatever she could reach.

"You're kidding. I'm not touching that thing."

"Jessica! Get over here!" Charlie commanded, and Jessica came reluctantly over.

"Ew, ew, ew." Jessica touched the suit, then recoiled. She gave Charlie a flat look and tried again, yanking her hands away as soon as she touched it. "Ew," she repeated quietly, then finally screwed her eyes shut and took hold of it.

Together they pulled, but nothing happened. "I think it's stuck," Jessica said. They shifted positions and finally heaved the mascot out of the cramped space. The fabric caught on stray nails and jagged wood, but Charlie kept pulling. At last the creature was out, splayed heavily on the ground.

"I definitely don't think Dave faked his own death," Charlie said.

"What if it's not him?" Jessica peered carefully into the face.

"It's him." Charlie looked at the dried blood soaked into the mascot's fingertips. "The spring locks might not have killed him right away, but this is where he died."

They could see Dave's body through the gaps in the costume, and the wide carved eyes of the mascot head showed through to his face. His skin was desiccated and shriveled. His eyes were wide open, his face expressionless and discolored. Charlie moved closer again. Her initial shock had passed, and now she was curious to see more of him. She probed carefully at first, in case some of the spring locks inside might still be waiting to snap, but it was clear that they'd already done their damage. The locks had been driven so deeply into his skin that the bases of each were flush against his neck; they looked like part of him.

Charlie studied the chest of the costume. There were large tears in the yellow fabric, which had gone green and pink with mold in patches. She grabbed hold of the sides and pulled the gap open as wide as she could. Jessica watched, fascinated, her hand over her mouth. Skewers of metal protruded through his entire body, dull and crusted with his blood. And there were more complex parts, twisted knots of gore with many layers of machinery that stuck out from his body. The suit's fabric was stiff with blood, too, yet the man didn't seem to have rotted, despite the year that had passed.

"It's like he's fused with the suit," Charlie said. She tugged at the mascot head, trying to pull it off, but gave up quickly. The gaping eyes stared up at her, behind which was the dead man's face. With the light directly on him, Dave's skin appeared sickly and discolored. Charlie felt a sudden rush of nausea. She pulled back from the corpse and looked up at Jessica.

"So now what?" Jessica said. "Did you want to give him a foot massage, too?" She abruptly turned her head away, gagging at her own joke.

"Listen, I have class in . . ." Charlie checked her watch. "About an hour. Did you still want to do some shopping?"

"Why can't I have normal friends?" Jessica groaned.

e are learning all the time. Hopefully at least some of you are learning right here in this class." Dr. Treadwell's students laughed nervously, but she continued over them; it had apparently not been a joke. "When we learn, our minds must decide where we will store that information. Unconsciously we determine what group of things it is most relevant to and connect it to that group. This is, of course, only the most rudimentary explanation. When computers do this, we call it an information tree . . ."

Charlie was only half listening; she knew this already and was taking her notes on autopilot. Since their expedition to Freddy's the day before, she hadn't been able to get the image of Dave's body out of her head: his torso and the gruesome lace of scars that had covered it. When he was alive, he'd shown them off to her, boasting of his survival. While he never told her what had happened, it must have been an accident. *He used to wear those suits all the time.* She could see him now, before all the murders, dressed as a yellow bunny and dancing merrily with a yellow bear . . . she shook her head suddenly, trying to get rid of the image.

"Are you okay?" Arty whispered. She nodded, waving him off.

*But the dead man in the field—that wasn't an accident. Someone forced him inside. But why?* Charlie restlessly tapped her fingers on her desk.

"That will be all for today." Dr. Treadwell set down her chalk and stalked off the auditorium stage with a purposeful step. Her teaching assistant, a flustered graduate student, scurried forward to collect the homework.

"Hey, do you have any time to go over some of this?" Arty asked Charlie as they gathered up their things. "I'm in a little bit over my head in this class."

Charlie paused. She'd promised to make up her first date with John, but she wasn't meeting him for over an hour. Now that she'd been to Freddy's, Charlie almost felt like she was on familiar ground, even if it was soaked in blood.

"I have some time now," she told Arty, who lit up.

"Great! Thanks so much, we can go work over at the library."

Charlie nodded. "Sure." She followed him across the campus, only half engaged as he explained his difficulties with the material.

They found a table, and Charlie opened her notebook to the pages she'd taken down today, pushing them across so Arty could see them.

"Actually, do you mind if I sit next to you?" he asked. "It's easier if we're both looking at the same thing, right?"

"Oh, yeah." Charlie pulled her notes back over as he came around and sat next to her, scooting his metal folding chair next to hers, just a few inches closer than she would have preferred. "So, where did you get lost?" she asked him.

"I was telling you on the way over," he said, with a hint of reproach in his voice, then cleared his throat. "I guess I understood the beginning of the lecture, when she was reviewing last week's material."

Charlie laughed. "So, basically you want to review everything new from today."

Arty nodded sheepishly. Charlie started from the beginning, pointing at her notes as she went. As she flipped through the pages, she noticed her own scribbles in the margins. Charlie leaned in closer, where harsh outlines of rectangles lined the bottom of the page. They were all colored in, like slabs of granite. She stared at them with a sensation of déjà vu: they were important. *I don't remember drawing that*, she thought uneasily. Then, *It's just doodles. Everybody doodles.*

She turned the page to the next segment of the lecture, and a strange alertness rose at the base of her neck, as if someone might be watching her. There were more doodles in the margins of this page, too, and the next one. All of them were rectangles. Some were large and some were small, some scribbled and some outlined in so solidly that her pen had wet the paper through and torn it. All of them were vertical, taller than they were wide. Charlie stared, tilting her head to see from different angles, until something pinged inside her.

*Sammy*, she thought, then, *Is this you? Does this mean something I don't understand?* Charlie glanced at Arty; he was staring at the paper, too. As she watched, he turned the page again. The next pages were the same. They were filled with neat, clear notes, but little rectangles were squashed into every available spot on the page: stuffed into the space between bullet points, crammed into the margins, and tucked away where lines came up short. Quickly, Arty flipped the page back. He looked up at her and smiled, but his eyes were wary.

"Why don't you try the first problem here?" Charlie suggested.

Arty bent over his worksheet, and Charlie stared down at her notebook. Her mind kept returning to her father's house, and the shapes she'd drawn only made the impulse stronger.

*I have to go back.*

"Are you okay?" Arty leaned in cautiously. Charlie stared down at her notebook. Now that she'd noticed the rectangles, they seemed more prominent than the notes; she could focus on nothing else. *I have to go back.*

Charlie shut the notebook and blinked hard. She ignored Arty's question, shoving the notebook into her backpack.

"I have to go," she said as she stood up.

"But I'm still stuck on the first problem," Arty said.

"I'm sorry, I really am!" she called over her shoulder as she hurried away. She bumped into two people as she passed the circulation desk but was too flustered to mutter an apology.

When she got to the door, she stopped, her guts twisting. *There's something wrong.* She hesitated, her hand suspended in the air, as if something was blocking her path. She finally took hold of the knob, and instantly her hand felt fused to it, as if by an electrical current. She couldn't turn it, and she couldn't let go. Suddenly, the knob moved on its own; someone was turning it from the other side. Charlie yanked her hand away and stepped back as a boy with an enormous backpack brushed past her. Snapping back into the moment, she slipped out before the door could swing shut again.

* * *

Charlie sped toward Hurricane, trying to calm herself as she drove. The windows were cracked open and wind was rushing in. She thought back to Treadwell's lecture earlier in the week. *At every moment, your senses are receiving far more information than they can process all at once.* Maybe that was Arty's problem in class. Charlie gazed at the mountains ahead, the open fields on either side. Watching them go by, she began to feel like some restraint had been loosened. She'd been spending too much time in her room or in class, and not enough out in the world. It was making her jumpy, exaggerating her natural awkwardness.

She rolled her window down farther, letting in the air. Over the field to her right a few birds were circling—no. Charlie stopped the car. *Something is wrong.* She got out, feeling ridiculous, but the last few days had put her on a hair trigger. The birds were too large.

She realized they were turkey vultures, and some of them were already on the ground, cautiously approaching what looked like a prone figure. *Could be anything.* She leaned against the car. *Probably just a dead animal.* After another moment, she turned back toward her car in frustration, but didn't get in.

*It's not a dead animal.*

She clenched her teeth and started to the spot the vultures were circling. As she got closer, the birds on the ground flapped their wings at the sight of her and soared away. Charlie dropped to her knees.

It was a woman. Charlie's eyes went first to her clothing. It was ripped up, just like the dead man Clay Burke had shown her.

She leaned over to check the woman's neck, though she knew what she would find. There were deep, ugly gouges from the spring locks of an animatronic suit. But before she could examine them closely, Charlie stopped, horrified.

*She looks just like me.* The woman's face was bruised and scratched, which obscured her features. Charlie shook her head. It was easier to imagine more of a resemblance than there really was. But her hair was brown and cut like Charlie's, and her face was the same round shape, with the same complexion. Her features were different, but not *that* different. Charlie stood up and took a deliberate step back from the woman, suddenly aware of how exposed she was in the open field. *Clay. I need to call Clay.* She looked up at the sky, wishing for a way to keep the vultures at bay, to protect the body. "I'm sorry," she whispered to the dead woman. "I'll be back."

Charlie started off to her car, then broke into a run, faster and faster across the field until she ran like something was right behind her. She got in and slammed the door, locking it as soon as she was inside.

Panting heavily, Charlie thought for a second. She was about halfway between Hurricane and the school, but there was a gas station just down the road where she could call Clay. With a last glance at the spot where the body lay, Charlie pulled out onto the road.

The gas station seemed to be empty. As she arrived, Charlie realized that she had never actually seen anyone fueling up here. *Is this a working gas station?* The place was old and shabby, which she had noticed in passing, but she'd never stopped to look around. The pumps looked functional, though not new, and there was no shelter above them. They simply stood on concrete blocks in the middle of a gravel driveway, exposed to the weather.

The little building attached to the station might have been painted white once, but the paint had worn down to reveal gray boards underneath. It seemed to be tilting slightly, slipping on its foundation. There was a window, but it was filthy, almost the same color gray as the building's outside walls. Charlie hesitated, then went to the door and knocked. A young man answered, about Charlie's age, wearing a St. John's College T-shirt and jeans.

"Yeah?" he said, giving her a blank stare.

"Are you—open?"

"Yeah." He was chewing gum and wiped his hands on a grimy rag. Charlie took a deep breath.

"I really need to use your phone." The boy opened the door and let her in. There was more space inside than she'd thought. In addition to the counter, there was a convenience store, though most of the shelves were empty and the line of refrigerators at the back was dark. The young man was looking at Charlie expectantly.

"Can I use your phone?" she asked again.

"Phone's for customers only," he said.

"Okay." Charlie glanced back at her car. "I'll get gas on the way out."

"Pump's broken; maybe you want something out of the cooler," he said, nodding at a grimy freezer with a sliding glass top and a faded patch of red paint that must once have been a logo. "We've got Popsicles."

"I don't want—fine, I'll take a Popsicle," Charlie said.

"Pick out any one you want."

Charlie leaned into the cooler.

Pale, glassy eyes stared back at her. Beneath them was a furry red muzzle, its mouth open and poised to snap.

Charlie screamed and hurtled backward, banging into the shelf behind her. Several cans fell off the shelf and rolled across the floor. The sound echoed in the empty space.

"What is that?" Charlie yelled, but the boy was cackling so hard he was gasping for breath. Peering back inside, Charlie realized that someone had placed a taxidermic animal in the cooler, maybe a coyote.

"That was great!" he finally managed to say. Charlie drew herself up, shaking with rage.

"I would like to use your phone now," she said coldly.

The boy beckoned her to the counter, all smiles, and handed her a rotary phone. "No long distance, though," he warned. Charlie turned her back and dialed, walking toward the cooler as the phone rang. She peered in the top, studying the stuffed canine from the high angle.

"Clay Burke here."

"Clay, it's Charlie. Listen, I need you to meet me. It's another . . ." She glanced at the young man behind the counter, who was watching her intently, not trying to hide the fact that he was listening. "It's like that thing you showed me before, with the cows."

"What? Charlie, where are you?"

"I'm at a gas station a few miles from you. Looks like someone painted an outhouse."

"Hey!" The boy behind the counter straightened for a moment, taking offense.

"Right, I know where you're at. I'll be right there." There was a click from the other end.

"Thanks for the phone," Charlie said begrudgingly, and left without waiting for a reply.

Charlie crouched again where the woman's body lay. She looked anxiously up the road for Clay's car, but it didn't appear. At least the vultures hadn't returned.

*I could just stay in the car until he gets here*, she thought. But Charlie didn't move from her spot. This woman had died horribly and been abandoned in a field. Now, at least, she didn't have to be alone.

The more Charlie looked at her, the harder it was to dismiss the resemblance. Charlie shivered, even though the sun was warm on her back. She was filling with a cold, crawling dread.

"Charlie?"

Charlie spun around to see Clay Burke, then sighed and shook her head.

"Sorry, I got here as fast as I could," he said lightly.

She smiled. "It's okay. I'm just on edge today. I think that's the third time I've jumped in the air when someone said my name."

Clay wasn't listening. His eyes were fixed on the body. He knelt carefully beside it, scrutinizing it. Charlie could almost see him filing every detail away. She held her breath, not wanting to disturb him.

"Did you touch the body?" he asked sharply, not looking away from the corpse.

"Yes," she admitted. "I checked to see if she had the same injuries as the man."

"Did she?"

"Yes. I think—I know she was killed the same way."

Clay nodded. Charlie watched as he got up and circled the woman, dropping down to look more closely at her head, and again at her feet. Finally, he turned his attention to Charlie again.

"How did you find her?" he asked.

"I saw birds—vultures—circling above the field. I went to check."

"Why did you go to check?" His eyes were hard, and Charlie felt a trickle of fear. Surely Clay didn't suspect her.

*Why wouldn't he?* she thought. *Who else would know how to use the spring locks? I bet he could come up with a million theories about me. Twisted girl avenges father's death. Acts out psychodrama. Film at eleven.* She took a deep breath, meeting Clay's eyes.

"I checked because of the body you showed me. It was in a field—I thought it might be another one." She kept her voice as steady as she could. Clay nodded, the steely expression slipping from his face, replaced by worry.

"Charlie, this girl looks like you," he said bluntly.

"Not that much like me."

"She could be your twin," Clay said.

"No," Charlie said, more harshly than she intended. "She looks nothing like my twin." Clay gave her a puzzled look, then comprehension dawned.

"I'm sorry. You had a twin, didn't you? Your brother."

"I barely remember him," she said softly, then swallowed. *All I do is remember him.* "I know she looks like me," she added weakly.

"We're right near a college town," Clay said. "She's a young white female with brown hair—you're not a rare type, Charlie. No offense."

"Do you think it's a coincidence?"

Clay didn't look at her. "There was another body found this morning," he said.

"Another girl?" Charlie drew closer.

"Yes, as a matter of fact. Been dead for a couple of days, probably killed two nights ago." Charlie looked down at him in alarm.

"Does that mean this is going to keep happening?"

"Unless you think we can stop it," he said. Charlie nodded.

"I can help," she said. She looked again at the woman's face. *She's nothing like me.* "Let me go to her house," she added abruptly, seized by a sudden impulse to prove it, to gather evidence that she and the victim were not the same.

"What? *Her* house?" Clay said, giving her a dubious look

"You asked me to help," Charlie said. "Let me help."

Clay didn't answer; instead he reached into the woman's pockets one by one, searching for her wallet. He had to move the body to do it, and she jerked a little as he did, like a ghastly puppet. Charlie waited, and at last he came back with her wallet. He handed Charlie her driver's license.

"Tracy Horton," she read. "She doesn't look like a Tracy."

"You got the address?" Clay scanned the road for police cars. Charlie read it quickly and handed the license back. "I'm going to give you twenty minutes before I radio this in," he told her. "Use it."

Tracy Horton had lived in a small house off a back road. Her nearest neighbors' houses were visible, but Charlie couldn't imagine they would have heard her scream. If she'd managed to scream at all. There was a small blue car in the driveway, but if Tracy had been taken from her home—since presumably she hadn't just been wandering through that field—it could easily have been hers.

Charlie pulled in behind the car and went to the front door. She knocked, wondering what she was going to do if someone answered. *I really should have thought this through.* She couldn't be the one to inform a parent, spouse, or sibling of the young woman's death. *Why did I assume she lived alone?*

No one answered. Charlie tried again, and when there was still no response, she tried the door. It was unlocked.

Charlie walked quietly through the house, not really sure what she was looking for. She glanced at her watch—ten of the twenty minutes had passed just driving here, and she had to assume that the police would get here faster than she did. *Why did I follow the speed limit the whole way here?* The living room and kitchen were clean, but they conveyed no information to her. Charlie didn't know what peach-painted walls said about a person, or the fact that there were three dining room chairs instead of four. There were two bedrooms. One had the sterile air of a guest room that was slowly being taken over by storage; the bed was made and clean towels were folded on the chest of drawers, but cardboard boxes filled a quarter of the room.

The other bedroom looked lived-in. The walls were green, the bedspread pale blue, and there were piles of clothing on the floor. Charlie stood in the doorway for a moment, and found she could not go inside. *I don't even know what I'm looking for.* This woman's life would be sifted through to the last grain by trained investigators. Her diary would be read, if she had one; her secrets would be revealed, if she had any. Charlie didn't need to be a part of it. She turned and walked quickly but quietly back to the front of the house, almost running down the front steps. Standing by the car, she checked her watch again. Six minutes before Clay called in the body.

Charlie went to the little blue car and peered inside. Like

the house, it was neat. There was dry-cleaning hanging in the back window, and a half-empty soda in the cup holder. She walked all around it, looking for something—mud in the tires, scratches in the paint, but there was nothing unusual. *Five minutes.*

She walked briskly through the unkempt grass that bordered the sides of the house. When she reached the backyard, she stopped dead. Before her were three huge holes in the ground, longer than they were wide. They looked like graves, but at a second glance they were too messy, their outlines poorly defined.

Charlie walked around them in a circle. They were lined up next to one another, and they were shallow, but the dirt at the bottom was loose. Charlie grabbed a stick off the ground and poked it into the middle hole: it went in almost a foot before it was stopped by denser soil. The dirt dug out of them was strewn messily all around. Whoever dug the holes had carelessly tossed it everywhere, not bothering to pile it up.

*Two minutes.*

Charlie hesitated for another moment, then lowered herself into the middle hole. Her feet sunk into the loose dirt and she fought to steady herself, catching her balance. It wasn't too deep. The walls came up to her waist. She knelt and put her palm against the wall of the grave—*the hole*, she reminded herself. The dirt was loose here, too, and the wall was rough.

Something had been hidden there, under the ground. *The air is growing thin. I am running out of oxygen, and I will die like this, alone, in the dark.* Charlie's throat seized; she felt as if she couldn't breathe. She climbed out of the hole and up onto the grass of Tracy Horton's backyard. Charlie took a deep breath, focusing all her attention on pushing away the panic. When she was free of it, she checked her watch.

*Minus one minute. He's already called them.* But something kept her there, something familiar. *The loose dirt.* Charlie's mind raced. *Something climbed out of these.*

From a distance, a siren was wailing; it would be here in no time. Charlie hurried to her car and pulled out of the driveway, taking the first corner without caring where it would take her. The holes stayed in her mind, the image like a stain.

harlie slowed her car. With half the cops in Hurricane converging on the area, now was not the time to be stopped for speeding. She was grubby with dirt from the dead woman's backyard, and had a nagging feeling there was something she was forgetting about.

*John*, she realized. She was supposed to meet him—she checked the clock on the dashboard—almost two hours ago. Her heart sank. *He'll think I stood him up. No, he'll think I'm dead*, she amended. Given the perilous history of their relationship, he'd probably think the second was more likely.

When she got to the restaurant where they had planned to meet, a small Italian place across town, Charlie ran in from the parking lot at full speed. She skidded to a stop in front of the teenage hostess, who greeted her with a flustered look.

"Can I help you?" she asked Charlie, taking a step back.

Charlie caught a glimpse of herself in the mirror behind the hostess counter. There were streaks of dirt on her face and clothes; she hadn't thought to clean up first. She quickly wiped her cheeks with her hands before answering the girl.

"I'm supposed to be meeting someone. A tall guy, brown hair. It's kind of . . ." She gestured vaguely at the top of her head, attempting to indicate the habitual chaos of John's hair, but the hostess looked at her blankly. Charlie bit her lip in frustration. *He must have left. Of course he left. You're two hours late.*

"Charlie?" A voice rang out. *John.*

"You're still here?" she cried, too loud for the quiet restaurant, as he appeared behind the hostess, looking profoundly relieved.

"I figured I might as well eat while I'm here." He swallowed what was in his mouth and laughed. "Are you okay? I thought you might . . . not be coming."

"I'm fine. Where are you sitting? Or are you still sitting? Well, I mean, you're obviously not sitting. You're standing. But I mean before you were standing, where were you sitting?" Charlie ran her fingers into her hair and clenched her fists against her scalp, trying to reassemble her thoughts. She mumbled an apology to the room, not sure who it was for.

John glanced around nervously, then gestured toward a table near the kitchen. There was a mostly empty plate with a half-eaten breadstick resting on it, a cup of coffee, and a second place setting, untouched.

They sat down and he looked at her appraisingly. Then John leaned across the table and asked in a low voice, "Charlie, what happened?"

"You wouldn't believe me if I told you?" she said lightly.

His face remained concerned. "You're filthy. Did you fall down in the parking lot?"

"Yes," Charlie said. "I fell in the parking lot and rolled down a hill and into a Dumpster, then fell out of the Dumpster and tripped on the way in. Happy? Stop looking at me like that."

"Like what?"

"Like you have the right to disapprove of me." John pulled back in his chair, his eyes wide. He blinked hard, and Charlie sighed.

"John, I'm sorry. I'll tell you everything. I just need some time; some time to collect my thoughts and to clean up." She laughed, an exhausted, shaken sound, then buried her face in her hands.

John leaned back and signaled for the waitress to bring the check. Breathing heavily, Charlie looked around the restaurant. It was almost empty. The hostess and the only other waitress were talking together near the door, with no apparent interest in anything their customers were doing. There was a family of four by the front window, the children just barely out of toddlerhood. One kept sliding out of his chair and onto the floor every time his mother turned her attention away. The other, a girl, was happily drawing on the tablecloth with markers. No one seemed to care what was going on. But the emptiness made Charlie feel exposed.

"I'm going to go clean up," she said. "Bathroom?" John pointed.

Charlie got up and left the table just as the waitress arrived to deliver his ticket. There was a pay phone in the hallway, and Charlie stopped at it, wavering. She craned her neck to see if John was watching, but from where she stood, she could only see a tiny corner of their table. Quickly, she called Clay Burke's office.

To her surprise, he answered. "You saw her backyard," he said. It wasn't a question.

"Can you give me the other addresses?" Charlie asked. "There could be a pattern—something."

"There sure could," he said drily. "That's why I raced back to the station instead of sticking around to measure the holes. You have a pen?"

"Hang on." The hostess was briefly absent from her station, and Charlie dropped the phone, letting it swing on its metal cord as she hurried to the podium and snatched a pen and a take-out menu. She rushed back. "Clay? Go ahead." He recited names and addresses, and she scribbled them dutifully in the margins of the menu. "Thanks," she said when he was done, and hung up without waiting for him to respond. She folded the menu and slipped it into her back pocket.

In the bathroom, Charlie washed off as much of the dirt as she could. She couldn't clean her clothing, but at least her face was scrubbed, and her hair was rearranged a little more neatly.

As she moved to exit the bathroom, an image flashed unbidden through her thoughts. It was the face of the dead woman.

*She could be your twin*, she heard Clay say, in his low, authoritative voice.

Charlie shook her head. *It's a coincidence. He's right. How many brown-haired, college-aged women are there around here? The first victim was a man. It doesn't mean anything.* She grabbed the doorknob to leave, but froze. It was just like in the library. Charlie released the knob and it spun slowly back into position, releasing a horrible creak as it moved.

*The costumes had been disturbed, and the creaking noise was so faint and careful she scarcely even heard it. Charlie looked up from her game: there was a figure in the door.*

Charlie glanced wildly around the room, pulling herself back to the present. With a swell of panic, Charlie pulled on the bathroom door, but it had somehow sealed shut. She mouthed words, but no sound came out:

*I know you're there. I'm trying to get to you.*

"I have to get inside!" she screamed. The door burst open, and Charlie fell into John's arms.

"Charlie!"

She collapsed to her knees. Charlie looked up to see the scattered handful of customers all staring at her. John glanced into the bathroom behind her, then quickly turned his attention back to Charlie, helping her to her feet.

"I'm okay. I'm fine." She shook loose of his hands. "I'm fine. The door was stuck. I felt hot." Charlie fanned at her face, trying to make a sensible story of it. "Come on, let's get to the car." He tried to take her arm again but she shook free. "I'm fine!" She dug her keys out of her pocket and walked straight for the door, not waiting for him. An old woman was openly staring at Charlie, her fork suspended in the air. Charlie returned her stare. "Food poisoning," Charlie said plainly. The woman's face went pale, and Charlie walked out the door.

When they got out to her car, John sat down in the passenger's seat and looked at Charlie expectantly. "You're sure you're okay?"

"It's been a rough day, that's all. I'm sorry."

"What happened?"

*Tell him what happened*, Charlie thought.

"I want to go to my dad's—my old house," she said instead, surprising herself. *Be honest*, her inner voice said harshly. *You know what kind of creature is doing this, and you know who built it. Stay focused.*

"Right," he said, his voice softening. "You haven't seen it since the storm." She nodded. *He thinks I want to see the damage.* She'd forgotten about the storm until now, but the sudden kindness in John's voice made her nervous. *Is there anything left?* She imagined the house razed to the ground and felt a sudden *wrongness*, like a part of her had been ripped away. She'd never thought of the house as anything but a house, but now, as she drove toward what was left of it, she felt a painful knot in her stomach. It was where all her clearest memories of her father were kept: his rough hands building her toys, showing her his new creations in his workshop, and holding her close when she was afraid. They'd lived there together, just the two of them, and it was the place where he had finally died. Charlie felt as if the joy, the sorrow, the love, and the anguish of their two lifetimes had poured off into the very bones of the old house. The idea of it being wrecked by a storm was an utter violation.

She shook her head and gripped the wheel tighter, suddenly aware of how angry she was. Her love of the house, even of her father, could never be simple. They had both betrayed her. But now there was a new monster out there. She clenched her jaw, trying to fight the tears that welled up in her eyes. *Dad, what did you do?*

As soon as they were out of the town center, Charlie sped up. Clay would be tied up dealing with the newest victim for a while, but eventually he would think to come to her father's house as well. She could only hope that she'd connected the dots first. *You're on the same side.* Charlie put a hand to her head and rubbed her temple. The impulse to guard her father's reputation from what was coming was visceral, but it was also nonsensical.

Less than a mile from the house they passed a construction site. It was set back too far from the road for Charlie to see what it was, though it looked abandoned at the moment.

"I did a little work over there when I first got here," John said. "Some huge demolition project." He laughed. "You have some weird stuff out here; you wouldn't know by looking at it." He studied the countryside for a moment.

"Isn't that the truth," Charlie said, not sure if there was something else she was supposed to say. She was still trying to calm herself. Finally, they came to her driveway. She pulled in with her eyes on the gravel, the house only a dark smudge in her peripheral vision. The last time Charlie had been here she'd run in and out without pausing to look at anything. All she'd wanted was Theodore, and she had grabbed him and gone. Now she regretted her haste, wishing for some final mental image. *You're not here to say good-bye.* She turned the car off, steeled herself, and looked up.

The house was surrounded by trees, and at least three of them had fallen, striking the roof directly. One had landed squarely on the front corner, crushing the walls beneath its weight. Charlie could see through the broken beams and crumbled drywall, into the living room. Inside there was only debris.

The front door was intact, though the steps to it were splintered and split. They looked as if they'd give way as soon as they bore weight. Charlie got out of the car and headed toward them.

"What are you doing?" John's voice was alarmed. Charlie ignored him. She heard his door slam, and he caught her arm, wrenching her back.

"What?" she snapped.

"Charlie, look at this place. That house is going to fall over any day now."

"It's not going to fall," she said flatly, but she did gaze up again. The house seemed to be listing to the side, though it must have been an illusion; surely the foundation itself couldn't have sunk. "I'll be out before I get killed, I promise," she said more gently, and he nodded.

"Go slow," he said.

They carefully climbed the steps to the porch, staying close to the sides, but the wood was sturdier than it looked. They could have taken three steps to the right and walked through the open wall, but Charlie took out her key and unlocked the door as John waited patiently, letting her go through the unnecessary ritual.

Inside, she paused at the foot of the stairs to the second floor. The holes in the ceiling were beaming down shafts of thin sunlight, dimming as the sun began to wane. It made the place feel almost like some sort of shrine. Charlie tore her eyes away from the holes and started upstairs to her bedroom.

As with the outdoor steps, she kept to the side, holding on to the bannister. The water damage was visible everywhere. There were dark stains and soft spots in the wood. Charlie reached out to touch a place where the paint had bubbled out from the wall, leaving a pocket of air.

Suddenly a cracking sound came from behind her and she spun around. John grabbed the bannister, struggling to hold on as the stair gave way under him. Charlie reached out, but John braced himself unsteadily. He hissed and gritted his teeth.

"My foot's stuck," he said, nodding down. Charlie saw that his foot had gone clear through the wood, and now the jagged edges dug into his ankle.

"Okay, hold on," Charlie said. She crouched down until she could reach him on the step below her, though the awkward angle made it hard to maintain her balance. The wood was only rotting in some places, while in others it was still intact. She grabbed the smaller pieces and pulled them cautiously back from John's foot, her hands growing raw with the rough and splintered surface.

"I think I've got it," John said finally, flexing his ankle.

She looked up and grinned. "And you thought *I* was going to get myself killed."

John gave her a weak smile. "How about we both make it out alive?"

"Right."

They made their way up the rest of the stairs much more slowly, each of them testing their weight before they took the next step. "Careful," John warned as Charlie reached the top.

"We won't be here long," Charlie said. She was much more aware of the danger now. The house's instability grew more obvious with each step they took; the very foundation seemed to wobble from side to side as they moved.

Her old bedroom was on the undamaged side of the house—or the side not struck by trees, at least. Charlie stopped in the doorway, and John came up behind her. The floor was strewn with glass. One window had been broken by something, and the shattered glass had blown into the room.

She took a deep breath, and it was then that she saw Stanley. The animatronic unicorn had once run on a track around her bedroom. Now he was lying on his side. Charlie went to him and sat down, pulling his head into her lap and patting his rusty cheek. He looked as if he'd been torn violently from his track. His legs were twisted, his hooves missing chunks. When she looked around the room she saw the missing pieces, still attached to the grooves in the floor.

"Stanley has seen better days." John smiled ruefully.

"Yeah," Charlie said absently, as she set the toy's head back on the floor. "John, can you turn that wheel?" She pointed to a crank soldered together at the foot of her bed. He complied, crossing the floor agonizingly slowly. Charlie bit back her impatience. He turned the crank and she waited for the littlest closet door to open, but nothing happened. John looked at Charlie expectantly.

She stood and went to the wall where the three closets stood, closed and apparently untouched by the weather. Even the paint was bright and immaculate. Charlie hesitated, feeling as if she might be disturbing something that no longer belonged to her, then forced the smallest door open.

Ella was there, the doll who had been the same size as Charlie when she was much younger. She, like Stanley, had once run around on a track, and she seemed to still be attached to it. She was entirely undamaged. Her dress was clean, and the tray she held in front of her was firm in her motionless hands. Her wide eyes had been gazing into the darkness since the last time Charlie saw her.

"Hi, Ella," Charlie said softly. "I don't suppose you can

tell me what I'm looking for?" She scanned over the doll quickly and brushed at her dress. "You just want to stay in here from now on?" Charlie studied the tiny frame of the door. "I don't blame you." She closed the closet door again without saying good-bye.

"So," she said, turning back to John. He seemed lost in thought, staring at something in his hand.

"What is that?" Charlie asked.

"A photo of you, when you were no bigger than her." John smiled and gestured toward Ella's door, then handed the picture to Charlie.

It looked like a school photo. A short, chubby girl gave a toothy grin for the camera—minus one tooth. Charlie smiled back at her. "I don't remember this."

"That doll is a little creepy, standing in the closet," John said. "I'm a bit on edge, I won't lie."

"Waiting for a tea party," Charlie said acerbically. "How sinister." She started to leave the room, but as her hand touched the doorframe, she paused. *Doors.* She stepped back through into her bedroom, and looked for a long moment at each of the rectangular closet doors. "John," she whispered.

"What?" John looked up, trying to follow Charlie's gaze.

"Doors," Charlie whispered. She took several long steps back to study the whole wall at once. The scribbles all over her notebooks had been shaped like dozens—hundreds—of rectangles. She drew them without thinking, as if they were pushing up through her mind, trying to break out of her subconscious. Now they had. "They're doors," she repeated.

"Yes. Yes, I see." John tilted his head curiously. "Are you okay?"

"Yes, I'm fine. I mean, I'm not sure." She ran her eyes over the wall of closets again. *Doors. But not* these *doors.*

"Come on, let's go look at the workshop," John said. "Maybe we can find something else there."

"Right." She gave a pained smile. She looked back once more at the three closets that sat in silence.

John nodded, and they went cautiously back down the stairs, testing each step before they took it. Outside, they stopped by the car. The workshop was invisible from the driveway, hidden behind the house. The backyard had once been surrounded by trees, a small wood that acted as a fence.

"Don't go into the woods, Charlie," she said, then smiled at John. "That's what he always told me, like something out of a fairy tale." They walked a bit farther, twigs snapping under their feet. "But the woods were only ten feet deep," she said, still peering into the trees as though something might leap out. As a child these trees had seemed impenetrable, a forest she might be lost in forever, if she dared to wander in. She started toward what remained of them, then stopped dead when she saw where some of the fallen trees had landed.

Her father's workshop had been crushed. A massive trunk

had hit the workshop's roof dead center, and others had come with it on all sides. The wall closest to the house was still standing, but it was bowed beneath the sagging roof.

It had been a garage when they moved in, and then it had become her father's world: a place of light and shadow that smelled of hot metal and burnt plastic. Charlie peered down at the rotting wood and broken glass with careful attention, looking for something she might otherwise miss.

"We're definitely not going in there," John said.

But Charlie was already lifting a piece of sheet metal that had once belonged to the roof. She threw it violently to the side, and it hit the ground with a resounding clang. John startled and kept his distance as Charlie continued to throw things. "What are you—what are *we* looking for?"

Charlie wrestled a toy from under the debris and threw it carelessly to the ground behind her, continuing to lift sheets of metal and toss them aside. "Charlie," John whispered, picking up the delicate toy and cradling it. "He must have made this for you."

Charlie ignored him. "There's got to be something else in here." She fought her way deeper into the workshop, toppling a wooden beam out of her way. Her hand slipped on the wood, and she realized it was wet; her arm was bleeding. She wiped her hand on her jeans. From the corner of her eye, she saw John set the toy carefully on the ground and follow her in.

Amazingly, there were still shelves and tables standing upright, with tools and shreds of fabric where her father had last set them. Charlie glanced at them for a passing moment, then swept her arm across the table nearest her, knocking everything to the ground. She didn't pause to see what had fallen before moving to the shelves. She began picking things off the nearest shelf one item at a time, inspecting them and throwing them to the ground. When the shelf was empty, she grabbed the board itself with both hands, wrenching at it violently, trying to pull it from the wall. When it didn't come loose, she began pounding at it with her fists.

"Stop!" John ran to her and grabbed her hands, pinning them to her sides.

"There has to be something here!" she screamed. "I'm supposed to be *here*, but I don't know what it is that I'm supposed to find."

"What are you talking about? There's a lot left. Look at this stuff!" He held the toy up to her again.

"This isn't about the storm, John. It's not about happy memories, or closure, or whatever you think I need. This is about monsters. They're out there, and they're killing people. And you and I both know that there is only one place they could have come from: here."

"You don't know that," John began. Charlie looked at him with a stony rage, stopping him short.

"I'm surrounded by monsters, and murder, and death, and spirits." At the last word her fury ebbed, and she turned away from John, surveying the workshop. She wasn't sure now what damage the storm had done, and what had been her. "All I can think about is Sammy. I *feel* him. Right now, I can feel him in this place, but he's—cut off. It doesn't even make sense. He died before my father and I moved here. But I know I'm here for a reason. There's something that I'm supposed to find. It's all connected, but I don't know how. Maybe something to do with the doors . . . I don't know."

"Hey, okay. We'll find it together." John reached out for her. Charlie's strength gave way and she let him pull her close, pressing her face into his shirt. "I know it's hard to see everything torn apart like this," he said. Charlie's anger drained away, fading into exhaustion. She rested her head on John's shoulder, wishing she could stay like this just a little longer.

"Charlie," John said with alarm, and Charlie came back to attention. He was looking over her shoulder, in the direction of the house.

The entire back face of the house had been torn open, as if someone had taken a massive hammer to it; inside was only dark.

"That's right under your room, isn't it? We could have fallen through the floor," John said.

"That should be the living room," Charlie said, wiping her sleeve across her face.

"Yeah, but it's not." John looked at her expectantly.

"That's not even a part of the house," she said. A sudden spark of hope revived inside her. Something was out of place. That meant there was something to find.

Charlie approached the chasm, and John didn't try to stop her as she climbed up several large slabs of broken concrete. John stayed a step behind her, close enough to catch her if she slipped. Charlie turned to him before entering. "Thank you," she said. John nodded.

"I've never seen this room before," Charlie whispered as she crept into the hollow space. The walls were made of dark concrete, and the room was small and windowless, a box jammed into the house and sealed away between the rooms. There were no decorations, and nothing to indicate what was stored here. Just a dirt floor and three large holes, deep and oblong like graves.

"Those don't look like storm damage," John said.

"They're not." Charlie went up to the edge of the nearest hole, looking down.

"Were you . . . expecting to find these?"

These holes were deeper than the ones she'd found at Tracy Horton's house. Perhaps it was the shadowy room, but these looked like real graves. They were a foot or so deeper than the ones she'd found before and partially filled with loose dirt.

John was standing patiently behind her, waiting for her answer.

"I've seen them before," she admitted. "Behind the house of a dead woman."

"What are you talking about?"

Charlie sighed. "There was another body. I found her today, in a field. I called Clay, and then I went to her house while he waited for the rest of the cops to show up. There were holes like this in her backyard."

"That's what you wouldn't tell me? Another body?" John sounded hurt, but his wounded expression lasted only seconds before it cleared. He started scanning the room again, his eyes intent on the walls and floor.

*That, and the fact that she looked like me*, Charlie thought.

"So what do you think the holes are?" he asked finally.

Charlie barely heard him. Her gaze had fixed on the blank concrete wall on the far side of the room. It was empty, whitewashed then left to turn gray with dust and mildew. But something drew her to it. Leaving John alone by the open graves, Charlie walked slowly to it, drawn there by a sense of sudden recognition. It was like she'd just remembered a word that had been on the tip of her tongue for days.

She hesitated, holding her hands out flat, less than an inch from the wall, uncertain what was holding her back. She steeled herself and placed her palms against the wall. It was cold. She felt a slight shock of surprise, as though she'd expected to feel warmth from the other side. John was speaking, but to her it was only murmurs in the distance. She turned her head and delicately placed her ear against the surface, closing her eyes. *Movement?*

"Hey!" John's voice broke her focus, waking her as if from a trance. "Over here!"

She turned. John was bent over the mound of dirt next to the farthest grave. Charlie started toward him, but he put up a hand to stop her.

"No, come around the other way."

She carefully made her way around the perimeter of the little room until she was beside him. At first she couldn't tell what he was trying to show her. Something was almost visible, veiled in a thin layer of dirt, so that it blended into the ground as if deliberately camouflaged.

But eventually she saw it—rusted metal, and the glint of a staring, plastic eye. She glanced at John, who just looked back at her. This was her territory now. Carefully, Charlie poked the mostly buried head of the thing with the toe of her sneaker, then yanked her foot back. The thing didn't move.

"What the heck is this?" John asked, glancing around the room. "And why is it in here?"

"I've never seen this before," Charlie said. She knelt, curiosity overtaking her fear, then used her hand to scrape aside some of the dirt, clearing off a little more of the creature's face. Behind her, John drew a sharp breath. Charlie just stared down. The creature had no fur, and its face was smooth. It had a short muzzle and oval ears sticking out from the sides of the head. It had the general appearance of an animal's head, though much larger than the animatronic animals from Freddy's. Charlie couldn't guess what kind of animal it was supposed to be. Running down the center of its face was a long, straight split, exposing wires and a line of metal frame. A thick plastic material was stuck to the face in large patches. Maybe it had been encased in it at some point.

"Do you recognize it?" John asked quietly.

Charlie shook her head. "No," she managed to say after a moment. "Something's wrong with it." She brushed back more dirt and found it came away easily. The thing had only been partially buried beneath the floor; that, or it had almost escaped. She started digging her hands into the dirt, trying to pry it out of what remained of its grave.

"You've got to be kidding me." John groaned as he knelt to help, getting his hands around any part of it he could. In one concentrated effort, they heaved it upward, managing to pull most of the torso out of the dirt. They let it drop, then fell back on the ground to study it while they caught their breath.

Like the face, the body was smoother than the animatronics that Charlie was used to. It had no fur, and no tail or other animal appendages. It was too large for a human being to wear, probably eight feet tall when standing. Still, Charlie couldn't shake the feeling that she recognized this creature. *Foxy.*

There was something sick about the creature, a weirdness that gripped her at the most basic, primal level and cried, *This is wrong.* Charlie closed her eyes for a moment. Her skin felt strange, like something was crawling all over it. *It's just an oversized doll.* She took a deep, deliberate breath, opened her eyes, and inched forward to examine the thing.

As her hand touched the creature, a wave of nausea hit her, but it lasted only a split second. She continued. She turned the head to the side, its joints resisting. The left side of its skull had been crushed. Charlie could see that the insides were broken, half the wires torn out. Just behind the eye, on the side that had been completely buried, a piece of the casing was missing. She could see a mass of plastic with a tangle of wires running in and out of it. Something had melted one of the circuit boards. Moving slowly down the body, Charlie examined its joints: one arm seemed fine, but on the other both the shoulder and elbow joints had been bent out of shape. Charlie looked up at John, who was watching her with a worried expression.

"Anything familiar?"

"I don't recognize it. It's not something my dad ever showed me," Charlie said.

"Maybe we should put it back in the ground and get out of here. This feels like it was a mistake."

"But on the inside . . ." Charlie ignored him. "The hardware, the joints—it's older technology. Maybe he made them earlier? I don't know."

"How can you tell?"

"I recognize some of this as my dad's work." She frowned and pointed at the creature's head. "But then a lot of it is foreign to me. Someone else may have had a hand in it. I'm not sure if my dad made it or not, but I have a feeling he's the one who buried it."

"I can't imagine it was designed to be onstage. It's hideous." John was noticeably nervous, and now he placed his hand on Charlie's arm. "Let's get out of here. This place gives me the creeps."

"'Gives me the creeps,'" Charlie said lightly. "Who says that? I'm going to try and get it the rest of the way out. I just want to see . . ." She moved away from John's touch, leaning down to dig again by the creature's buried torso.

"Charlie!" John cried, just as a metal shriek rang out.

The animatronic's arms lifted, and its chest opened like an iron gate. Its metal pieces slid out of place to reveal a dark, gaping pit where sharp spikes and spring locks were just barely visible. It was a trap waiting to be triggered. Yet, disorientingly, something else about it had transformed at the same time. Its artificial skin took on a luminescence, and its movements were fluid and sure. Its casing suddenly appeared to have skin and fur, though they were blurry, flickering like a trick of the light.

Charlie jumped backward, but it was too late: the thing had her in its grip and lifted her high into the air. It was pulling her toward it. She beat against its bent and damaged arm, but the other arm steadily forced her closer to the chest cavity. John stumbled backward for a moment, bending forward with one hand over his mouth, as if struck by a wave of nausea.

Charlie struggled to break free, but her strength was no match for the creature. Out of the corner of her eye she could see John lunging toward the beast. He grabbed its head, wrenching at it, trying to force it sideways. Beneath Charlie, the animatronic began to spasm, a stuttering, uncontrolled movement. The creature's grip came loose and its arms swung around wildly. Charlie struggled to get to her feet, but her legs slid in the dirt. The creature seized her again, and its cold fingers drew her closer.

Charlie braced her shoe against the ground, trying to give herself leverage, but she was being pulled down by an overwhelming force. Suddenly she was face-to-face with the beast, her shoulder already inside its chest cavity. The thing pressed her closer, then suddenly it jerked and released her. She rolled away and heard the sound of snapping spring locks. The creature convulsed on the ground in front of her, headless. Charlie looked at John. He was holding the thing's head in his hands, his eyes wide with shock. He dropped it and kicked it across the floor.

"Are you okay?" John scrambled to her. Charlie nodded, staring at the broken animatronic head. It still seemed alive. Its fur bristled and skin moved, as if there were muscle and sinew underneath.

"What the heck just happened?"

John raised both hands in surrender.

Charlie carefully picked up the massive head and flipped it upside down, peering into it through the base where John had torn it off the neck.

"Ugh." John bent over, his hands on his knees. His face was pale. He stifled a retching sound.

Charlie started toward him, surprised. "What's wrong with you? You've seen worse than this."

"No, it's not that. I don't know what it is." He straightened, then stumbled toward the wall, bracing himself. "It's like there's some horrible smell in the air, but without the smell."

Charlie held her finger to her ear, listening. There was a tone in the air, so high-pitched and quiet it was almost imperceptible. "I think something is still . . . on," she said.

She set the giant head on the ground. John had a hand to his ear, listening, but when she looked at him he shook his head.

"I can't hear anything."

Charlie returned to the body of the creature and peered into its gaping chest cavity. "Are you okay?" she asked half-heartedly, not taking her eyes off the robot.

"Yeah, I feel better back here." He heaved and she turned. John's face was strained, and his arm was tight across his stomach. "I think it's passing," he said, then doubled over, barely getting out the last syllable.

"This thing." Charlie clenched her teeth and jerked her weight back and forth, trying to wrestle something loose from inside the chest cavity.

"Charlie get away from it!" John took a step toward her, then swayed back, as if he were tethered to the wall. "There is something *really* wrong with that thing."

"Now *this* I've seen before," Charlie said as she pulled the object out at last. It was a flat disc, about the size of a half-dollar coin. She held it up to her ear. "Wow, that's really high-pitched. I can barely hear it. The sound is why you feel sick."

Charlie wedged her fingernail into a small groove on the side of the object and flipped a thin switch. John took several deep breaths, then stood upright again slowly, testing himself. He looked at Charlie. "It stopped," she said.

"Charlie," John whispered, nodding toward the beast on the ground. Charlie looked, and a shock went through her.

The illusion of fur and flesh was gone. It was nothing more than a broken robot with unfinished features.

John picked up the head once again, turning it to face them. "That thing, it did something," John said, nodding toward the device in Charlie's hands. "Turn it back on." He lifted the creature's head a bit higher and stared into its lifeless round eyes.

*Are you sure that's a good idea?* she was about to say, but curiosity got the better of her. John could handle a little more nausea. She slipped her nail back into the groove and flipped the tiny switch. Before their eyes, the fractured and worn face became fluid and smooth, warping into something lifelike. John dropped the head and jumped backward.

"It's alive!"

"No, it's not," Charlie whispered, flipping the switch off again. She cradled the strange device in her hands, gazing down at it, mesmerized. "I want to know more about this. We have to get back to the dorm." She got to her feet. "I've seen something like this. When I came back here for Theodore, I grabbed a bunch of stuff and put it in a box to study later. I know I saw something like this."

For a long moment, John said nothing. Charlie felt a surge of shame. He was looking at her the way Jessica had, the way he had when he first saw her experiment. The little disc in Charlie's palm felt suddenly like the most vital thing in the world. She closed her hand on it.

"Okay, then," John said plainly. "Let's go." His tone was calm, and it caught Charlie off guard. John was being deliberately agreeable. She wasn't sure exactly why, but it was reassuring nonetheless.

"Okay." Charlie smiled.

# CHAPTER SEVEN

hen they got back to the college, Charlie headed for the dorm.

"Hey, slow down!" John struggled to catch up.

"You have that disc?"

"Of course." He patted his pocket.

"I know I've seen something like this before," she said. "I'll show you." She glanced at John as she let him into the room she shared with Jessica, but his face remained impassive. He'd already seen the mess. But John didn't look in the direction of Charlie's desk and the covered faces.

"You can clear off the chair," Charlie said as she shoved a stack of books out of the way. She crawled under the bed and emerged a moment later with a large cardboard box. John was standing beside the chair, looking perplexed. "I said you can clear it off," she said.

He laughed. "Clear it off to where?"

"Right." The chair had a stack of books on the seat, and a stack of T-shirts draped over the back. Charlie grabbed the shirts and threw them onto the bed. She set the box on the bed and settled herself cross-legged behind it, so that John would be able to look through it, too.

"So what is all of this?" He leaned slowly over the box as Charlie rummaged through it, pulling parts out one by one and setting them in a straight line on the bed.

"Stuff from my dad's house: electronics, mechanical parts. Things from the animatronics, from his work." She glanced at him nervously. "I know I said that I just went back for Theodore, and I did. But I may have grabbed a few things on the way out. I wanted to learn, and these classes—John, you know some of the tech my father was working with was ancient. It's practically ridiculous now. But he was making it up as he went along; he thought of stuff that's still unique, that no one else has thought of yet. I wanted all of it. I wanted to understand it. So, I went back to get what I could."

"You stripped the house for parts, I get it." John laughed as he picked up Theodore's severed paw and considered it for a moment. "Even your favorite toy? Don't you think that's a little . . . heartless?"

"Is it?" Charlie picked up a piece from the box, a metal

joint, and weighed it in her hands. "I took Theodore apart because I wanted to understand him, John. Isn't that the most loving thing there is?"

"Maybe I should reconsider this whole dating thing," John said, wide-eyed.

"He was important to me because my father made him for me, not because he was stitched up to look like a rabbit." She discarded the joint, setting it next to her on the bed. She turned her attention to the box, picking up pieces one by one and setting them in a row. She was sure she'd recognize what she needed when she saw.it.

Charlie looked at circuitry and wires, metal joints and plastic casings, examining each piece carefully. Something would cry out to her, just like the animatronic beast had done, with that raw sense of *wrongness*. But after a while her neck grew sore from bending over the box. Her eyes were beginning to glaze over. She discarded the piece of metal tubing in her hand, tossing it onto the growing pile on her bed. At the clanking sound, John looked up.

"Where do you even sleep?" he asked, gesturing not only to the growing pile of electronic and mechanical parts, but to the clothing and books, and the smaller piles of electronic and mechanical parts.

Charlie shrugged. "There's always room for me," she said mildly. "Even if just barely."

"Yeah, but what about when you're married?" John's face

flushed before he'd even finished the sentence. Charlie looked up at him, one eyebrow hinged slightly higher than the other. "Someday," John said hastily. "To someone. Else." His face grew grimmer. Charlie felt her eyebrow lift higher of its own volition. "So, what are we looking for again?" John furrowed his brow and scooted his chair closer to the bed, peering into the box.

"This." Spotting a glimmer in the pile, Charlie took hold of a small disc and carefully placed it in the palm of her hand. She held it out so John could see. It looked just like the metallic disc they'd found in the body of the animatronic, but one side of it had been damaged, revealing a curious metal framework inside. Several wires extended, connecting to a black keypad not much larger than the disc itself.

"Funny." Charlie chuckled to herself.

"What?"

"The last time I held this, I was more interested in the keypad." She smiled. "This part is a common diagnostic tool. Someone must have been testing it."

"Or trying to find out what it was," John added. "That thing doesn't look like anything else in the box; just like that monster we found doesn't look like anything your dad made. I mean, it *kind of* looked like Foxy, but not the one your dad made. This was some sort of twisted version of Foxy."

She pulled a heavy metal joint from the box. "This doesn't belong here, either."

"What's wrong with it?"

"It's meant to be an elbow, but look." She bent the joint all the way over, then all the way back the other way, then looked at John expectantly.

He looked blank. "So?"

"My father wouldn't have used this. He always put stops so that the joints couldn't do things humans can't do."

"Maybe it's not finished?"

"It's finished. It's not just that, though, it's . . . it's the way the metal is cut, the way it's put together. It's like—you write things, right? So, you read other people's work?" He nodded. "If I ripped up some books and gave you a big pile of pages, and asked you to pick out the ones by your favorite author, could you do that, just based on the style?"

"Yeah, of course. I mean, I might be wrong about a few, but yeah."

"Well, it's the same thing here." She held the heavy piece up again to make her point. "My dad didn't *write* this."

"Okay, but what does it mean?" John asked. He unplugged the broken disc from the diagnostic keypad and took the second disc from the monster out of his pocket. He fiddled with it briefly, then managed to unhinge one side of it. Frowning with concentration, he attached the wires from the keypad to the new disc. When he was finished, he hesitated. "I don't want to flip any of the switches," he said. "I don't think my stomach can take it."

"Yeah, don't touch anything yet. After what happened at the house, we shouldn't assume that we know what any of this does." Charlie set the box on the floor and started shuffling through the parts again, looking at the patterns, trying to see something in them. "There has to be something else in here that I'm missing."

"Charlie," John said. "Sorry to interrupt your conversation with yourself, but look." He passed her the broken disc he'd just unhooked. "Look on the back."

The back had once been smooth, but it was scratched a lot since it was first made. Charlie stared at it for a minute, then finally saw it: there was writing along one edge. She had to bring the piece of plastic close to her face to make the letters out. They were tiny, and written in an old-fashioned, flowing script. They read: *Afton Robotics, LLC.* Charlie dropped the disc immediately.

"Afton? William Afton? That's my father's old partner. That's—"

"That's Dave's real name," John finished. Charlie sat silently for a moment, feeling as if something very large and unwieldy had been shoved into her head.

"I thought he was just a business partner for Freddy's," she said slowly.

"I guess he did a bit more than that."

"He's dead, though. It's not like we can ask him questions. We have to figure out what's happening now." She grabbed the cardboard box and swept the extraneous pieces—the pieces that had been her father's—into it, then shoved it back under the bed. John ducked out of her way as she maneuvered around the small space.

"And how do you think we should do that?" he asked. "What *is* happening now? There have been two bodies so far, both killed by something like what we just found."

"Three bodies," Charlie said, flushing slightly. John covered his face with his hands for a moment and took a deep breath.

"Okay, three. Are you sure it's not four?"

"I didn't see the third one. Clay just told me about it, after she was found. It had been out for a few days—she was the first one, I think."

"So why them? Are these robots just going on a killing spree? Why would they do that? Charlie, is there anything else about this that you're not telling me?" Charlie bit her lip, hesitant. "I'm serious. I'm in this with you, but if I don't know what's happening, I can't help you."

Charlie nodded. "I don't know if it means anything. Clay said it was just a coincidence. But the woman I found in the field—John, she looked like me."

His expression went dark. "What do you mean, looked like you?"

"Not exactly like me. Brown hair, same size, sort of. I don't know, if you described me to someone and asked them to pick me out of a crowd, they might come back with her. There was just this awful moment when I looked down at her, and it was like looking at me."

"Clay said it didn't mean anything?"

"He said it's a college town; there are a lot of brown-haired girls around. One of the other two victims was a man, so . . ."

"Probably a coincidence then," John offered.

"Yeah," Charlie said. "I guess it was just . . . unsettling."

"There must be something else that's linking them together. Another person, a job, a location maybe." John looked toward the window. Charlie caught him smiling, and John's expression sobered, looking suddenly self-conscious.

"You're enjoying this," she said.

"No." He shrugged. "I wouldn't put it that way. I don't want any more bodies. But—it's a mystery, and it's an excuse to spend some time with you." He smiled, but quickly made his face serious again. "So what about the bodies? Where were they found?"

"Well." Charlie brushed the hair off her face, slightly distracted. "They were all found in fields, miles apart. The first one—the one they just found—was over on the far side of Hurricane, and the girl I found today was left by the side of the road between Hurricane and here."

"Where on the road? How far from here?"

"About halfway . . ." Suddenly her eyes widened. "Forget

the fields. Or don't forget them, but they're not the point, or at least not the whole point. The holes were behind the woman's house. They take them from their homes. That's where they're starting; it's where we should start, too." She headed for the door, and John followed.

"Wait, what? Where are we going?"

"My car. I want to look at a map."

When they got to the car, Charlie pulled a stack of papers out of the glove compartment and rifled through them, then pulled out a map and handed it to John.

"Give me a pen." She held out her hand, and John pulled two from his front pocket, handing her one. Charlie spread the map out on the hood of the car and they bent over it.

"The woman's house was here," she said, circling the spot. "Clay gave me the addresses of the others." She pulled the now slightly grubby menu from her pocket and handed it to John. "You look for that one," she said quietly.

Even though they both knew the area, tracing the streets for the victim's houses took longer than Charlie had expected.

"Found it," John announced.

"1158 Oak Street is right . . . there." She circled the point and stepped back.

"What's that?" John said, pointing to something scribbled in the margin. Charlie picked up the corner of the map and her heart skipped. It was another drawing of a rectangle. She didn't remember making it. *It's a door. But what door?* She stared down at it. It had no knobs or latches, nothing to indicate how she would get inside. Or where it was. *What good is it to know what I'm looking for, if I don't know why, or how to find it?*

"Just a doodle," she said sternly, to redirect his attention. "Come on, concentrate."

"Yeah," John said. At least the pattern was instantly clear; the houses made a crooked line from Hurricane toward St. George, truncated halfway between.

"They're all about the same distance apart," Charlie said, a swell of dread rising in her chest. John was nodding as if he understood. "What does it mean?" she asked urgently.

"They're moving in a specific direction, and traveling roughly the same distance between." He paused. "Killing."

"Who's killing who?" A voice rang out behind them.

Charlie gasped and whirled around, her heart pounding. Jessica was behind her, holding a stack of books to her chest. Her eyes were wide and a grin of excitement broke across her face.

"We were just talking about the movie we saw last night," John said with a casual smile.

"Oh yeah, okay." Jessica gave him a quick look of faux seriousness and glanced at Charlie. "So, Charlie, what's the map for?" she asked, gesturing at it elaborately. "Oh, does it have to do with Freddy's?" she said with excitement in her voice. John looked at Charlie suspiciously.

"Did she tell you?" Jessica looked to John, and John looked back at Charlie, eager to hear the rest.

"Jessica, now probably isn't the best time," Charlie said feebly.

"We went to Freddy's yesterday," Jessica said in a hushed tone, although no one else was around.

"Oh, really? Funny, Charlie didn't mention that. Was that before or after all that shopping?" John folded his arms.

"I was going to tell you," Charlie murmured.

"Charlie, sometimes I think you're just trying to get yourself killed." John put his hand over his face.

"So what's the map for?" Jessica repeated. "What are we looking for?"

"Monsters," Charlie said. "New . . . animatronics. They're murdering people, seemingly at random," she continued, not fully convinced of what she'd just said.

Jessica's face grew grave, but her eyes still held a twinkle of eagerness as she walked around the side of the car to dump her books on the backseat. "How? Where did they come from? Freddy's?"

"No, not Freddy's. They came from my dad's house, we think. But they weren't his, Jessica. He didn't build them. We think it was Dave . . . Afton . . . whatever his name is." The words had come tumbling out all at once, nonsensical, and John stepped in to translate.

"She means that—"

"No, I get it," Jessica cut in. "You don't have to talk to me like I'm uninitiated. I was at Freddy's last year, too, remember? I've seen some crazy things. So, what are we going to do?" She looked at Charlie, her game face on. She looked far more together than Charlie felt.

"We don't know what any of it means for sure," John said. "We're still figuring it out."

"Why didn't you tell me?" Jessica asked. Charlie looked up at her hesitantly.

"I just didn't want it to be like last time," she said. "There's no need to put everyone at risk."

"Yeah, just me." John smirked.

"I get that," Jessica said. "But after what happened last time . . . I mean, we're in this together."

John leaned back against the car, glancing around for anyone who might be listening.

"So . . ." Jessica stepped around her to look at the map. "What are we doing?"

Charlie leaned in and squinted at the distance key on the map. "There's about three miles between each location." She studied the map again for a moment, then drew another circle. "That's my house—my dad's house." She looked up at John. "Whatever is out there killing people came from there. They must have . . ." Her voice trailed off.

"When the storm broke the wall," John muttered.

"What?" Jessica asked.

"A section of the house was sealed until the storm broke through."

With firm strokes, Charlie drew a straight line from her father's house, through the three houses of the victims, and continued the line across the map. "That can't be right," Jessica said when she saw where the line finally ended. John peered over Charlie's shoulder.

"Isn't that your college?" he asked.

"Yeah, it's our dorm." The excitement had left Jessica's voice. "That doesn't make any sense."

Charlie couldn't take her eyes off the paper. It felt a little like she had drawn the path to her own death. "It wasn't a coincidence," she said.

"What are you talking about?"

"Don't you get it?" She let out a faint laugh, unable to stop herself. "It's me. They're coming for me. They're *looking* for me!"

"What? Who are *they*?" Jessica looked to John.

"There were three empty . . . graves at her dad's house. So, there must be three of them out there somewhere."

"They move at night," Charlie said. "I mean they can't walk around in the daylight. So they find a place to bury themselves until nightfall."

"Even if you're right, and they're coming for you," John

said, bending down and trying to catch her eye, "now we know they're coming. And going by this, we can at least guess where they might go next."

"So, what are you saying? What does that matter?" Charlie heard her own voice break.

"It matters because those things are out there, right now, buried in someone's yard. And when the sun goes down they're going to kill again, in the most horrible way possible." Charlie said nothing, her head bowed. "Look." John straightened out the map and pushed it into Charlie's lap, so she couldn't help but see it. "Somewhere in here." He pointed to the next circled area on the line. "We can stop them if we can find them first," John said with urgency.

"Okay." Charlie took a breath. "We don't have much time, though."

John grabbed the map, and they all got into the car.

"Just tell me where to go," Charlie said grimly.

John peered down at the map. "So this is where we need to be?" he confirmed, pointing to the fifth circle, and Charlie nodded. He turned the map and squinted. "Turn left out of the parking lot, then take the next right. I know this place. I've driven past it. It's an apartment complex. It's pretty run-down from what I remember."

Jessica leaned forward, poking her head between the front seats. "Those circles don't look too precise; it could be anywhere in the area."

"Yeah, but I'm guessing it's going to be the place with the three fresh graves in the backyard," John said.

Charlie glanced at each of them for a second before fixing her eyes back on the road. There was safety in numbers. Last year when they were trapped at Freddy's together, Jessica was the one who had gotten them inside the restaurant in the first place. She was brave, even when she didn't want to be, and that meant more than whatever notion of romance John was entertaining.

"Charlie, turn right!" John exclaimed. She yanked the wheel, barely making the turn. *Focus. Imminent murder first, everything else later.*

Before them lay sprawling fields, lots marked out and prepared for construction and future development but never finished. Some had never even begun. Slabs of concrete were stacked here and there, almost completely obscured by overgrowth. A few lots away, steel beams had been erected to make a foundation that was never filled in. The place had decayed before it was completed.

In the farthest lot back was a cluster of what seemed to be finished apartment complexes. Grass and weeds grew rampant around them, however, climbing up their very walls; it looked like years of growth. It was hard to tell whether anyone lived inside. Years ago, the city had been diligently preparing for a population boom, one that never arrived.

"Are there even people out here?" Jessica was gazing out the window.

"There must be. There are parked cars." John craned his neck. "I think those are cars. I don't know where we're supposed to look, though."

"I think we just have to drive around." Charlie slowed the car as they traversed the road leading toward the buildings.

"Maybe not," John said. "I bet it's somewhere near the edge of the development. Most people would probably call the police if they saw eight-foot monsters digging holes in someone's backyard. There is a lot of visibility out here."

"Of course," Charlie said with dread in her voice. "They're buried, out of sight, and strategically placing themselves so as not to be found." She looked at John expectantly, but he just stared back. "They're intelligent," she explained. "I think I would have liked it better if they were just roaming the streets mindlessly. At least then someone could call the national guard or something." Charlie kept her eyes on the fields.

They drove around the outer edges of the development slowly, looking at the yards of each house. Some of the buildings looked abandoned, the windows boarded up or torn out completely, opening the apartments to the elements. The storm had done its damage, but little had been done to repair it. A tree had fallen across one cul-de-sac, blocking a building off completely. But it didn't look like anyone was trying to get in or out; the tree rotted where it lay. There was litter strewn in the abandoned streets, collecting in the gutters and bolstering the curbs. Maybe one apartment in five had curtains in the window.

Occasionally they passed a parked car or a toppled tricycle on the patchy grass. No one came outside, though Charlie thought she saw a curtain pull shut as they drove past. In two backyards there were aboveground pools filled by rainwater, and one had a large trampoline, its springs rusted and its canvas torn.

"Just a second." Charlie pulled to a stop, leaving the car running as she approached a tall wooden fence. It was too high to climb, but there was a single board that hung loose off its nail near the base. She squatted down and pried it away to peek inside.

Two round black eyes glared at her.

Charlie froze. The eyes belonged to a dog, a massive thing, which started to bark, its teeth gnashing and its chain clanking. Charlie slammed the board back in place and walked to the car. "Okay, let's keep going."

"Nothing?" Jessica asked dubiously, and Charlie shook her head. "Maybe they didn't make it this far."

"I think they did," Charlie said. "I think they're doing exactly what they mean to." She pulled the car over to the shoulder of the winding road and looked at the apartment buildings on either side. "This could have been a nice place to live," she said softly.

"Why are we stopping?" John looked confused.

Charlie leaned back in her seat and closed her eyes. *Locked in a box, a dark and cramped box, can't move, can't see, can't think. Let me out!* Her eyes flew open, and she grabbed the handle of the car door in a panic. She pulled against it hard.

"It's locked," John said. He leaned across her to pull up the button lock.

"I know that," she said angrily. She got out and closed the door. John moved to follow her, but Jessica placed her hand on his shoulder.

"Leave her alone for a minute," she said.

Charlie leaned over the trunk, propping her chin on her hands. *What am I missing, Dad?* She stood up straight and stretched her arms over her head, turning her whole body slowly to study her surroundings.

There was an empty lot beyond the development, not far from where they were. It was marked out with telephone poles, only one of which had wires. A breeze dragged the loose wires through the dirt, scattering gravel. It didn't look like it had ever been paved. There was a coil of barbed wire as tall as Charlie, sitting uselessly in a corner. Empty cans and fast-food wrappers littered the ground, the paper quivering and the cans rattling in the slight wind, like they sensed something awful. The wind rushed up behind Charlie and blew past her, straight toward the field, rustling the papers and cans and sending waves across the patches of brown grass. *Something wrong is planted there.*

Filled with a new energy, Charlie opened the car door just enough to lean inside.

"That lot. We have to go look."

"What do you see? It's kind of out of the way," John said.

Charlie nodded. "You said it yourself. If an eight-foot monster is digging up the neighbor's backyard, someone's going to notice. Besides, I just have . . . I have a feeling."

Jessica got out of the car and John followed at her heels. Charlie already had the trunk open. She pulled out a shovel, the big Maglite flashlight she always kept close by, and a crowbar.

"I've only got one shovel," she explained, making it clear she was keeping it for herself. Jessica took the flashlight and made a practice swing with it, as if hitting an invisible assailant.

"Why would you even have a shovel?" Jessica asked in a suspicious tone.

"Aunt Jen," John said by way of explanation.

Jessica laughed. "Well, you never know when you might have to dig up a robot."

"Come on," Charlie said, tossing John the crowbar and starting off. He caught it with ease and jogged beside her, leaning in so Jessica wouldn't hear.

"How come I don't get the shovel?"

"I figure you can swing a crowbar harder than I can," Charlie said.

He grinned. "Makes sense," he said confidently, gripping the crowbar with new purpose.

When they reached the edge of the lot, John and Jessica stopped, looking down at the ground before them, as though scared of what they might step on. Charlie went ahead across the loose dirt, gripping the shovel tightly. The field was mostly barren soil, studded with large mounds of gravel and dirt that had been left for so long that grass had begun growing on them.

"This must have been the dumping ground for when they were building," John said. He took a few steps into the lot, avoiding a broken glass bottle.

At the opposite edge was the tree line. Charlie studied it carefully, tracking its path back in the direction they'd come.

John knelt beside a pile of gravel and carefully poked at it with his crowbar, as though something might leap out. Jessica had wandered toward a cluster of bushes. She crouched to pick something up, then quickly dropped it and wiped her hands on her shirt. "Charlie, this place is disgusting!" she cried.

Charlie had reached the tree line and began walking alongside it, studying the ground.

"See anything?" John yelled from the other side of the lot.

Charlie ignored him. Deep grooves in the dirt extended from the trees, snaking around the bushes. The large rocks nearby were freshly marked with gashes and scrapes. "Not exactly footprints," Charlie whispered as she followed the grooves in the soil. Her foot touched soft ground, a sudden contrast to the hard-packed dirt of the rest of the lot. She stepped back. The dirt at her feet was discolored, familiar.

Charlie struck her shovel into the ground and started to dig, the metal rasping noisily on the gravel mixed in with the dirt. Jessica and John ran toward her.

"Careful," John warned as he approached. He hefted the crowbar in his hands like a baseball bat, ready to strike. Jessica hung back. Charlie saw that her knuckles were white on the flashlight's handle, but her face was calm and determined. The dirt was loose and came away easily. At last the blade of the shovel struck metal with a hollow *clunk*, and they all jumped. Charlie handed the shovel to John and knelt in the mess of scattered earth, brushing away the dirt with her hands.

"Careful!" Jessica said, her voice higher-pitched than usual, and John echoed her.

"This was a horrible idea," he murmured, scouting the area. "Where's a police car when you need one? Or any car?"

"It's still day for a little while longer," Charlie said absently, focused on the ground as her hands ran through it, prying away rocks and clods of dirt, digging to find what lay beneath.

"Yeah, it's day. It was also day when that twisted Foxy attacked you earlier, remember?" John said more urgently.

"Wait, WHAT?" Jessica exclaimed. "Charlie, get away from there! You didn't tell me that!" She turned on John accusingly.

"Look, a LOT has been going on, okay?" John raised his hands, palms out.

"Yeah, but if you're going to sign me up for this stuff, then you need to tell me about things like that! You were attacked?"

"Sign you up for this? You had one foot in the car at the first mention of murder! You practically invited yourself."

"Invited myself? You talk like I crashed your date, but you didn't exactly fall over yourself to refuse my help." Jessica planted her hands on her hips.

"Charlie," John sighed. "Can you please talk to—OH JEEZ." He jumped backward, and Jessica followed suit as soon as she looked down. Beneath them, gazing up from the loose dirt, was an enormous metal face, staring toward the sun. Charlie didn't say anything. She was still busy scooping away the soil from the edges, revealing two rounded ears on the sides of its head.

"Charlie. Is that . . . Freddy?" Jessica gasped.

"I don't know. I think it was supposed to be." Charlie heard the anxiety in her own voice as she stared down at the large, lifeless bear with its perpetual smile. The crude metal frame was covered with a layer of gelatinous plastic, giving it an organic appearance, almost embryonic.

"It's huge." John gasped. "And there's no fur . . ."

"Just like the other Foxy." Charlie's hands were getting sore. She cleared the hair from her face and stood up.

It was Freddy, but somehow not. The bear's eyes were open, glazed over with the inanimate look of lifelessness Charlie knew so well. This bear was dormant, for now.

"Charlie, we have to go," John said with a tone of warning. But he didn't move, still staring downward. He knelt beside the face and began to claw at the dirt above its forehead, clearing the earth away until he saw it: a filthy, battered black top hat. Charlie felt a smile tugging at her mouth, and she bit her lip.

"We should call Burke," Jessica said. "Now."

They all turned back toward the development as the wind rose again, rushing past them and making waves in the tall grass. The earth was still, and the sun was sinking lower behind the rolling hills in the distance.

harlie tossed her keys to John. "You go. There's a gas station a few miles back the way we came. You can call from there." He nodded, jangling the keys in his hand.

"I'll stay with you," Jessica said instantly.

"No," Charlie said, more forcefully than she intended. "Go with John." Jessica looked confused for a moment but finally nodded and headed off toward the car.

"Are you sure?" John asked. Charlie waved her hand at him dismissively.

"Someone needs to stay with it. I'll keep my distance. I promise. I won't disturb . . . it."

"Okay." Like Jessica, John hesitated for a moment. Then they left Charlie alone in the empty lot. After a minute, she heard the engine start, and the noise of the car faded as they drove off down the empty streets. She sat at the top of the mound where she had uncovered the misshapen bear and gazed down at it.

"What do you know?" she whispered. She stood and paced slowly over the other two plots of disturbed soil, wondering what lay beneath. The bear was frightening, misshapen, an imitation of Freddy created by someone else. It was a strange variation, into which her father had never breathed life. *But William Afton—Dave—did*. The man who designed these things was the same man who had stolen and murdered her brother.

A thought surfaced, a question that had visited her many times before: *Why did he take Sammy?* Charlie had asked herself, the wind, and her dreams that question endlessly. *Why did he take Sammy?* But she had always meant, *Why not me? Why was I the one who lived?* She stared down at the soil beneath her, envisioning the bear's strange, embryonic face. The children murdered at Freddy Fazbear's had lived on after death, their spirits lodged somehow inside the animatronic costumes that had killed them. Could Sammy's spirit be imprisoned somehow, behind a large, rectangular door?

Charlie shivered and stood up, suddenly wanting to put as much distance as possible between her and the twisted Freddy buried in the soil. The image of his face came to her again, and this time it made her skin crawl. Did the other two mounds hide similar creatures? Was there a malformed rabbit hidden in the dirt just there? A chicken clutching a cupcake to its grotesque chest? *But the thing that tried to kill me—tried to envelop me—it was designed to kill. There could be anything buried down there, waiting for nightfall.* She could look, dig up the other two mounds to see what lay slumbering beneath. But as soon as she thought it she could almost feel the lock of metal hands on her arms, forcing her inside that deathly, cavernous chest.

Charlie took a few deliberate steps back from the mounds, wishing just a little that she had allowed Jessica to stay.


"How has your visit with Charlie been?" Jessica asked in a conspiratorial tone as they made the final turn out of the development and onto the main road.

John didn't take his eyes off the road. "It's been fun to see her again. You, too," he added, and she laughed.

"Yes, you've always loved me. Don't worry, I know you're here to see her."

"I'm here for a job, actually."

"Right," Jessica said. She turned and looked out the window. "Do you think Charlie's changed?" she asked abruptly.

John was silent for a moment, picturing the bedroom Charlie had turned into a scrap heap and Theodore, ripped apart and strewn in pieces. He thought of her tendency to

retreat into herself, losing whole minutes as if she were stepping briefly out of time. *Do I think she's changed?*

"No," he said finally.

"I don't think she has, either." Jessica sighed.

"What did you find at Freddy's?" John asked.

"Dave," Jessica said plainly, waiting for a moment before
looking at John. "Right where we left him."

"And you're sure he was dead?" John looked down.

Jessica swallowed hard, suddenly seeing the body again.
She pictured the discolored skin and the costume that had
sunken into his rotting flesh, fusing the man to the mascot
in a grotesque eternity.

"He was dead all right," she said hoarsely.

The gas station was just up ahead. John parked in the small
lot and got out of the car without waiting for Jessica. She followed at his heels.

"What a dump." Jessica spun, marveling at the surroundings. "Surely there was a better place to . . ." Jessica stopped
short, suddenly seeing the teenage boy behind the counter.
He was staring into space, watching something just behind
them and to the left.

"Excuse me," John said. "Do you have a public phone?"
The boy shook his head.

"No, not public," he said, gesturing to it.

"Could we use it? Please?"

"Customers only."

"I'll pay for the call," John said. "Look, this is important." The boy looked at them, his eyes finally focusing, as if only just registering their presence. He nodded slowly.

"Okay, but you have to buy something while she makes the call." He shrugged, helpless against the rules of management.

"John, just give me the number," Jessica said. He dug it out of his pocket and handed it to her. As she went behind the counter, John scanned the shelves impatiently, looking for the cheapest item available.

"We have Popsicles," the kid said.

"No, thanks," John said.

"They're free." He pointed at the cooler.

"Well, how's that going to help me if they're free?"

"I'll let it count as a purchase." The boy winked.

John clenched his jaw and lifted the lid of the cooler, jerking slightly at the sight of the taxidermy coyote hidden inside.

"Brilliant. Did you stuff that yourself?" he asked loudly.

The boy laughed, a sudden, snorting sound. "Hey!" he yelled as John grabbed the carcass by the head and yanked it out of the cooler. "Hey! You can't do that!" John marched to the door, out into the parking lot, and hurled the dead thing into the road. "Hey!" The boy screamed again and ran out into the street, disappearing into a cloud of dust.

"John?" Jessica hurried out from around the counter. "Clay's on his way."

"Great." He followed her out to the car.

Charlie was still walking in circles, glancing up at the horizon every few seconds. She felt like a sentry, or the keeper of a vigil. She couldn't stop imagining the animatronics buried there, whatever they were. They weren't in boxes, not even shielded from the dirt; it would sink into their every pore and joint, it would fill them. They could open their mouths to scream, but the relentless dirt would just flow in, too fast for sound to escape.

Charlie shivered and rubbed her arms, looking up at the sky. It was turning orange, and shadows from the weeds began stretching out across the ground. Giving the mounds a sideways glance, she walked with deliberate steps to the other side of the lot where the only telephone pole with wires stood. They hung down from it like the branches of a weeping willow, dragging in the dirt. As Charlie got closer she saw small, dark shapes by its base. She approached slowly: they were rats, all lying stiff and dead. She stared down at them for a long moment, then whirled, startled, at the sounds of cars.

John and Jessica had returned, and Clay was just behind them. He must have already been in the area.

"Watch out for that pole," Charlie said by way of greeting. "I think the wires are live."

John laughed. "No one touch the wires. Glad you're okay."

Clay didn't speak; he was busy examining the patches of dirt. He walked around them as Charlie had, peering at them from every angle, then finally came to a stop when he'd made a full circle. "You dug one of these up?" he asked, and Charlie could hear the strain behind his level voice.

"No," John said hastily. "We just uncovered part of it, then covered it back up."

Clay looked down again. "I'm not sure if that makes it better or worse," he said, his eyes still on the mounds.

"It looked like Freddy," Charlie said urgently. "It looked like a strange, misshapen Freddy. There was something wrong with it."

"What was wrong?" Clay asked gently. He looked at her with serious eyes.

"I don't know," Charlie said helplessly. "But there's something wrong with all of them."

"Well, they're murdering people," Jessica offered. "I'd count that as something being wrong with them."

"Charlie," Clay said, still focused on her, "If you can tell me anything else about these things, then now's the time. We have to assume that, as Jessica told me over the phone, they're going to kill again tonight."

Charlie dropped to her knees in the place where they had dug up the twisted Freddy, and began digging again.

"What are you doing?" John protested.

"Clay needs to see it," she muttered.

"What in the . . ." Clay inched forward to study the face, then took a long step back to observe the disturbed plots of earth, measuring the size of the things buried at their feet.

"We have to evacuate these buildings," John said. "Otherwise, what are we going to do when these things get up? Ask them to go back to bed? There aren't that many apartments in this area that actually have people living in them. There's only one building in the whole block," he said, pointing, "maybe two, that looked occupied."

"Okay, I'm going to go check it out and see who's home. Keep watch over these things." Clay studied the row of buildings and made his way toward them.

"So we wait," John said.

Charlie continued watching the skyline. Dark clouds were rolling over the sun, making it appear as though night had fallen early.

"Do you hear that?" Jessica whispered.

Charlie knelt beside the metal face half-buried in the ground and turned her ear to it. "Charlie!" John startled. She lifted her head and stared at the face again. It had changed from one moment to the next. Its features had smoothed over, become less crude. She looked up at John, her eyes wide. "It's changing."

"Wait, what? What does that mean?" Jessica said, looking horrified.

"It means something is very wrong," he said. Jessica waited for him to explain.

"We're not at Freddy's anymore," was all he offered.

Clay returned from across the field.

"Everyone into the car," he said.

"My car?" Charlie asked.

Clay shook his head. "Mine." Charlie was about to protest, but Clay gave her a stern look. "Charlie, unless your car has a siren and you've had high-speed pursuit training, stand down." She nodded.

"What did you tell them?" Jessica asked suddenly.

"I told them there was a gas leak in the area," Clay said. "Scary enough to get them out, not so scary as to start a panic." Jessica nodded. She looked almost impressed, like she was taking mental notes.

They piled into Clay's car, Jessica quickly claiming the front seat, though Charlie suspected that she just wanted to leave her alone next to John. The cruiser sat at the edge of the lot, as far from the mounds as they could be without edging onto the road. As the sun sank below the horizon and the final streaks of light bled away into darkness, a single streetlight flickered on. It was old, the light almost orange, and it sputtered at intervals, as if it might fail at any moment. Charlie watched it for a while, empathizing.

John was busy staring out across the field, unblinking, but as the hour passed he began to slouch in his seat. He let out a yawn, then quickly brought himself back to alertness. An elbow poked him in the ribs and he turned to find Charlie with a mess of wires in her lap, studying something carefully. "What are you doing?" he asked, then turned his gaze back to the field.

"I'm trying to see what exactly this thing does." Charlie had the metal disc firmly in her hand. It was the one they'd wrestled from the monster that day. She was trying to connect it properly to the diagnostic tool's small keypad and display.

"Okay, John, don't puke on me." She smiled, her finger ready to flick the switch.

"I'll do my best," he grumbled and tried to concentrate on the dimly lit field.

"What is that?" Jessica whispered.

"We found it inside the animatronic that attacked us today," Charlie was eager to explain. Jessica leaned in closer to see. "It emits some kind of signal; we don't know what it is."

"It changes what those things look like." John turned his head from the window with a nauseated look.

"It changes our *perception* of what they look like," Charlie corrected.

"How?" Jessica seemed captivated.

"I'm not sure yet, but maybe we can find out." Charlie dug her nail into the groove and pulled the switch. "Ugh, I can hear it already."

John sighed. "And I can feel it."

"I can't . . ." Jessica tilted her head to listen. "Maybe I can. I don't know."

"It's very high-pitched." Charlie was busy turning small knobs on the handheld display, trying to get a readout from the device.

"It gets into your head." John rubbed his forehead. "This morning it almost made me sick."

"Of course," Charlie whispered. "It gets into your head."

"What?" Jessica turned toward her.

"These readings looked nonsensical at first. I thought something was wrong."

"And?" John said impatiently when Charlie suddenly went silent.

"In class we learned that when the brain is overstimulated, it fills in gaps for you. So, say you pass a red hexagonal sign on the road, and someone asks you what words were on it. You'd say 'STOP.' And you'd imagine that you saw it. You'd be able to picture that stop sign the way it should have been. That is, of course, if you were properly distracted and didn't notice an obviously blank sign. This thing distracts us. Somehow it makes our brains fill in blanks with previous experiences, the things we think we *should* be seeing."

"How does it do that? What's in the actual signal?" John glanced back again, only half listening.

"It's a pattern. Sort of." Charlie leaned back, letting her arms relax, the device cradled in her hands. "The disc emits five sound waves that continuously vary in frequency. First they match one another, then they don't; they go in and out of harmony, always on the edge of forming a predictable sequence, then branching away."

"I don't understand. So, it's *not* a pattern?" John said.

"It's not, but that's the whole point. It almost makes sense, but not quite." Charlie paused, thinking for a moment. "The tone fluctuations happen so fast that they're only detected by your subconscious. Your mind goes mad trying to make sense of it; it's immediately overwhelmed. It's like the opposite of white noise: you can't follow it, and you can't tune it out."

"So the animatronics aren't changing shape. We're just being distracted. What's the purpose of that, though?" John had turned away from the window, giving up the pretense of ignoring the conversation.

"To earn our trust. To look more friendly. To look more real." As the possibilities stacked up, a grim picture began to form in Charlie's mind.

John laughed. "To look more real, maybe. But they certainly don't strike me as friendly."

"To lure kids closer," Charlie continued. The car got quiet.

"Let's just focus on getting through the night, okay?" Clay said from the front seat. "I can't call this in as is. Right now it's just buried junk in a field. But if you're right, and something starts moving out there . . ." He didn't finish. John leaned against the car door, propping his head against the window so he could keep watching.

Charlie leaned her head back, letting her eyes close for just a few moments. Across the field, the orange bulb continued to flicker with a hypnotic pulse.

Minutes passed, and then almost another hour. Clay glanced at the teenagers. They had all fallen asleep. Charlie and John were awkwardly leaning on each other. Jessica had curled up with her feet on the seat beneath her and her head resting on the narrow window ledge. She looked like a cat, or a human who was going to wake up with neck problems. Clay shrugged his shoulders up and down, seized with the odd alertness he always felt when he was the only one awake. When Carlton had been a baby, he and Betty would take turns getting up with him. But while Betty had been exhausted by it, barely making it through the following day, Clay had found himself almost energized. There was something about walking through the world when no one else was stirring. It made him feel as if he could protect them all, as if he could make everything all right. *Oh, Betty.* He blinked, the orange streetlight suddenly shimmering as his eyes moistened. He took a deep breath, regaining control. *There was nothing I could say, was there?* Unbidden, the memory of their last conversation—their last fight—reared in his mind.

*"All hours of the night. It's not healthy. You're obsessed!"*

*"You're as consumed by your work as I am. It's something we have in common, remember? Something we love about each other."*

*"This is different, Clay. This worries me."*

*"You're being irrational."*

*She laughed, a sound like breaking glass. "If you think that, then we're not living in the same reality."*

*"Maybe we're not."*

*"Maybe not."*

The light changed. Clay glanced around, fully focused on the present again. The orange streetlight was fading, the flickering growing faster. As he watched, it gave a final heroic burst and went dark.

"Damn it," he said aloud. Jessica stirred in her sleep, making a small protesting noise. Quietly, but quickly, Clay exited the car, grabbing the flashlight from its place beside his seat. He closed the door and started toward the mounds, his frantic light shaking out across the field until it disappeared.

Charlie roused. Her heart was racing, but she couldn't tell if it was from the sudden awakening, or from the remnants of a dream she could no longer recall. She shook John.

"John, Jessica. Something's going on." Charlie was out of the car and running before they could answer, heading toward the mounds. "Clay!" she called. He jumped at the sound of her voice.

"They're gone." Charlie gasped, stumbling on the upturned earth. Clay was already running toward the apartment nearest him. "Go back to the car," he barked over his shoulder. Charlie ran after him, glancing back, trying to spot John and Jessica. Charlie's eyes weren't adjusted yet and Clay's flashlight seemed to sink into the darkness ahead of him. Charlie could only follow the sounds of his footsteps as he charged through the shallow grass.

She finally came to a brick wall and sprinted around it to the front of the apartment. Clay was at the door already. He banged against it and impatiently peered into the nearest window. No one answered; no one was inside.

A scream cut through the night, and Charlie froze. It was high-pitched and human, reverberating off the walls of the houses. It came again. Clay aimed his light in the direction of the sound.

"We missed someone!" he shouted. He darted around the side of the house, running blindly back across the field. The scream seemed to be in motion, making its way rapidly toward the black trees.

"Over here!" Charlie cried, breaking from behind Clay and running toward an indistinct movement in the dark.

"Charlie!" John's voice cut distantly through the night, but Charlie didn't wait for him. The sound of gravel under her feet was deafening. She came to an abrupt stop, realizing she'd lost her bearings. "Charlie!" someone yelled in the distance. The rest was lost in the rustle of the trees as a night wind swept through. She tried to keep her eyes open as grains of sand pelted her face. Then the wind finally calmed, and there was another rustle of branches nearby, this one unnatural. Charlie stumbled toward the sound, holding her arms in front of her until she could see again.

Then it was there. Just at the edge of the tree line, a misshapen figure stood hunched in the darkness. Charlie stopped short a few yards away, struck still, suddenly aware that she was alone. The thing lurched to the side, then stepped toward her, revealing a sleek snout. A wolf's mane ran over the top of its head and down its back. It was stooped over, one arm twisted downward while the other flailed up. Perhaps its control over its limbs was uncertain. It was looking at Charlie, and she met its eyes: they were piercing blue and self-illuminating. Yet while the eyes held a steady light, the rest of the creature was in flux, morphing in a disorienting fashion even as she watched. One moment it was a groomed and agile figure covered in silver hair, the next a tattered metal framework, partly coated in rubbery translucent skin. Its eyes were stark white bulbs. The creature flinched and convulsed, finally settling on its crude metal appearance. Charlie drew in a sharp breath, and the wolf broke its stare.

It spasmed alarmingly, doubling over. Its chest split open, folding outward like a horrid metal mouth. The parts made a grinding, abrasive sound. Charlie stifled a scream, rooted to the spot. It lurched again, and something fell from inside it, landing solidly on the ground. The wolf toppled forward beside it, shuddered, and went still.

"Oh no." Clay arrived from behind Charlie, staring at the human body that lay writhing in the grass.

Charlie remained motionless, captivated by the wolfish pinpoints of light that stared back at her. The thing tucked its head down, suddenly flowing again with a silver mane. It folded its long, silken ears, and slunk backward, disappearing into the woods. There was a rustling in the trees, and then it was gone.

No sooner had Jessica arrived than Clay was forcefully shoving the light into her hands. "Take it!" Clay knelt by the body doubled over in the grass and checked for a pulse. "She's alive," he said, but his voice was hard. He bent over her, looking for something else.

"Charlie!" It was John, tugging at her shoulder. "Charlie, come on, we have to get help!"

John took off running and Charlie followed more slowly, unable to take her eyes off the woman who seemed to be dying on the ground. Clay's voice faded into the darkness behind them.

"Miss, are you all right? Miss? Can you hear me?"

# CHAPTER NINE

**P**rofessor Treadwell seemed restless. Her face was calm as ever, but as the students worked, she paced back and forth across the auditorium stage, the heels of her shoes making a repetitive click. Arty poked Charlie, nodded toward the professor, and quickly mimed screaming. Charlie smiled and turned back to her own work. She didn't mind the sound. The professor's sharp, regular steps were like a metronome, marking the time.

She reread the first question: *Describe the difference between a conditional loop and an infinite loop.* Charlie sighed. She knew the answer; it just seemed pointless to write it down. *A conditional loop happens only when certain conditions* she started, then scratched it out and sighed again, staring out over the heads of the other students.

She could see the face of the wolf again, shimmering back and forth between its two faces: the illusion and the frame beneath it. Its eyes stared into her own, as if reading something deep inside her. *Who are you? Who were you supposed to be?* she thought. She had never seen it before, and it worried her. Freddy Fazbear's Pizza didn't *have* a wolf.

Charlie had a near-photographic memory, she'd realized last year. It was the reason she had such recall of even her early childhood. But she didn't remember the wolf. *That's silly*, she told herself. *There's plenty you don't remember.* And yet her memories of her father's workshop were so strong: the smell, the heat. Her father bent over his workbench, and the place in the corner where she didn't like to look. It was all so present within her, so immediate. Even the things she didn't remember without prompting, like the old Fredbear's Family Diner, had been instantly familiar as soon as she'd seen them. Yet these creatures had no foothold in her memory. She didn't know them, but they clearly knew her.

*Why were they entombed in the back of the house like that? Why not just destroyed?* Her father's deep attachment to his creations had never outweighed his pragmatism. If something didn't work, he dismantled it for parts. He had done the same with Charlie's own toys.

She blinked, suddenly recalling.

*He held it out to her, a little green frog with horn-rimmed glasses over its bulging eyes. Charlie looked at it skeptically.*

"No," she said.

"Don't you want to see what he does?" her father protested, and she crossed her arms and shook her head.

"No," she mumbled. "I don't like the big eyes." Despite her protests, her father set the frog on the ground in front of her and pressed a button hidden beneath the plastic at its neck. It rotated its head from side to side, then suddenly leaped in the air. Charlie screamed and jumped back, and her father rushed to pick her up.

"I'm sorry, sweetheart. It's okay," he whispered. "I didn't mean for it to startle you."

"I don't like the eyes," she sobbed against his neck, and he held her for a long moment. Then set her down and picked up the frog. He put it on his workbench, took a short knife from the shelf, and sliced its skin along its entire length. Charlie clapped a hand over her mouth and made a small, squeaking sound, watching wide-eyed as he carelessly peeled the green casing off the robot. The plastic split with a loud cracking noise in the quiet workshop. The frog's legs kicked helplessly.

"I didn't mean it," she said hoarsely. "I'm sorry, I didn't mean it! Daddy!" She was speaking aloud, but it was mostly air. Her voice was somehow constrained, like in dreams where she tried to scream, but nothing came out. Her father was intent on his work and didn't seem to hear her.

The stripped-down robot lay prone before him on the bench. He prodded it and it made a horrible twitch, its back legs kicking out uselessly, repeating the motion of its leap into the air. It tried again, more frantically, like it was in pain.

"Wait. Daddy, don't hurt him," Charlie mouthed, trying and failing to force out the sound. Her father selected a tiny screwdriver and began to work at the frog's head, deftly unscrewing something on each side. He removed the back of the skull to reach inside. Its whole body convulsed. Charlie ran to her father's side and grabbed his leg, tugging at the knee of his pants. "Please!" she cried, her voice returning.

He disconnected something, and the skeleton went completely limp. Joints that had been stiff collapsed into a slump of parts. The eyes, which Charlie had not even noticed were lit, dimmed, flickered, and went dark. She let go of her father and moved back into the recess of the workshop, putting both hands over her mouth again so that he would not hear her cry as he began to methodically dismantle the frog.

Charlie shook her head, pulling herself back to the present. The child's guilt still clung to her, like a weight in her chest. She gently pressed her hand there. *My father was pragmatic,* she thought. *Parts were expensive, and he didn't waste them on things that didn't work.* She forced her mind to the problem at hand.

*So why would he have buried them alive?*

"Buried who alive?" Arty hissed, and she turned, startled.

"Shouldn't you be busy doing something?" she said hastily, mortified to have spoken aloud.

The creatures had been buried in a chamber like a mausoleum, hidden in the walls of the house. Her father hadn't wanted to destroy them for some reason, and he had wanted them nearby. *Why? So he could keep an eye on them? Or did he even know they were there? Did Dave somehow hide them there without his knowledge?* She shook her head. It didn't matter. What mattered was what the creatures were going to do next.

She closed her eyes again, trying to envision the wolflike creature. She'd only seen it for that moment, as it disgorged the woman inside it and hovered between states, its illusion flickering like a faulty lightbulb. Charlie held on to the image, kept it frozen in her mind. She'd been fixated first on the victim, then on the wolf's eyes, but she had still seen the rest of it. Now she pictured the scene, ignoring the wolf's gaze, ignoring the panic that had seized her, the others shouting and running around her. She watched it happen again and again, picturing the chest sliding open one tooth-like rib at a time, then the woman falling out.

She realized she had a better picture of the same thing stored away: the creature in the tomb, just before it tried to swallow her. She visualized its chest opening, searching her mind to see what lay beyond the hideous mouth, inside the cavernous chest. Then she bent her head over her exam book and began to draw.

"Time," called one of the graduate students. The other three began to march up the aisles, collecting blue books one by one. Charlie only had half a sentence in answer to the first question, and it was crossed out—the rest of the book was a mess of mechanisms and monsters. Just before the teaching assistant reached her, she quietly tucked the book under her arm. She exited the row, blending in with the students who had already finished. She didn't speak to anyone on the way out, drifting more than walking, focused on her own thoughts as her body carried her aimlessly down the familiar hallway. She found a bench and sat. She looked around at the passing students, chatting to one another or lost in thoughts of their own. It was as if a wall had risen up, circling only her, completely isolating her from everything around her.

She opened her book again, to the page where she'd spent her test time scribbling. There, staring back at her, were the faces she understood: the faces of monsters and murderers, with blank eyes that pierced right through her, even from her own sketches. *What are you trying to tell me?* She stood, clenching her book, then took one last look at her surroundings.

It felt as though she were saying good-bye to a chapter of her life, another passage that would become nothing more than a haunting memory.

"Charlie," John's voice said from nearby. She glanced around, trying to find him through the thick flow of students exiting the building.

She finally spotted him off to the side of the stairs. "Oh, hey," she called and made her way over. "What are you doing here? Not that I'm not glad to see you, I just thought you had to work," she added hastily, trying to settle the whirling thoughts in her head.

"Clay called me. He tried your dorm, but you were here I guess. The woman we . . . from last night. She's going to be okay. He said he went to the next area, the next spot on the map, and drove around." John glanced at the crowd of students streaming past them and lowered his voice. "You know, the next place they're going to—"

"I know," Charlie said quickly, forestalling the explanation. "What did he find?"

"Well, it's a lot of empty space and fields mostly. One plot for future development, but it's vacant. He thinks we should focus on tomorrow instead. He has a plan." Charlie looked at him blankly.

"We're going to have to fight them," he said at last. "We both know that. But it won't be tonight."

Charlie nodded. "So what do we do tonight then?" she asked helplessly.

"Dinner?" John suggested.

"You can't be serious." Charlie's tone dropped.

"I know there's a lot going on, but we still need to eat, right?"

Charlie stared at the ground, collecting her thoughts. "Sure. Dinner." She smiled. "This is all pretty awful. It might be nice to get my mind off it, even if just for an evening."

"Okay," he said, and shifted awkwardly. "I'm going to run home and change then. I won't be long."

"John, none of this has to involve you," Charlie said softly. She gripped the straps of her backpack with both hands, as if they were tethering her to the ground.

"What are you talking about?" John looked at her, his self-consciousness gone.

"It doesn't have to involve anybody. It's me they're looking for."

"We don't know that for sure," he said, and put a hand on her shoulder. "You have to get that out of your head for a while. You'll drive yourself crazy." John smiled briefly, but he still looked worried. "Try to do something relaxing for a bit, take a nap or something. I'll see you for dinner, okay? Same restaurant at seven?"

"Okay," she echoed. He looked at her helplessly and gave a distressed smile, then turned and went.


Jessica was gone when Charlie got back to the dorm. She closed the door behind her with a sense of relief. She needed quiet. She needed to think, and she needed to move. She looked around, paralyzed for a moment. Her system of piling everything up as she used it was functional day-to-day, but when searching for something she hadn't touched in weeks, the system broke down.

"Where is it?" she muttered, scanning the room. Her eyes lit on Theodore's head, lying tumbled up against the leg of her bed. She picked it up and brushed off the dust, stroking his long ears until they were clean, if matted and patchy. "You used to be so soft," she told the rabbit's head. She set it on the bed, propped up on her pillow. "I guess I did, too," she added and sighed.

"Have you seen my duffel bag?" she asked the dismembered toy. "Maybe under the bed?" She got down on her knees to check. It was there, all the way at the far side, crushed by a pile of books and clothing that had fallen through the space between the bed and the wall. Charlie wriggled under the bed until she could snag the strap, then dragged it out and set it on top.

It was empty—she'd dumped out the contents as soon as she arrived, a harbinger of the messy habits to follow. She grabbed her toothbrush and toothpaste and zipped them into the bag's side pocket.

"I lied to John," she said. "No, that's not right. I let him lie to me. He has to know it's me they're coming for. We all do. And this isn't going to stop." She picked up clothing from what she thought was the clean pile, pulling out a T-shirt and jeans, socks and underwear, and shoving them emphatically into her bag as she spoke. "Why else would they be coming in this direction?" she asked the rabbit. "But . . . how would they even know?" She threw two textbooks into the bag and patted her pocket, reassuring herself that the disc and the diagnostic keyboard were there. She zipped up the bag and tilted her head, meeting Theodore's plastic eyes.

"It's not just that," she said. "This thing . . ." She measured the disc in her hand and studied it anew. "It made John sick. But it sings a song to me." She broke off, unsure of what that meant about her. "I don't know if I've ever known anything with quite such certainty," she said quietly. "But I have to do this. Afton made them. And Afton took Sammy. When I was with John, I could feel . . . something in the house. It had to be him; it was like the missing part of me was *there*, closer than it had ever been. I just couldn't quite reach it. And I think those monsters are the only things in the world that might have answers."

Theodore stared back at her, unmoved.

"It's me they want. No one else is going to die because of me." She sighed. "At least I have you to protect me, right?" She slung the bag over her back and turned to go, then paused. She grabbed Theodore's head by the ears and held him up to her own eye level. "I think today I need all the support I can get," she whispered. She shoved him into her bag, then hurried out of the dorm to her car.

The map was in the glove compartment. Charlie took it out and spread it in front of her, glancing at it momentarily then putting it away with confidence. She drove slowly out of the lot. Though she passed people and other cars on her way, she felt as though she was just part of the background, unseen to the world. By the time she and her car slipped out of sight, she'd already be forgotten.

The sky was cloudy; it gave the world a sense of waiting. It seemed like Charlie had the road to herself, and peacefulness overtook her. She'd been preoccupied with isolation today, but the speed and openness were comforting. She didn't feel alone. The tree line seemed to race across the field when she watched it from the window, an illusion made by the speeding car. She began to feel as though there were something in the woods matching her speed, darting through the blur of branches, a silent companion, someone coming to tell her everything that she ever wanted to know. *I'm coming*, she whispered.

The street dwindled from a highway to a country road, then to a gravel path. It rose up a long hill, and as Charlie slowly ascended, she could see clusters of houses and cars in distant, more populated areas. She turned a corner and left it all behind: there were no more houses, no more cars. The rows of trees had been replaced with lines of stumps and piles of brush, accompanied by the occasional blank billboard that, presumably, would someday announce what was to come. Slabs of concrete and half-paved driveways interrupted the countryside, and an abandoned bulldozer sat in the distance. Charlie took Theodore's head from her bag and set it on the passenger seat.

"Stay alert," she said.

Then she saw it: a single ranch-style house stood at the center of it all, surrounded by bulldozed land and the bare rib cages of half-built houses jutting from the ground. It was out of place: painted, fenced, and even planted with flowers in the garden. That's when it made sense. *A show house.*

The road stopped a few yards into the development, replaced by worn-down tracks in the dirt where the machinery came in and out. Charlie slowed the car to a stop. "Even you can't follow me this time," she said to the rabbit's head, then got out and closed the door, giving Theodore a smile through the window.

Charlie walked the trail slowly. The hulking, unfinished frames of the houses seemed to watch her reproachfully as she trespassed. The gravel crunched under her feet in the silence. There wasn't even a breeze; everything was still. She stopped when she reached higher ground and surveyed her surroundings for a moment. Everything was disturbed. Everything was upturned. She glanced above her as a single bird passed overhead, barely visible from its soaring height. Her eyes returned to the wasteland. "You're here somewhere, aren't you?"

At last she reached the lone finished house. It was set at the center of a neat square of perfectly trimmed grass, towering above its stooped, half-constructed neighbors. Charlie stared at the lawn for a moment before realizing that it must be fake, just like whatever furniture was inside.

She didn't try the door right away, instead going around to the backyard. It was laid out in a neat square of AstroTurf, just like the front, but here the illusion had been ruined. Ragged strips of grass had been torn up. The place radiated a sense of distress, now eerily familiar. Charlie just stared for a moment, certainty pulsing through her. She clenched her jaw, then went back around to the front door. It opened easily, without even a whisper of sound, and Charlie went inside.

It was dark in the house. She flipped a light switch experimentally, and it illuminated the whole place in an instant. A fully furnished living room greeted her, complete with leather chairs and a couch, and even candles on the fireplace mantle. She started to close the front door behind her, then hesitated, leaving it ajar. She walked farther into the living room, where there was an L-shaped couch and a wide-screen TV. *I'm surprised it hasn't been stolen*, she thought. But when she went closer she saw why—it wasn't real. There were no cords or cables coming from it. The whole place had a surreal quality, almost of mockery.

She walked slowly into the dining room, her feet clapping against the polished hardwood floor. Inside was a beautiful, mahogany dining set. Charlie bent over to look at the underside of the table. "Balsa wood," she said, grinning to herself. It was a light, airy wood, made for model airplanes, not furniture; she could probably lift the table over her head if she wanted to. Down a short hallway from the dining room was a kitchen with gleaming new appliances, or at least imitations of them. There was also a back door in the kitchen. She unlocked it and pushed it open halfway, leaning outside and looking again at the expansive, tortured landscape. There were several stone steps here, leading down into a small garden. She stepped back inside, being sure to leave the door hanging slightly open.

There was a second long hall off the living room. This led to bedrooms and a small room fashioned into an office or den, complete with tall bookshelves, a desk, and an inbox tray full of empty file folders. Charlie sat down in the desk chair, finding herself enchanted by the utterly surface imitation of life. She spun the chair once, then stood again, not wanting to get distracted. There was a door to the outside here, too, though it was oddly placed beside the desk. Charlie opened it, fiddling with the latch until she was sure it would stay open. She continued on her way, walking through the house systematically, unlocking and opening each window she came to. Then she went down to the basement, where a storm cellar hung over a set of steep stone stairs. She opened that as well, leaving the doors gaping wide. Outside, dark had fallen.

There were several bedrooms, each furnished and made up with bright curtains and silk sheets, and a large bathroom with marble sinks. Charlie turned the faucet to see if there was water, but nothing happened, not even the grinding of pipes trying and failing. There was a master bedroom with an enormous bed, a guest room that somehow looked even less lived-in than the rest of the house, and a nursery with a life-size menagerie painted on the wall and a mobile hanging above a crib. Charlie glanced inside each, then went back into the master bedroom.

The bed was wide and covered in a light canopy of white mosquito netting. The covers were white as well, and the moon shone through the window to illuminate the pillows. It had an uncanny effect, as if whoever slept there would be on display. Charlie went to the window and leaned out, breathing in the soothing, cool night air. She looked up at the sky. It was still cloudy; there were only a few stars visible. She'd been moving with such grim, impulsive energy until now, but this part would be agonizing. Long hours might pass before anything happened, and all she could do was wait. A nervous fluttering had begun to fill her stomach. She wanted to pace, or even to run away, but she closed her eyes and clenched her jaw. *It's me they want.*

At last, Charlie pulled herself away from the window. She'd packed pajamas in the bag out in the car, but this sterile house full of props and imitations felt too strange for her to actually dress for bed. Instead she just took off her sneakers and considered her bedtime rituals complete. She laid down on the bed and tried to conjure her nightmares, gathering up those final moments with Sammy and holding them close to her like a talisman. *Hold on*, she thought. *I'm coming.*

John checked his watch. *She's just running late. But she was late last time, too.* The waitress caught his eye, and he shook his head. *Of course, last time she showed up covered in filth.* He'd already called her dorm room, but the phone just rang and rang. He'd seen what he'd thought was an answering machine when he was there, but realized only as he was waiting for it to pick up that it could have been one of Charlie's projects, or some piece of discarded junk. The waitress refilled his water glass, and he smiled at her.

She shook her head. "Same girl?" she asked gently.

John let out an involuntary laugh. "Yes, same girl," he said. "But it's okay. She's not standing me up, she's just . . . busy. College life, you know."

"Of course. Let me know if you want to order." She gave him another look of pity and went away. He shook his head.

Suddenly, he saw Charlie's hands on her backpack straps, holding on so tight that her knuckles had gone white. *They're coming for me*, she'd said. Charlie wasn't the type to wait around patiently for something to happen to her.

He got up and walked urgently to the pay phone at the back of the restaurant. Clay picked up on the first ring.

"Clay, it's John. Have you heard from Charlie?"

"No. What's wrong?"

"Nothing," John said reflexively. "I mean, I don't know. She was supposed to meet me, and she's—twenty-four minutes late. I know it's not a lot, but she said something earlier that's bothering me. I think she might do something stupid."

"Where are you?" John gave him the address. "I'll be right there," Clay said and hung up before John could reply.

# CHAPTER TEN

For the first few minutes, Charlie kept her eyes shut, feigning sleep, but after a little while they began to flutter of their own accord. She squeezed her eyes shut, trying to force them to stay closed, but it became unbearable. She opened them into the darkness and at once felt relief.

The house had grown cool with night. The open window let in fresh, clean air. She breathed deeply, trying with each exhalation to make herself calm. She wasn't anxious so much as impatient. *Hurry up*, she thought. *I know you're out there.*

But there was only silence, and stillness.

She took the disc out of her pocket and looked at it. It was too dark to see any details, not that there was anything on it she hadn't already memorized. A little light shone in from the moon outside, but the shadows in the corners were deep, like there was something hidden there eating up the light. She rubbed the side of the disc with her thumb, feeling the bumps of the letters. If she didn't know they were there, they'd be scarcely noticeable.

*Afton Robotics, LLC.* She'd seen pictures of William Afton, the man who Dave had been: pictures of him with her father, smiling and laughing. But she only remembered him as the man in the rabbit suit. *My father must have trusted him. He must not have suspected. He would never have built a second restaurant with the man who murdered one of his children. But those creatures—he had to have known they were buried beneath our house.* Charlie clenched her teeth, stifling a sudden delirious urge to smile. "Of course there was a secret robot graveyard under my bedroom," she murmured. "Of course that's where it would be." She covered her face in her hands. All the threads were tangling in her mind.

She pictured it unwillingly. *The creature in the doorway. At first he was a shadow, blocking the light, then he was a man in a rabbit suit, and even then it didn't occur to Charlie to be afraid. She knew this rabbit. Sammy hadn't even noticed him yet. He continued to play with his toy truck, running it back and forth hypnotically across the floor. Charlie stared up at the thing in the doorway, and a coldness began to gather in the pit of her stomach. This was not the rabbit she knew. Its eyes shifted back and forth subtly between the twins, taking its time: making its choice. When the eyes settled on Charlie, the cold feeling spread all through her, then he looked away again, at Sammy, who still hadn't turned around. Then a sudden movement, and the costumes on their hangers all leaped together, covering her so she couldn't see. She heard the toy truck hit the ground and spin in place for a moment, then everything was still.*

*She was alone, a vital part of her cut away.*

Charlie sat up, shaking herself to try and set the memories loose. She'd grown accustomed to sharing a room with Jessica. It was a long time since she'd been completely alone with her thoughts in the dark.

"I forgot how hard it is to be quiet," she whispered, her voice as soft as breath. She glared down at the strange disc in her hand, as if it was bringing these visions on her. She tossed it across the room and into a dark corner, out of sight.

Then she heard it. Something was inside the house.

Whatever it was, it was being cautious. She heard creaks from somewhere distant, but they were slow and muted. Silence followed; whatever moved was hoping the sound would be forgotten. Charlie crept from the bed and approached the door carefully, pushing it farther open and leaning out agonizingly slowly, until she could see deep into the living room, and the dining room beyond that. A part of her kept returning to the thought that she was in someone else's house, that she was the intruder.

"Hello?" she called, almost hoping for an answer, even an

angry one demanding to know what she was doing there. Maybe John would answer, happy to have found her, and come running from the darkness.

Only silence returned her call, but Charlie knew she wasn't alone anymore.

Her eyes widened, her heartbeat drumming in her throat, making it hard to breathe. She took careful steps over the stone tiles, down the short hall to just outside the living room, where she stood to listen again. A clock chimed the hours in a different room. Charlie walked to the edge of the living room and stopped again. She could see most of the house from here, and she scanned the area for anything out of place. Doorways surrounded her like gaping mouths, breathing night air from the windows she'd opened.

There was a long hall leading from the farthest corner of the living room to a different bedroom. It was one of the few places she didn't have a clear line of sight into. She edged around the leather sofa in front of her and across the circular rug that filled the room. As she walked, she could see more of the hall slowly revealing itself. It stretched out, farther and farther.

Charlie stopped midstep. She could see into the far bedroom now. It was full of windows and blue moonlight, and there was something obstructing her view, something she hadn't noticed while she was moving. Now its silhouette was unmistakable. Charlie carefully looked around again, her eyes adjusting to her surroundings. To her right, another large door led down a single step and into the large den. Bookcases stretched up to the ceiling, and a putrid air emanated from inside. Beyond the bookcases was another shadow that didn't belong. Charlie bumped into a lamp and startled. She hadn't even realized she was moving backward.

The front door was open wide. Charlie nearly bolted toward it to escape, but she stopped herself. She took a breath and stepped softly back toward the bedroom, checking over her shoulder as she went. She went back to the bed, sliding her bare feet on the wood floor so her steps would make no sound, and eased herself slowly onto the mattress, cautious to keep the springs from creaking. Charlie lay back, closed her eyes, and waited.

Her eyes twitched, every instinct she had shouting the same thing: *Open your eyes! Run!* Charlie breathed steadily in and out, trying to make her body go limp, trying to look asleep. *Something is moving.* She counted the steps. *One, two, one, two—no.* They were slightly asynchronous: there was more than one of them. Two, maybe all three, were inside the house. One set of footsteps passed her door, and she let her eyes flutter open for an instant, just in time to see an indistinct shadow cross before the crack in the door.

Another set of footsteps sounded like they were in the side hallway, while a third . . .

She screwed her eyes shut tight. The steps fell still outside her door. Her breath was shuddering; she almost hiccupped as she inhaled and she bit her lips together. The door was gliding open. Her lungs tightened, pressing her for air, but she refused. She hung on to that single breath as if it were the last one she'd ever get. *I'll find you.* She clenched her fists, determined to remain still.

The footsteps were through the door now, crossing the floor with a heavy tread. She kept still. The air above her stirred, and through her closed eyelids, the darkness grew even darker. Charlie opened her eyes, and breathed in.

The space above her was empty; nothing was looking down at her.

She turned her head slowly, peering into the open hall to her left. The noises had all stopped.

Suddenly the blankets were yanked off her, pulled from the foot of the bed. Charlie shot up and finally saw what had come for her. An enormous head rested its chin at her feet. It looked like something from a carnival game, its eyes rolling from side to side, clicking each time they moved. A pitch-black top hat was perched on its head, cocked slightly to one side, and the giant cheeks and button nose gave him away immediately. *Freddy.*

It was no longer the sleek and featureless head she had unearthed in the abandoned lot. His head was lively and full of movement, covered in wavy brown fur and bouncy cheeks. Yet there was something disjointed about it all, as though every part of his face was moving independently.

Charlie fought to remain still, but her body was acting of its own accord, squirming and pulling to get away from the mouth opening up toward her. Freddy's face slid across the bed like a python. His head lost its shape as it folded outward, taking hold of her feet and beginning to swallow, moving slowly upward as she fought not to scream or fight. A giant arm reached up and clapped the side of the bed, shaking the room as it anchored itself and pulled the giant torso higher. Freddy's jaw made motions of chewing as the distorted face pulled Charlie's legs inside it. His cheeks and chin dislocating further. It no longer resembled a living thing.

Panic took hold and Charlie screamed. She clenched her fists, but there was no longer a face to strike. There was only a squeezing and spiraling vortex of fur, teeth, and wire. Before she could struggle further, her arms were pinned to her side, trapped inside the thing. Only her head remained free. She gasped for a last breath, then was violently scooped up, consumed by the creature.

Clay Burke stopped the car without slowing down. The brakes screeched as they fishtailed in the dirt. John was out of the car before Clay had gotten it under control, running up the hill toward the house.

"Around back," Clay said, catching up to John, his voice low and tight. They made their way around the house to the back door, which was gaping open. "Check that way." Clay gestured to his right as he ran left. John stuck close to the wall, peering into doorways as he passed them.

"Charlie!" he cried.

"Charlie!" Clay echoed, entering the master bedroom.

"CHARLIE!" John ran from room to room, moving faster. "CHARLIE!" He arrived at the front door. He swung it wide open and stepped outside, half expecting to catch someone fleeing the scene.

"Clay, did you find her?" he shouted as he raced back inside.

Clay walked briskly back into the living room, shaking his head. "No, but she was here. The bed was unmade and there was dirt all over the floor. And these . . ." He held up Charlie's sneakers. John nodded grimly, only now noticing the trails of dirt strewn through the house. He glanced again to the front door.

"She's gone," John said, his voice catching in his throat. He looked at the older man. "Now what?" he asked.

Clay just stared at the floor, and said nothing.

# CHAPTER ELEVEN

lay!" John repeated. His alarm grew as the older man stared down at the dirty floorboards, apparently lost in thought. John put a hand on his arm, and Clay startled. He looked as if just he'd realized he wasn't alone. "We have to find her," John said urgently.

Clay nodded, springing back to life. He broke into a run and John followed close at heel, barely making it into the passenger's seat before Clay started the engine and took off, speeding down the half-made road.

"Where are we going?" John shouted. He was still struggling to close the door against the wind. It flapped like a massive wing, pulling against him as Clay swerved down the hill. Finally John yanked it shut.

"I don't know," Clay said grimly. "But we know about

how far they can get." He drove wildly back down the hill and out to the main road, flipping on his police lights. They went less than a mile before he turned quickly onto a small, unpaved lane.

John's shoulder banged hard against the door. He gripped his seat belt as they barreled down the trail, high brush scraping the sides of the car and thumping the windshield.

"They have to come through here," Clay said. "This field is right in the middle of the path between that house and the next area on the map. We just have to wait for them." He stopped the car abruptly and John jerked forward.

Together they got out of the car. Clay had stopped at the edge of an open field. There were trees scattered here and there, and the grass was tall, but there were no crops, and no livestock grazed. John walked out into the open, watching the grass ripple like water in the wind.

"You really think they'll come by here?" John asked.

"If they keep moving the direction they've been going," Clay said. "They have to."

Long minutes passed. John paced back and forth in front of the car. Clay positioned himself closer to the middle of the field, ready to run in any direction at a moment's notice.

"They should have been here by now," John said. "Something's wrong." He glanced at Clay, who nodded.

The sound of a car engine rose from the distance, growing louder. They both froze. Whoever it was, they were coming fast; John could hear branches whipping against the car's body in an irregular percussion. After a few seconds the car shot out from the lane and screeched to a halt.

"Jessica." John walked toward the car.

"Where's Charlie?" Jessica asked, stepping out onto the grass.

"How did you find us?" Clay demanded.

"I called her," John put in quickly. "From the restaurant, right after I talked to you."

"I've been driving all over the place. I'm lucky I found you. Why are we stopped here?"

"Their route crosses through here," John explained, but she looked skeptical.

"What does that mean? How do you know?"

John glanced at Clay, neither of them looking confident.

"They have her already, right?" Jessica said. "So why would they keep going toward her dorm?" Clay closed his eyes, putting a hand to his temples.

"They wouldn't," he said. He looked up at the sky, the wind battering across his upturned face with a raw touch.

"So they could be going anywhere now," Jessica added.

"We can't predict what they're doing anymore," John said. "They got what they wanted."

"And she wanted this? She planned this?" Jessica said, her voice rising. "What's *wrong* with you, Charlie?" She turned back to John. "They might not have even wanted *her*. It could have been anyone! So why did she have to go up there, like some kind of—of—"

"Sacrifice," John said quietly.

"She can't be dead," Jessica muttered, her voice shaky even under her breath.

"We can't think like that," John said sternly.

"We'll form a perimeter," Clay said. "Jessica, you and John take your car and start driving that way." He pointed. "I'll loop back the other direction. We'll make circles and hope we catch them. I can't think of any other way." He looked at the teenagers helplessly. No one moved, despite Clay's new plan. John could feel it in the air; they had all surrendered. "I don't know what else to do." Clay's voice had lost its strength.

"I might," John said abruptly, the idea forming even as he spoke. "Maybe we can ask them."

"You want to ask them?" Jessica said sarcastically. "Let's call them and leave a message. 'Please call us back with your murderous plot at your earliest convenience!'"

"Exactly," John said. "Clay, the mascots from Freddy's: Are they *all* gone? When you say you threw them out, what does that mean? Can we get access to them?" He turned to Jessica. "They helped us before, or at least they tried to, once they stopped trying to kill us. They might know something, I don't know, even if they're on a scrap heap somewhere, there must be something left. Clay?"

Clay had turned his face up to the sky again. Jessica gave him a sharp look. "You know, don't you?" she said. "You know where they are."

Clay sighed. "Yeah, I know where they are." He hesitated. "I couldn't let them be dismantled," he went on. "Not knowing what they are, who they had been. And I didn't dare let them be casually tossed out, considering what they're capable of doing." Jessica opened her mouth, about to ask a question, then stopped herself. "I . . . I kept them," Clay said. There was a rare note of uncertainty in his voice.

"You what?" John stepped forward, suddenly on guard.

"I kept them. All of them. I don't know about asking them any questions, though. Ever since that night, they haven't moved an inch. They're broken, or at least they're doing a good impression of it. They've been sitting in my basement for over a year now. I've been careful to leave them alone. It just seemed like they shouldn't be disturbed."

"Well, we have to disturb them," Jessica said. "We have to try to find Charlie."

John scarcely heard her. He was staring searchingly at Clay.

"Come on," Clay said. He set off toward his car with a heavy look, as if something had just been taken from him.

John and Jessica exchanged a glance, then followed. Before they reached Jessica's car, Clay was already heading toward the main road. Jessica stepped on the gas, catching up just as Clay made a sharp right turn.

They didn't speak. Jessica was intent on the road, and John was slouched in his seat, thinking things through. Ahead of them, Clay had switched on his flashing lights, though he left off the siren.

John stared into the darkness as they drove. Maybe he'd spot Charlie just by chance. He kept his hand loose on the door handle, ready to jump out, to run and save her. But there were only endless trees, scattered with the orange windows of distant houses, which hung on the hills like Christmas lights.

"We're here," Jessica said, sooner than John had expected.

John pushed himself upright and peered out the window.

She made a left turn and slowed the car down, and as she did John recognized it. A few yards ahead was Carlton's house, surrounded by a cove of trees. Clay pulled into the driveway and they came in behind him. Jessica stopped the car inches from his bumper.

Clay jangled his keys nervously as they approached the house; he looked like an altered man, no longer the assured police chief in control of every situation. He unlocked the door, but John hung back. He wanted Clay to go in first.

Clay led them into the living room, and Jessica made a noise of surprise. Clay gave her a sheepish look. "Sorry for the mess," he said.

John glanced around. The room was mostly the same as he remembered, full of couches and chairs all fanned around a fireplace. But both couches were piled with open files and stacks of newspapers, and what looked like dirty laundry. Six coffee mugs sat crowded together on a single end table. John's heart sank as he noticed two bottles of whiskey lying on their sides between an armchair and the hearth. He cast his eyes around quickly, spotting two more. One had rolled under a couch; the other was still half-full, sitting beside a glass with a distinct yellow tinge. John snuck a look at Jessica, who bit her lip.

"What happened here?" she asked.

"Betty left," Clay said shortly.

"Oh."

"I'm sorry," John offered. Clay waved a hand at him, staving off further attempts at comfort. He cleared his throat.

"She was right, I guess. Or at least she did what was right for her." He forced a laugh and gestured at the mess that surrounded him. "We all do what we have to do." He sat down in a green armchair, the only seat completely free of paperwork and debris, and shook his head.

"Can I move these?" John asked, pointing to the papers that filled the couch opposite Clay. Clay didn't respond, so John stacked them up and put them to one side, careful not to let anything fall. He sat, and after a moment so did Jessica, though she eyed the couch as if she thought it might be carrying the plague.

"Clay—" John started, but the older man started talking again, as if he'd never stopped.

"After all of you left—after all of you were safe—I went back for them. Betty and I had decided it might be a good time for Carlton to get out of town for a while, so she took him to stay with her sister for a few weeks. To be honest, I don't remember if she suggested it, or if it was me who put the idea in her mind. But as soon as I saw them pull down the driveway and out of sight, I got to work.

"Freddy's was locked up. They'd taken away Officer Dunn's body and completed their search, under my careful guidance, of course. They took some samples, but nothing else had been removed from the premises, not yet. They were waiting on me to give the go-ahead. The place wasn't even under guard—after all, there was nothing dangerous inside, right? So, I waited for things to calm down. Then I drove to St. George and rented a U-Haul.

"It was raining when I picked up the truck, and by the time I got to Freddy's there was a full-on thunderstorm, even though the forecast had been clear. I had keys this time; all the locks were police-issue now, so I just walked right into the place. I knew where I would find them—or at least, I knew where I'd left them and prayed they were still here. They were all piled together in that room with the little stage."

"Pirate's Cove," Jessica said, her voice barely a whisper.

"I half expected them to be gone, but they were sitting patiently, like they'd been waiting for me. They're immense, you know. Hundreds of pounds of metal and whatever else was in there, so I had to drag them one by one. I loaded them all up eventually. I figured I would bring them down through the storm cellar, but when I got back home the lights were on and Betty's car was in the driveway. She'd come back from her trip early, it seemed."

"What did you do?" Jessica asked. She was hunched over, her chin in her palms. John shook his head, mildly amused. She was enjoying the story.

"I waited across the street. I watched the lights, staking out my own house. When the last light went out, I pulled into the driveway and started dragging those things again, lowering them down into the cellar one by one. I drove the truck back to St. George and came back home, all without anyone seeing me. It would have never worked if I hadn't had the cover of thunder and lightning to mask what I was doing. When I came in, I was soaking wet and my whole body ached. All I wanted was to go upstairs to bed, next to my wife . . ." He cleared his throat. "But I didn't dare. I took a blanket and I slept in front of the basement door, just in case something tried to come out."

"Did it?" Jessica asked. Clay shook his head slowly back and forth, like it had taken on extra weight.

"In the morning, they were exactly the way I'd left them. Every night after that, I went down there when Betty was asleep. I watched them, sometimes I even . . . talked to them, trying to provoke them somehow. I wanted to make sure they weren't going to kill us in our sleep. I went back over the case files, trying to figure out how we'd missed Afton. How had he managed to come back without anyone suspecting?

"Betty could tell something was wrong. A few weeks later, she woke up and came looking for me—she found me, and them." Burke closed his eyes. "I don't remember exactly how the conversation went, but the next morning she was gone again, and this time she didn't come back."

John shifted on the couch restlessly. "They haven't moved since then?"

"They're just sitting there like broken dolls. I don't even think about them anymore."

"Clay, Charlie's in danger," John said, standing. "We have to go see them."

Clay nodded. "Well, then let's go see them." He stood and gestured toward the kitchen.

The last time John had stood in the Burkes' kitchen was the morning after they'd all escaped from Freddy's. Clay had been making pancakes and kidding around. Betty, Carlton's mother, was sitting next to her son as if she were afraid to leave his side. They were all giddy with relief that the ordeal was over, but John could tell that each of them, in their own particular ways, was struggling with other emotions, too. Someone might stop talking in midsentence, forgetting the rest, or stare for several moments at the empty air in front of them. They were all just barely recovering. But the kitchen had been bright. Light sparkled off the counters, and the smells of coffee and pancakes were reassuring, a connection to reality.

Now, John was struck hard by the contrast. There was a rank smell, and he could see immediately what it was: the counters and table were strewn with dirty dishes, all crusted with leftover meals. Most had scarcely been eaten. There were two more empty bottles in the kitchen sink.

Clay opened the door to what looked like a closet, but turned out to be the basement steps. He flipped a light switch, illuminating a dim bulb right above the stairs, and motioned them in. Jessica started forward, but John put a hand lightly on her arm, stopping her. Clay went first, leading their descent, and John followed, guiding Jessica behind him.

The stairs were narrow and a little too steep. Each time John stepped down he felt a slight lurch, his body unprepared for the distance. Two steps down the air changed: it was damp and moldy.

"Watch out for that one," Clay said. John looked down to see that one of the boards was missing. He stepped over it carefully and turned, offering Jessica a hand as she made the awkward jump. "One of many things that's on my to-do list," Clay said offhandedly.

The basement itself was unfinished. The floor and walls were nothing but the unpainted inner surface of the foundation. Clay gestured to a dark corner where the boiler lurked heavily. Jessica gasped.

They were all there, lined up in a row against the wall. At the end of the line, Bonnie slumped against the boiler. The gigantic rabbit's blue fur was stained and matted, and his long ears drooped forward, almost obscuring his wide, square face. He still held a red bass guitar in one enormous hand, though it was battered and broken. Half of his bright red bow tie had torn off, giving his face a lopsided look. Beside him sat Freddy Fazbear. His top hat and matching black bow tie were undamaged, their material only a little scuffed. And though his brown fur was bedraggled, he still smiled for an absent audience. His blue eyes were wide and his eyebrows raised, like something exciting was about to happen. His microphone was missing, and he held his arms out stiffly before him, grasping at nothing. Chica leaned against Freddy, her head drooping to the side. The weight of her yellow body—inexplicably covered in fur, not feathers—seemed to rest entirely on him. Her long, orange chicken legs were splayed out in front of her, and for the first time John noticed the silver talons on her feet, inches long and sharp as knives. The bib she always wore had been torn. It had read: LET'S EAT!!!, but it was faded by time, along with the damp and mildew of the basement.

John squinted at her. Something else was missing.

"The cupcake," Jessica said, echoing his thoughts.

Then he spotted it. "There on the floor," he said. It was sitting alone beside Chica, almost huddled, its evil grin maniacal and pathetic.

Set a little apart from the three was the yellow Freddy, the one that had saved all their lives. He looked like Freddy Fazbear, and yet he did not. There was something different about him besides the color, but if someone had asked John what it was, he knew he wouldn't be able to name it. Jessica and John looked at it for a long moment. John felt a sense of quiet awe as he studied the yellow bear. *I never got to thank you*, he wanted to say. But he found he was too scared to approach it.

"Where's—" Jessica started, then cut herself off. She pointed to the corner where Foxy was propped against the wall, clothed in shadows but still visible. John knew what he would see: a robotic skeleton covered with dark red fur, but only from the knees up. It had been tattered even when the restaurant was open. Foxy had his own stage in Pirate's Cove. As John peered at him now, he thought he could see more places where the fur covering was ripped, and the metal frame showed through. Foxy's eye patch was still fixed in place above his eye. While one hand drooped at his side, the arm with the large, sharpened hook was raised above his head, poised for a downward slash.

"Is this how you left them?" John asked.

"Yep. Exactly how I left them," Clay answered, but he sounded suspicious of his own words.

Jessica approached Bonnie cautiously and crouched down to make her eyes level with the enormous rabbit. "Are you in there?" she whispered. There was no response. Jessica reached out slowly to touch his face. John watched, tensing, but as Jessica petted the rabbit, not even dust stirred in the mildewed basement. Finally she straightened and took a step back, then looked helplessly at John. "There's nothing—"

"Shh," he interrupted. A noise caught his attention.

"What is it?"

John bent his head, craning closer to the sound, though he couldn't tell exactly where it was coming from. It was like a voice on the wind, words swept away before he could catch them, so that he couldn't be sure it was a voice at all. "Is anyone . . . here?" he murmured. He looked at Freddy Fazbear, but as he tried to focus his attention, the sound situated itself. He turned to the yellow Freddy suit.

"You're here, aren't you?" he asked the bear. He went to the animatronic and crouched in front of it, but he didn't try to touch it. John looked into its shining eyes, searching for any of the spark of life he had seen that night, when the golden bear entered the room and they all knew as irrefutable fact that Michael, their childhood friend, was inside. John couldn't remember precisely how that knowledge had come: there was nothing behind the plastic eyes, nothing different physically. It was just pure certainty. He closed his eyes, trying to call it back. Maybe by recalling that essence of *Michael*, he could conjure him again. But he couldn't catch it, couldn't sense the presence of his friend as he had that night.

John opened his eyes and looked at all the animatronics one by one, remembering them alive and mobile. Once, the children stolen by William Afton had watched him back from inside. Were they still inside now, dormant? It was horrible to think of them moldering down here, staring into the darkness.

Something flickered in the yellow bear's eye, almost imperceptibly, and John drew in a sharp breath. He glanced behind, checking for a light that might have glanced off the hard plastic surface, but there was no obvious source. *Come back*, he pled silently, hoping to see the spark again.

"John." Jessica's voice pulled him back to reality. "John, I'm not sure that this was a good idea." He turned toward her voice, then stood, his legs cramping. How long had he been there, staring into the blind eyes of the mascot?

"I think there's still someone in there," he said slowly.

"Maybe so, but this doesn't feel right." She looked down from John toward the suits again.

Their heads had moved; they tilted up unnaturally, facing John and Jessica.

Jessica screamed and John heard himself shout something unintelligible, leaping back as if he'd been stung. They were all looking directly at him. John took three experimental steps to the left, and they appeared to track him: their eyes stayed fixed on him, and him alone.

Clay had grabbed a shovel and was holding it like a baseball bat, ready to strike. "I think it's time to go." He stepped forward.

"Stop, it's okay!" John exclaimed. "They know that we aren't enemies. We're here because we need their help." John opened his palms toward the creatures.

Clay lowered the shovel, though he kept it in his hand. John looked at Jessica, who nodded rapidly.

John turned back to the mascots. "We're here because we need your help," he said again. They gazed back at him blankly. "Remember me?" he asked awkwardly. They continued to stare, as frozen in their new poses as they'd been before. "Please listen," he went on. "Charlie, you remember her, right? You must. She's been taken by . . . creatures like you, but not like you." He glanced at Jessica, but she was watching anxiously, trusting this to him.

"They were animatronic suits, buried under Charlie's house. We don't know why they were there." He took a deep breath. "We don't think they were built by Henry; we think they were built by William Afton."

As soon as John said the name, the robots all began to shudder, convulsing where they sat. It was as if their machinery was being jump-started by a current too powerful for their systems to absorb.

"John!" Jessica cried. Clay stepped forward and grabbed John by the shoulder.

"We have to get out of here," Jessica said urgently. The mascots were seizing wildly, their arms and legs jerking. Their heads banged against the back wall with painful clanks. John stood rooted to the spot, torn between the impulse to run *to* them, to try and help, and the urge to run away.

"Go, now!" Clay shouted over the noise, pulling John backward. They made their way back up the basement stairs, Clay followed behind with the shovel raised defensively. John watched the mascots convulsing on the ground until they were out of sight.

"We need your help to find Charlie!" he shouted one last time, as Clay slammed the basement door and snapped three shiny new deadbolts shut.

"Come on," Clay said. They followed him, chased by hideous clanking and banging noises, only slightly muffled by the floor beneath. He led them back through the living room to a small study branching off from it, where he shut the door and bolted it.

"They're coming up," John said, pacing and watching the ground beneath his feet. Metal ground against metal; something crashed like it was slammed against the wall. The echo reverberated through the floor.

"Block the door," Clay ordered, grabbing one side of the desk in the corner. John grabbed the other side as Jessica cleared a path for them, yanking two chairs and a lamp out of the way. They dropped it in front of the door as, beneath them, something scraped across the concrete like it was being dragged.

Heavy footsteps shook the foundation of the house. The high-pitched whine of malfunctioning electronics filled the air, almost too high to hear. Jessica rubbed her ears. "Are they coming for *us*?"

"No. I mean, I don't think so," John said. He looked to Clay for reassurance, but Clay's eyes were on the door. The whine intensified and Jessica clapped her hands over her ears. The footsteps grew louder. There was a noise like cracking wood.

"At the door," Clay whispered. There was a loud thud, and then another. John, Jessica, and Clay sank down behind the desk, as if it would better hide them. Another thud resounded, then a sound of splintering wood. The earth-shaking footsteps came closer. John tried to count them, to see if the creatures were all together, but there was too much overlap. They layered one over another, rattling his teeth and shaking through his chest. It felt like the sound alone might break him to pieces.

Then, quickly, the footsteps faded and were gone. For a long moment no one moved. John gasped to breathe, realizing only now that he'd been holding his breath. He looked at the others. Jessica's eyes were closed, and she gripped her hands together so tightly that her fingertips had gone white. John reached out and touched her shoulder and she jumped, her eyes flying open. Clay was already standing, tugging at the desk. "Come on, John," he said. "Help me get this out of the way."

"Right," he said unsteadily. Together they shoved it aside and hurried out into the hall. The front door stood wide open to the night. John rushed out to look.

The grass outside had been torn up where the mascots shuffled through it. The tracks were obvious and easy to follow, leading straight into the woods. John broke into a run, chasing after them, Clay and Jessica at his heels. When they reached the cover of trees they slowed. In the distance, John saw a blur of movement for only an instant, and he motioned the others to hold back. They would follow, but they didn't dare be seen by whatever was leading the way.

# CHAPTER TWELVE

The world thundered around Charlie, shaking her rhythmically back and forth, strange objects digging harder into her each time she was jostled. Charlie opened her eyes, and remembered where she was. Or rather, what she was inside. The awful image of the malformed Freddy sucking her into its mouth like some kind of snake hit her, and she closed her eyes again, biting her lips together so that she wouldn't scream. The thuds were footsteps, she realized: the animatronics were on the move.

Her head throbbed with each blow, making it hard to think straight. *I must have been knocked unconscious when it threw me in here,* she thought. The torso of the thing was connected to the head by a wide neck, which was almost level with her own, though its head stretched up another foot above her. It was like looking at the inside of a mask: the hollow of a protruding snout, the blank spheres that were the backs of the eyes. When she carefully tilted her head up, she could even see the bolt that attached the black top hat.

Charlie's legs were cramped and bent at odd angles, wedged between pieces of machinery. She must have been stuck this way for some time, but she had no way of knowing how long. Her arms were constrained, suspended away from her body into the arms of the suit. Her whole body was covered in small points of pain, bruises and cuts from tiny pieces of plastic and metal that deepened each time they banged against her. Charlie could feel blood trickling down her skin in half a dozen places. She itched to wipe it away but had no idea how much she could struggle without triggering the springs. Her mind flashed to the first murder victim, the lacerations that covered his body almost decoratively. She thought of Dave's screams as he died, and the bloated corpse beneath the stage at Pirate's Cove. *That can't be me. I can't die like that!*

Charlie had told Clay what she knew about the spring-lock suits. The animatronic parts were either recoiled, making room for a person inside to use it as a costume, or fully extended, so the mascot would work as a robot. But that was what Charlie knew from Fredbear's Family Diner— this creature was different. She was inside a cavity made for a human being, but the suit was moving with complete autonomy. Its insides were full of metal architecture and wires, all except for the space that Charlie occupied.

The animatronic lurched unexpectedly to the side, and Charlie was smacked against the jagged wall again with greater force. She cried out this time, unable to help herself, but there was no break in Freddy's stride. Either the creature hadn't heard, or it didn't care. She clenched her teeth, trying to quell the pounding in her head.

*Where are we going?* She craned her neck this way and that, looking through the holes in the animatronic's battered suit. There were only a few holes, small and on either side of the thing's torso. All she could make out was the forest: trees rushing by in the darkness as they hurried to their mysterious destination. Charlie sighed in frustration, tears welling up. *Where are you? Am I getting closer to you? Sammy, is it you?*

She gave up looking for hints outside and stared straight ahead at the inside of the suit. *Stay calm*, Aunt Jen's voice said in her head. *Always stay calm. It's the only way to keep your head clear.* She stared up into the mask, at the inside-out features of the twisted Freddy.

Suddenly, the blank spheres rolled back and the eyes flipped in, staring straight down at her with an impassive, plastic gaze. Charlie screamed and jerked back. Something behind her snapped, lashing a whiplike piece of metal into her side. She froze in terror. *No, please no.* Nothing else triggered, and after a moment she cautiously settled herself in place, trying not to meet the shiny blue eyes above her. Her side where the piece of metal had hit her shocked with pain each time she breathed. She wondered, alarmed, if a rib had broken. Before she could be sure, the animatronic lurched to the side again, and Charlie fell with it, hitting her head so hard that the blow reverberated through her body. Her vision darkened, closing to a tunnel, and as she faded into unconsciousness again, all she could see were Freddy's watching eyes.

John's lungs were beginning to burn, his legs turning rubbery as they ran on and on through the forest. They had been running for what felt like hours, though he knew it couldn't be. That was just his exhaustion playing tricks on his mind. The trail had faded. When they entered the forest, the trees had been their guide. They followed ripped, ragged bark and broken branches, and even torn roots where massive, careless feet had stepped.

But the signs had grown farther between, then stopped entirely. Now John ran on in the direction the creatures seemed to have been headed.

Truthfully, he might have been lost.

As he darted around trees, trekked up and down small hills, and stumbled on uneven ground, John began to lose his sense of direction entirely. Ahead of him, Jessica ran confidently onward. He followed, but for all he knew they could be running in an endless circle.

Behind him, Clay's steps were slowing, his breathing heavy. Jessica, a few paces ahead, doubled back, jogging in place as she waited for them to catch up.

"Come on, guys, we're almost there!" she said energetically.

"Almost where?" John asked, struggling to keep his tone even.

"I'm just trying to be encouraging," she said. "I was on my high school cross-country team for three years."

"Well, I was always more of a heavy-lifter, you know," John panted, suddenly defensive.

"Clay, come on, you can do it!" Jessica called. John glanced back. Clay had stopped running and was doubled over with his hands on his knees, taking gasping breaths. With relief, John slowed to a walk and turned back. Jessica let out a frustrated sound and followed him to Clay.

"Are you all right?" John asked.

The older man nodded, waving him back. "Fine," he said. "Go ahead, I'll catch up."

"There's nowhere to 'go ahead' to," John said. "We're running blind. When's the last time you saw tracks?"

"A while back," Clay said, "but they were heading this way, and it's all we have to go on."

"But it's nothing to go on!" John's voice rose in frustration. "There's no reason to think they went this way!"

"We're losing them," Jessica said urgently. She was still running in place, her ponytail bouncing like a little nervous animal behind her. Clay shook his head.

"No, we've already lost them."

Jessica stopped running, but she kept shifting from one foot to the other. "So now what?"

Something rustled in the trees ahead of them. Jessica grabbed John's arm, then released it quickly, looking embarrassed. The sound came again, and John started toward it, raising a hand to signal the others to stay. He made his way cautiously through the trees, glancing back once and noting that Jessica and Clay were close behind, despite his attempt to keep them back.

A few feet farther on, the trees broke into an open field; they had reached the far side of the woods. Jessica gasped, and a split second later John saw it. Halfway across the clearing a figure stood in the darkness. It was almost featureless and flat, scarcely distinct from the shadows. John squinted, trying to get hold of the image, to assure himself he was really seeing it. Heavy, black electrical wires stretched above the field like a canopy, but besides the wires, the field was clear. Though it was dark, there was no way for them to sneak closer to the figure without being seen.

So John straightened his shoulders and began to walk slowly and openly toward it.

The field was untended, and tall grass brushed John's knees as he walked. Behind him, Jessica and Clay made rustling sounds with every step. The wind whipped the grass against their legs, blowing more ferociously with each step they took. Almost halfway across the field, John stopped, puzzled. The figure was still there, but it seemed as far away from them as when they'd started. He glanced back at Jessica.

"Is it moving?" she whispered. He nodded and started walking again, not taking his eyes from the shadowy figure. "John, it looks like . . . Freddy?"

"I don't know what it is," John answered cautiously. "But I think it wants us to follow."

*I can't breathe.* Charlie coughed and gagged, coming suddenly awake. She lay on her back, dirt pouring down onto her. It filled her mouth, clogging her nose and covering her eyes. She spat, shaking her head and blinking rapidly. She tried to raise her hands but couldn't move them. She remembered suddenly that they were trapped inside the arms of the suit and would be mutilated if she struggled to free them.

*Buried alive! I'm being buried alive.* She opened her mouth to scream and more dirt fell in, hitting the back of her throat and making her gag again. Charlie could feel her pulse in her throat, choking her from the inside as surely as the dirt from outside. Her heart was beating too fast and she felt light-headed. She took faster breaths, trying in vain to fill her lungs, but she only stirred up the dirt and inhaled it. She spat, gargling at the back of her throat to catch it before she swallowed, and turned her head to the side, away from the soil that fell like rain. She took a shuddering breath that shook her chest, and then another. *You're hyperventilating*, she told herself sternly. *You have to stop. You have to calm down. You need your head clear.* The last thought came in Aunt Jen's voice. She stared at the now-familiar side of the suit and took deep breaths, ignoring the dirt settling in her ear and sliding down her neck, until her fluttering heart slowed, and she could breathe almost normally again.

Charlie closed her eyes. *You have to get your arms free.* She concentrated all her attention on her left arm. Her T-shirt left the skin of her arms bare against the suit, so she could feel everything that touched her. With her eyes still closed, Charlie began to draw a map. *There's something at the shoulder joints on either side, and a space just below. Spikes in a line all the way down to my elbow on the outside, and the inside has—what is that?* She rocked her arm slowly, gently, back and forth against the objects, trying to envision them. *They're not spring locks.* She froze, focusing again on the place where the arm joined the torso. *THOSE are spring locks. Okay, I'll get to it. Hands.* She flexed her fingers slightly: the sleeves were wide, and her hands—which reached roughly to the creature's elbows—were less constrained than anything else. She spat out dirt again, trying not to notice that it was still pouring in steadily, piling up all around her. *Breathe. While you still can.* She clenched her jaw, envisioning the sleeve that encased her arm, and slowly began to work her way out of it. She dipped down her shoulder, rotated forward, held her breath—and pulled her arm three inches out. Charlie let out a shuddering sigh. Her shoulder was free of the spring locks. *That was the hardest part. The rest of my arm won't touch them if I'm careful.* She kept going, avoiding the things she thought might snap or stab her. When she was halfway out, her elbow at the shoulder seam, she twisted her arm too quickly and heard a snap. She stared horrified at the suit's shoulder, but it wasn't the spring lock. Something smaller inside had triggered, and now she could feel the burn of a fresh cut. *Okay. It's okay.* She got back to work.

Minutes later, her arm was free. She flexed it back and forth in the small space, feeling a little like she had never had an arm before. *Now the other one.* She wiped her face with her hand, smearing away the dirt, closed her eyes, and began again with her right arm.

The second sleeve took less time to get out of, but fatigue and the growing mounds of dirt around her made Charlie careless. Twice she triggered small mechanisms that bruised her painfully, but didn't break her skin. She yanked herself free too fast, bumping the spring locks and only barely snatch-ing her hand away before they cracked open. The arm jumped and jolted as the robotic skeleton inside it unfolded with a noise like firecrackers. Charlie clutched her hand to her chest, cradling it against her pounding heart as she watched. *That could have been . . . It wasn't. It wasn't me. Focus. Legs.*

Her legs weren't pinned in place as her arms had been. They'd simply been awkwardly positioned, wedged between metal rods that ran through the body of the mascot. Without the weight of her body resting on them, she was able to maneuver. Cautiously, Charlie lifted her right leg into the air, pulling it over the rod and into the center of the torso. Nothing triggered, and she did the same with her left.

Her limbs freed, Charlie looked down the length of the animatronic, at the door to the chest cavity. The latch was on the outside, but these creatures were old; their parts were rusted and weak. She reached out and put her hands against the metal, feeling for springs and other devices. She couldn't quite see from where her head was stuck, and she couldn't move down safely. *Unless.*

The dirt had piled up almost a foot on either side of her head, and it covered the lower half of her body. Charlie abandoned the door momentarily, and began to slowly move the dirt. She lifted her head slightly and brushed at the mound with her hands, pushing soil into the space she left. She rocked her body back and forth, using her hands to sweep dirt under her, until she lay on it like a thin bed. It wouldn't protect her from the suit if she triggered it, but it would give her an extra cushion, make it slightly harder for her to jostle something and be skewered alive. She glanced at the arm of the suit that had been triggered, now filled with metal spines and hard plastic parts. A shiver went down her back.

Now she inched down until she could see the chest plates, placed her hands in the center, and began to push upward with all her might. After a moment they came apart and a rush of dirt cascaded in. Charlie coughed and turned her head, but she kept pushing as the dirt rained down on her. She managed to get the plates a foot apart, then crouched beneath them and paused for a moment. *How deep am I?* she thought for the first time. If she'd been buried six feet down, she might be escaping only to suffocate in the home stretch. *What else am I going to do?* Charlie closed her eyes, took a deep breath, and held it. Then she pressed herself up to the doors and began to claw her way out of the grave.

The dirt wasn't packed tightly, but it still took effort: she scratched and scraped at it with her bare hands, wishing for a tool as her fingernails split and bled. As she hacked at the dirt, her lungs began to burn and clench, trying to get her to breathe. She scrunched her face up as hard as she could and scratched harder. *Are you out there? I'm coming, but help me, please, I have to get out of this. Please, I can't die here, buried ali—*

Her hand broke the surface, and she drew it back in shock. *Air.* She gasped gratefully until she no longer felt starved of oxygen. Then she closed her eyes and battered her fists at the tiny hole above her head, breaking the sides until it was large enough to wriggle through. Charlie stood up, her feet still planted in the chest cavity of the suit. There had been little more than a foot of dirt covering her. She braced her feet on the half-open doors and clambered out of the hole, hauling herself up. She collapsed beside it, shaking with exhaustion. *You're not safe yet*, she scolded herself. *You have to get up.* But she couldn't bring herself to move. She stared, horrified, at the hole she had escaped from, her face wet with tears.

Time passed, minutes or hours; she lost track completely. Finally mustering her strength, Charlie pushed herself up to a sitting position, wiping her face. She couldn't tell where she was, but the air was cool and still. She was indoors, and somewhere in the distance was the sound of rushing water. With the adrenaline gone, her head ached again, throbbing along with her heartbeat. It wasn't just her head—everything hurt. She was covered in bruises, her clothing was stained with blood, and now that she wasn't suffocating, she was aware again of the stabbing sensation in her rib cage every time she inhaled. Charlie prodded her ribs, trying to feel if anything seemed out of place. The bruises were already brightly colored, especially where parts of the suit had struck her, but nothing was broken.

Charlie stood up, the pain receding enough to at least move and get her bearings. As she looked around, her blood went cold.

It was Freddy Fazbear's Pizza.

*It can't be.* The wave of panic rose again. She glanced around wildly, backing up, away from the hole in the ground. *The tables, the carousel in the corner, the stage—the tablecloths are blue.* "The tablecloths at Freddy's weren't blue," she said, but her relief was quickly washed away by confusion. *Then what is this place?*

The dining room was larger than the one at Freddy's, though there were fewer tables. The floor was black and white tile, except for large patches where the tiles were missing, revealing plots of packed dirt. It was oddly incongruous with everything else, which looked finished and brand-new, if dusty. As she turned to the opposite wall, she saw that she was being watched. Large plastic eyes stared back from the dark, glaring down at Charlie, seeming to identify her as an intruder. Fur and beaks and eyes stood poised like a small army halfway up the wall.

For a long moment she stood stock-still, bracing herself. But the animatronics didn't move. Charlie took a small step to one side, then the other; the eyes did not track her. The creatures looked forward, unseeing, at their fixed points. Some of their faces were animals, and some seemed to be painted like clowns. Others appeared disturbingly human.

Charlie moved closer and saw what it was they were perched on. All along the wall, arcade games and carnival attractions were lined up, each with its guardian beast or a giant face mounted on top. Their mouths were wide open, as if they were all laughing and cheering some invisible spectacle. As Charlie peered through the darkness, she saw that the animals were unnaturally posed, their bodies twisted in ways no animal should be able to twist. She scanned the wide-mouthed faces again and shivered. With their bodies so torturously bent, they looked like they were screaming in pain.

Charlie took deep breaths. As she calmed herself she realized that there was music playing through the speakers overhead. It was quiet; familiar, but she couldn't name it.

She approached the nearest of the games. A massive, contorted birdlike creature with a wide, curved beak presided over a large cabinet with a fake pond. Rows of ducks sat still in paper water, waiting for rubber balls to knock them down. Charlie looked up again at the creature perched on top of the game. Its wings stretched wide, and its head was thrown upward in the midst of an elaborate dance. It cast a shadow in front of the game, right where the player would stand. Charlie turned, not stepping any closer. Besides the duck pond, there were three arcade consoles lined up next to one another, their screens dusty. Three large chimpanzees squatted atop them, the tips of their toes gripping the edges above the screen. Their arms were raised, frozen in motion, and their teeth were bared in mirth, rage, or fear. Charlie stared for a moment at the teeth; they were long and yellow.

Something about the arcade games nagged at her. She looked them up and down carefully, but nothing tripped her memory. None were turned on, and none of them were games she had ever seen before. She wiped the dust from the screen of the central console, revealing a glossy black screen. Her face, distorted in the curved glass, showed only a little bruising and a few visible cuts. Charlie self-consciously smoothed her hair.

*Wait*. At Freddy's Pizza, ghostly images had been burned into the arcade screens after years of play. She pressed a couple of buttons experimentally. They were stiff and shiny—untouched.

"That's why it feels so empty," she said to the chimp above her. "No one's ever been here, have they?" The great ape didn't respond. Charlie glanced around. There was a doorway to her left, the bluish glow of an unseen black light emanating from the room beyond. Charlie went toward the light, through the door, and into another room of games and attractions. Here, too, they were all guarded by mascots, some more identifiable than others. Charlie staggered for a moment and put her hand on her forehead. "Strange," she whispered, regaining her balance. She looked back the way she'd come. *It must be the light making me dizzy*, she thought.

"Hello?" someone called faintly in the distance. Charlie whirled around as if someone had shouted in her ear. She held her breath, waiting for it to come again. The voice had been high and scared, a child. The sudden impression of life in this place shook her, as if waking her from a dream.

"Hello!" she called back. "Hello, are you all right? I won't hurt you." She glanced around the room. The sound of rushing water was louder here, making it hard to judge how far away the voice had come from. She moved quickly through the room, ignoring the wide-eyed creatures and the strange and garish games. A simple, skirted table in the corner caught her attention, and she went to it swiftly. Charlie crouched down, careful to keep her balance, and lifted the cloth. Eyes stared back at her and she startled, then steadied herself.

"It's okay," she whispered, flipping the cloth up over the table. The glimmer of the eyes faded with the rush of light. There was no one there after all.

Charlie put her hands on her forehead and pressed hard for a moment, trying to ward off the growing pain in her temples.

She went through another door, now unsure which way she'd come from, and discovered the source of the running water. Springing from the center of the wall to her left was a waterfall. It cascaded down over a rock face protruding several feet out, and joined with a riverbed below. The water rushed from a wide pipe only partly concealed by the rock.

The stream below was maybe three feet wide. It crossed the room, splitting the floor in two, and disappeared into the open mouth of a cave.

Charlie watched it for a moment, mesmerized by the water. After a moment, she noticed a narrow gap in the rock face behind the waterfall, just big enough for a person to walk through. "Hello?" Charlie called again, but only half-heartedly; here the white noise of the water was louder than anywhere else. She realized after a second that it was a recording, overpowering the sound of the actual water.

She surveyed the rest of the room: except for the water-fall and the little river it was empty, but she noticed the floor had a gray border. *No, it's a path.* It was narrower than a sidewalk, paved with square gray cobblestones. It ran along-side the curved wall, tracing the way to the waterfall, and led through a narrow passage under the fall itself. Charlie crouched down to touch the stones: they felt like hard plastic given a rough finish. The path was likely there for a time when the place would be filled with other attractions; she could probably just walk straight across the room. *Probably.*

Charlie stepped onto the cobblestones carefully, expecting them to give way under her weight, but they held. The man-ufactured coarseness of the rocks' surface was sharp—it hurt a little to walk on it. Charlie dutifully followed the walkway, keeping close to the wall. She had a vague sense that step-ping off onto the open floor might be dangerous.

When she reached the waterfall, she went to the gap and gingerly touched the rock surface. It was the same plastic as the cobblestones. Like the path, the cliff was hard plastic, solid, but because it looked like rocks it felt insubstantial when she touched it. Charlie took her hands away and wiped them on her jeans. She stepped carefully sideways, scooting through the hole behind the waterfall. The cavern was only a few feet long, but she stopped for a moment at the center. She felt trapped in the darkness, though she could see light on either side. *Trapped.* Her chest tightened, and she screwed her eyes shut. *Calm down. Focus on what's around you*, she thought. Charlie took a long, steadying breath and listened.

Standing beneath the waterfall, the tape recording was muffled. She thought she could hear the water itself, rushing over her head and spilling down in front of her, though she couldn't see it. There was something else as well, quiet but distinct. From above her, or maybe behind, Charlie could hear the cranking of gears. A machine was churning the water, keeping it flowing in a giant cycle, making the whole thing work. The sound of the machine at work calmed her; the rising panic subsided, and she opened her eyes.

She took another sideways step, moving closer to the light, and stubbed her toe on something hard. A shock of pain jolted her. The object tipped over, making a sloshing sound as it fell. Grinding her teeth, she waited a moment for her toe to stop hurting, then maneuvered herself into a crouch. It was a fuel can. *For the waterfall,* she realized as the machinery ground on overhead. There were several more, all neatly arranged along the wall, but this one had been in the middle of the path. If she had been going faster, she would have fallen over it. Charlie set it firmly beside the others, and stepped quickly into the other half of the room.

"Hello?" The voice again, this time a little louder. Charlie stood up straight, immediately on alert. It had come from ahead. She didn't respond this time but moved carefully toward it, staying on the path and keeping close to the wall.

The hallway opened out into another room. The lights were dimmer here. In the corner opposite Charlie was a small carousel, but there seemed to be little else. Charlie scanned the room, and then her breath caught. The child was there, motionless, almost hidden in the shadows in the far corner of the room.

Charlie approached slowly, apprehensive of what she might find. She blinked and shook her head hard, her dizziness resurging. The room seemed to spin around her. *Who are you? Are you all right?* she wanted to ask but kept silent. She stepped closer, and the figure came into focus. It was just another animatronic, or perhaps just a normal doll, made to look like a little boy selling balloons.

He was perhaps four feet tall, with a round head and a round body, his arms almost as long as his stout legs. He wore a red-and-blue striped shirt, and a matching propeller beanie on his head. He was made of plastic, but his shiny face had something old-fashioned about it. Its features mimicked fairy-tale dolls carved from wood. His nose was a triangle and his cheeks were made rosy with two raised circles of dusky pink. His blue eyes were enormous, wide, and staring, and his mouth was open in a grin that bared all his even white teeth. His hands were fingerless balls, each gripping an object. In one he held a red and yellow balloon nearly half his size on a stick. In the other he raised a wooden sign reading BALLOONS!

He was nothing like the creatures Charlie's father had made, nothing even like the animatronics that had kidnapped her. They were horrible, but she recognized them as twisted copies of her father's work. This boy was something new. She circled around him, tempted to poke and prod, but she held back. *Don't chance triggering anything.*

"You're not so bad," Charlie murmured, cautious not to take her eyes off him. He just kept grinning, wide-eyed, into the darkness. Turning her attention to the rest of the room, Charlie looked thoughtfully at the carousel, the only thing there besides the boy. She was too far away to make out the animals.

"Hello?" said the voice, right behind her. She spun back just in time to see the boy turn toward her with a single, swinging step. Charlie screamed and ran back the way she came from, but beneath her feet the dirt began to stir. It jolted, as if something were bumping upward. She scrambled backward as the dirt rose again, and something broke through the surface.

Charlie ran for the carousel, the only cover in the room. She ducked behind it, lying down on her stomach so her body would be hidden behind its base. She stared down at the ground and listened to muffled scratches and beating sounds as some creature climbed free of its grave. The spinning sensation took hold of her again. The black-and-white tiles swam beneath her. She tried to push herself up to peek over the carousel, but her head felt leaden. The weight of it held her down, threatening to pin her back to the ground. *There's something wrong with this room.* Charlie gritted her teeth and yanked her head up; she scrambled to her feet, steadying herself against the carousel, and ran back the way she came, not looking back.

The room with the games and the harsh black light was dizzying as well, and it sprawled out in all directions. Everything seemed farther apart than before, the walls miles away. Her mind was numb. She fumbled to remember where she was, unable to tell which way was which. She stumbled forward, and another mound of earth rose ahead of her. Something glimmered. Her eyes lit on the silhouettes of arcade machines, their reflective surfaces acting as beacons in the dark.

She staggered toward them, her head swaying, so heavy she could hardly stay upright. The walls were crawling with activity. Small things skittered disjointedly all over the ceiling, but she couldn't see what they were—they were wriggling *under* the paint. The surface undulated chaotically. There was a strange ringing in the air, and though she only now registered it, she realized it had been sounding all along. She stopped in her tracks and looked desperately for the source, but her vision was clouding and her thoughts were slow. She could barely name the things she saw. *Rectangle*, she thought fuzzily. *Circle. No. Sphere.* She looked from one indistinct shape to another, trying to remember what they were called. The effort distracted her from staying on her feet, and she fell to the ground again with a hard thud. Charlie was sitting upright, but her head dragged at her, threatening to pull her over.

*Hello?* A voice called again. She put her hands on her head, forcing it back, and looked up to see several children standing around her, all with plump little bodies and broad smiling faces. *Sammy?* She moved toward them instinctively. They were blurred, and she couldn't see their features. She blinked, but her vision didn't clear. *Don't trust your senses. Something is wrong.*

"Stay back!" Charlie screamed at them. She forced herself unsteadily to her feet and stumbled toward the shadows cast by the arcade towers. There, at least, she might be hidden from whatever worse things lurked in the room.

The children went with her, rushing in trails of color around her and sweeping in and out of view. They seemed more to float than walk. Charlie kept her eyes on the towers; the children were distracting, but she knew there was something worse nearby. She could hear the sickening grind of metal, and plastic twisting, and a rasping noise she recognized. Sharp feet scraped against the floor, digging grooves into the tile.

She crouched low, fixing her eyes on the nearest open door, and was struck with a certainty that this was the way she had come. She crawled desperately toward it, moving as fast as she could without fully standing. Finally, she collapsed under her own weight and lay flat on the tile again. *You have to get up, now!* Charlie let out a scream and clambered to her feet. She ran headlong into the next room, barely keeping her balance, and skidded to a stop. The room was full of dining tables and carnival games; it was where she'd started, but something had changed.

All the eyes were tracking her. The creatures were moving, their skin stretching organically, their mouths snapping. Charlie ran for the dining table in the center of the room, the largest one with a tablecloth that almost reached the floor on all sides. She slid to the ground and crawled under it, curling herself into a ball and pulling her legs tight against her. For a moment, there was only silence, and then the voices began again. *Hello?* a voice called from somewhere nearby. The tablecloth rustled.

Charlie held her breath. She looked at the thin gap between the tablecloth and the floor, but she could see only a sliver of the black-and-white tile. Something shot by, too fast to see, and she gasped and drew back, forgetting to be silent. The cloth rustled again, swinging gently inward. Someone outside was prodding it. Charlie maneuvered herself onto her hands and knees, feeling as if she had too many arms and legs. The cloth moved again, and this time a swirl of color appeared and vanished in the gap. *The children.* They had found her. The tablecloth swung again, but now it was moving on all sides, jouncing up and down as the children brushed against it. The strange, colorful trails of movement appeared and vanished all around the edges of her hiding place, surrounding her like a wall of living paper dolls.

*Hello? Hello? Hello?* More than one spoke at a time now, but not in a chorus. Their voices overlapped until the word became a meaningless layer of sound, blurred like the floating children themselves.

She turned her face to the side. One of the children stared back—it was under the cloth and gazing at her with a fixed grin and motionless eyes. Charlie jumped up, banging her head on the tabletop. She looked around wildly. She was surrounded: a smiling, blurry face was staring at her from every side. *One, two, three, four, four, four.* She turned in an awkward circle on her hands and knees. Two of the children feinted at her, making little jumps as if they were about to spring. She turned again, and the next one leaped at her, swimming under the cloth in a bright streak of blue and yellow. Charlie froze. *What do I do?* She scrabbled at her sluggish brain, trying desperately to revive it. Another sweep of color whooshed at her, all purple, and her brain awoke: *RUN.*

Charlie scrambled to the tablecloth on her hands and knees and grabbed it, yanking it off the table as she stood. She threw it down behind her and ran, not looking back as someone called again, *Hello?*

She raced toward a sign propped up in the middle of the room, knocking it over behind her as she ran past. Then a shadow near the stage caught her attention, and she swerved. She tripped over a chair and just barely managed to catch herself on another table. Her head was still too heavy. It jerked her forward, and she shoved the table aside, managing to stay upright. She arrived at the stage, and in the shadow there was a door.

Charlie fumbled with the knob, but it was spongy, too soft to turn. She grabbed it with both hands, putting the whole force of her body behind it, and it moved at last: the door opened. She hurried through and slammed it shut behind her, feeling for some kind of latch. She found one and snapped it shut, and as she did her hand brushed a light switch.

A bulb flickered for a moment, then came on dimly, a single glowing strand of orange illuminating the room. Charlie stared at it for a minute, waiting for the rest of the light. No more appeared.

She leaned back against a cabinet beside the door and slid down to sit, putting her hands on her temples and trying to shove her head back to a normal size. The relative darkness steadied her. She stared down at the floor, hoping whatever was happening to her was almost over. She looked up, and the room shifted nauseatingly. *It's not over.* Charlie closed her eyes, took a deep breath of the stale air, and opened them again.

*Fur. Claws. Eyes.* She clapped a hand over her mouth to stop herself from screaming. A jolt of adrenaline cut briefly through the fuzziness. The room was full of creatures, but she couldn't make sense of them. The dark fur of a simian arm lay on the floor, inches from her feet, but out of it spilled coils and bare wire. The rest of the ape was nowhere to be seen.

There was something large and gray right in front of her, a torso with arms and webbed, amphibious hands, but there was no head. Instead, someone had balanced a large cardboard box where the neck would have been. Past the torso were standing figures, a phalanx of shadows. As she stared at them, they resolved into something comprehensible. They were unfinished mascots, as distorted as the ones outside.

A rabbit stood at the back. Its head was brown like a jackrabbit and its ears were swept back, but its eyes were just empty holes. The rabbit's body was hunched to the side, and its arms were short, held up as if in surrender. Two metal frames stood in front of it. One was headless, and the other topped with the head of a red-eyed, slavering black dog, whose fangs stuck out from its mouth. Charlie kept her eyes on it for a moment, but it didn't move. Beside it—

Charlie cringed and ducked her head, covering her face with her arms. Nothing happened. Cautiously, she lowered her hands and looked again.

It was Freddy—the misshapen Freddy that had been buried. Charlie glanced at the door, then back at Freddy. He stared straight ahead, his eyes blank and his hat askew. *It can't be him*, she told herself. *It's just another costume.* But she shrank back, trying to make herself smaller.

Something delicately stroked the top of her head. Charlie screamed and yanked herself away. She turned to see a disembodied human arm on the shelf above where she'd been sitting. Its hand stuck out at just the right height to brush her head. Other arms were stacked beside it and on top of it, some covered in fur and others not. Some had fingers, some simply ended, cut off at what would have been the wrist. The other shelves were stacked with similar things: one with pelts of fur, another with piles of detached feet. One just had dozens of extension cords tangled up in an ugly nest.

From outside the door Charlie heard the voice again. *Hello?* The doorknob rattled. She squeezed past the mutilated arcade games and chopped-off parts, gritting her teeth as she crawled over soft things that squelched beneath her weight. As she stepped back, her shoulder crashed into one of the standing metal frames, the headless one. It rocked on its ungrounded feet, threatening to topple. She tried to pull away, but the frame followed, swaying for a moment as she fought to free her hands. She yanked them back and ducked as more metal frames came crashing to the ground.

She squatted down beside one of the large arcade cabinets. The plastic casing was cracked so badly the words and pictures were entirely obscured. Right beside her, inches away, were Freddy's stocky legs. Charlie huddled down, pressing against the game as if she could blend in with it. *Don't turn around*, she thought, eyeing the motionless bear. The dim light seemed to be moving like a spotlight. It glinted off the dog's red eyes, then the gleaming tusk, then off something sharp-cornered at the back of the rabbit's hollow socket.

Just out of her line of sight, something moved. Charlie whipped her head around, but there was nothing there. From the corner of her eye, she saw the rabbit straighten its spine. She turned frantically back toward it but found it hunched in its same agonized posture as before. Slowly,

Charlie looked around her in a half circle, keeping her back pressed against the console.

*Hello?* The doorknob rattled again. She closed her eyes and pressed her fists to her temples. *No one's here, no one's here.* Something rustled in front of her, and Charlie's eyes snapped open. Scarcely breathing, she watched as Freddy came alive. A sickly twisting sound filled the room, and Freddy's torso began to turn. *Hello?* Her eyes shifted to the door for a split second, and when she looked back again Freddy was still. *I have to get out of here.*

She took a moment to measure the path, looking first to the door, then to Freddy in front of her, mapping a blurry route. At last she went, looking down at her hands and nothing else as she crawled steadily around the motionless legs of the standing animatronics, and past the half-bestial games. *Don't look up.* Something brushed against her leg as she passed it, and she pressed on, her head down. Then something grabbed her ankle.

Charlie screamed and flailed, trying to kick herself free, but the iron grip tightened. She looked frantically over her shoulder: Freddy was crouched behind her, the light glinting off his face and making him seem to smile. Charlie yanked her foot back with all her strength, and Freddy pulled even harder, dragging her closer. Charlie grabbed the leg of a pinball game and hoisted herself up to her knees. As Freddy tried again to drag her back, the game shook and rattled like it was about to fall. Clutching at it with all her might, Charlie jerked her body up and forward. Freddy's claws tore her skin as she wrenched herself free, and the pinball machine collapsed under her weight.

Freddy lurched forward. That horrible mouth unhinged again like an enormous snake. He crouched down, coming toward her in a sinuous motion. She scrambled over the broken game toward the door. Behind her, something rustled and scraped, but she didn't look back. Her hand on the doorknob, Charlie stopped as the room around her swayed. The noise behind her grew louder, closer, and she turned to see Freddy crawling toward her in a predatory crouch. His mouth was widening. Dirt poured out of it in a steady stream.

"Hello? Charlie?" came a voice from outside. But this voice was different; it wasn't the animatronic child. Charlie fumbled at the knob, the spinning sensation in her head worsening as Freddy came slowly, purposefully closer. The room swayed again, and her hand closed on the knob and turned it. She shoved the door open and stumbled into the light.

"Charlie!" someone cried, but she didn't look up. The sudden brightness was piercing, and she held up a hand to shield her eyes as she forced the door shut again. The ringing hadn't stopped while she was in the closet, but now it was louder. It filled her ears like a skewer, plunging into her swollen brain. She fell to her knees, wrapping her arms around her head, trying to protect it. "Charlie, are you okay?" Something touched her, and she shied away, her eyes screwed shut against the light. "Charlie, it's John," the voice said, cutting through the awful noise, and something in her went still.

"John?" she whispered, her voice raspy. The dust from the grave had settled in her throat.

"Yeah." She turned her head and peered up through the shield of her arms. Slowly, the blazing light calmed, and she saw a human face. *John.*

"Are you real?" she asked, uncertain what kind of answer would convince her. He touched her again, a hand on her arm, and she didn't pull away. She blinked, and her vision cleared a little. She looked up, feeling as if she were opening herself to attack. Her eyes lit on two more people, and her halting mind slowly named them. "Jessica . . . ? Clay?"

"Yeah," John said. She put her hand on his and tried to focus. She could see Jessica, who was doubled over, her hands over her own ears.

"The noise," Charlie said. "She hears the noise, too. Do you?" It grew louder, drowning out John's response, and Charlie grabbed his hand. *Real. This is real.* "The children!" she cried out suddenly, as a swath of undulating colors rose from underneath the tables. They flew, their feet not touching the ground, their bodies leaving comet-like trails of color behind them. "Do you see?" Charlie whispered to John.

"Jessica!" he shouted. "Look out!" Jessica straightened, dropping her hands, and yelled something indistinct. The children converged on her in a swarm, dancing around her, darting in close, then back out again, as if it were a game, or an ambush. Two rushed on Clay, who stared them down until they shriveled and swirled back to join the circle around Jessica.

"The lights!" Jessica cried, her voice rising above the painful ringing noise. "Clay, it's coming from the lights on the walls!" She pointed up, where Charlie could just make out a long row of decorative colored lights, evenly spaced.

A gunshot cut through the clamor, and Charlie gripped John's hand tighter. Jessica's hands were on her ears again. The children were still in motion, but it was a nervous, shimmering movement. They'd stopped in place. Clay stood with his back to them all, his gun pointed at the wall. Charlie watched, wide-eyed, as he took aim again, and shot out the bulb of the second light fixture. The room dimmed slightly, and he moved on to the third, then the next, then the next. As one shot rang out after another, Charlie's head began to equalize, like whatever stuff had filled her to the point of bursting was slowly being drained. The room darkened, one bulb at a time. *Bang.* She looked up at John, and his face was clear. "It's really you," she said, her voice still choked with dust. *Bang.*

"It's really me," he agreed.

*Bang.*

The children's shimmering slowed, giving glimpses of arms and legs and faces. Jessica took her hands from her ears.

*Bang.*

Clay shot the last light, and the children stopped shimmering. They wavered briefly on the edge of solidity, a sickening ripple of lights in a scattered harmony, and then they were still. The room was silent. It was still lit by the overhead lights, but all the others were dead. Jessica looked around her, bafflement and horror taking turns on her face. The children were no longer children. They were wind-up toys, plastic boys in striped shirts, wearing plastic smiles and propeller beanies, and offering balloons.

"Jessica, come here," Clay said in a low voice, holding out his hand. She stepped toward him, glancing warily at the balloon boys as she moved between them. He took her hand to help her through, as if he were pulling her out of a chasm. Charlie slowly let go of John's hand and put hers to her temples, checking to make sure everything was still there. Her head no longer ached; her vision was clear. Whatever had come over her was gone.

"Charlie," Jessica said. "Are you all right? What's going on in here? I feel . . . drugged."

"These things aren't real." Charlie steadied herself and slowly got to her feet. "I mean, they're real, but not how we're seeing them. This whole place is an illusion. It's twisted somehow. Those things . . ." She gestured toward the wall where Clay had shot out the lights. "Those things are like the disc we found. They emit some kind of signal that distorts how we see." Charlie shook her head. "We have to get out of here," she said. "There's something worse here than these."

She pushed over a balloon boy, and it toppled easily. Its head popped off as it hit the ground, and it rolled across the floor. *Hello?* it muttered, much quieter than before.

ohn prodded the plastic balloon boy's head with his toe. It rolled a little farther, but did not speak again.

"Charlie?" Jessica said shakily. "Where are they? The big ones."

"I don't know. My head is still spinning." Charlie glanced around quickly, then drew closer to the others as they surveyed the room. Everything had changed when Clay shattered the fixtures. The realistic beasts and vicious-looking creatures were gone, replaced with strange, hairless versions of themselves. They no longer had eyes, only smooth, raised bumps of blank plastic.

"They look like corpses," John said softly.

"Or some kind of mold," Clay said thoughtfully. "They don't look finished."

"It's the lights," Charlie said. "They were creating an illusion, like the chip."

"What are you talking about?" Jessica said. "What chip?"

"It's—it's some kind of transmitter, embedded in a disc," Charlie said. "It scrambles your brain, cluttering it with nonsense so that you see what you expect to see."

"Then why don't they look like that?" Clay pointed to posters on the walls depicting a very cheerful Freddy Fazbear with rosy cheeks and a warm smile.

"Or that." John had found another, depicting Bonnie jovially strumming a bright red guitar so shiny it looked like it was made from candy.

Charlie looked thoughtful for a moment. "Because we didn't come here first." She walked toward the posters. "If you were a little kid and you saw the cute commercials, then saw these posters and toys and all that stuff, then I think that's exactly what they would have looked like."

"Because you already have those images in your head," John said. He tore the Freddy poster off the wall and stared at it momentarily before letting it fall to the ground. "But we know better. We know they're monsters."

"And we're afraid of them," Charlie said.

"And so we're seeing them for exactly what they are," John concluded.

Clay went up to the arcade mascots again, his gun still

drawn. He walked back and forth in front of the displays, looking at them from different angles.

"How did you find me?" Charlie asked suddenly. "You showed up like the cavalry—just in time. How did you know I was here? How did you know any of this was here?"

No one answered right away. John and Jessica looked to Clay, who was casting his eyes around the room purposefully; he looked like he was searching for something specific. "We followed . . ." He trailed off.

Charlie looked at each of the three of them in turn. "Who?" she demanded. But just as she spoke, the closet door burst open, banging against the wall with a ringing clatter. The twisted Freddy who had taken Charlie came crashing out, his mouth still unhinged and swinging unnaturally. He was a nightmarish version of the Freddy they'd known as kids, with searing red eyes and the musculature of a monster. He turned his elongated head from side to side wildly, his jaw bouncing in place.

"Run!" Clay yelled, waving his arms and trying to usher them together toward the door. Charlie was rooted to the ground, unable to take her eyes off the maw of the beast.

"Wait!" Jessica cried suddenly. "Clay, these aren't possessed like the others—they're not the lost children!"

"What?" he said, momentarily stopping his frantic movement and looking thoroughly confused.

*"Shoot it!"* Jessica screamed. Clay clenched his jaw, then raised the gun and aimed at Freddy's gaping mouth. He fired once. The shot was only a few feet from Charlie's ear, and it was deafening. Freddy jerked back, the python-like jaw contracting, and for a split second his image blurred and distorted. The unnaturally stretched mouth began to close, but before it could, Clay fired again, three more times in quick succession. With each shot the creature seemed to glitch: it blurred, sputtering around the edges. Freddy's mouth curled in on itself, not quite closing but shrinking inward, as the bear hunched forward around its wounds. Clay fired one last time, aiming for Freddy's head. Finally, the animatronic toppled forward, a misshapen heap on the ground.

Freddy's image flickered like static on a television screen. The color faded from his fur, then everything that made him *Freddy* winked out, leaving only a smooth plastic figure in his place. It looked like the rest of the animals in the room, a blank mannequin stripped of its characteristics. Charlie approached the thing that had been Freddy cautiously. The ringing in her ears was beginning to fade. She crouched down next to the creature, tilting her head to the side.

"It's not like the other mascots from Freddy's," she said. "These aren't made of fur and fabric, they're made of us—by twisting our minds." The words came out with a revulsion she hadn't expected.

"Charlie," John said softly. He stepped forward, but she ignored him. She touched the creature's smooth skin. It felt like something between plastic and human skin: a strange, malleable substance that was a little too soft, a little too slick. The feeling of it made her nauseous. Charlie leaned over the body, ignoring her disgust, and plunged her fingers into one of the bullet holes. She dug around in the slippery, inorganic stuff of the chest cavity, pretending not to hear Jessica and Clay's protests, and then she found it. Her fingers touched the disc, which was bent in half, almost broken. Charlie pried out a second piece of metal that was wedged beside it.

She stood up and held it out to the others; a bullet rested in her palm.

"You shot the chip," she said. "You killed the illusion."

No one spoke. In the momentary quiet, Charlie was suddenly aware of the racket they had just made, in this place so accustomed to stillness. The silence was broken by a clicking sound: the noise of claws on tile.

They all whirled to see, and from what had appeared to be a dark and empty corner, a wolflike figure split away from the shadows and stalked toward them, upright but hunched forward, as if uncertain whether to walk as a beast or a human.

They backed away as one. Charlie saw Clay about to trip on Freddy's collapsed body. She shouted, "Look out!" He stopped, turning to see, and his eyes widened at something behind Charlie.

"There!" he cried, and fired a shot into the dark. They turned: an eight-foot, misshapen Bonnie, the rabbit counterpart to the creature on the floor, was blocking the doorway behind them. Its head was too large for its body, with eyes glowing white-hot in the dark. Its mouth was open, revealing several rows of gleaming teeth. Clay fired again, but the bullet had no effect.

"How many bullets do you have left?" John said, measuring up the two threats still in the room.

Clay fired off three more shots at Bonnie, then lowered the gun.

"Three," he said dryly. "I had three." From the corner of her eye, Charlie saw John and Jessica draw closer together, moving a little behind Clay. She stayed where she was as the others retreated, transfixed by the two advancing figures: the wolf and the rabbit. She started to walk toward them.

"Charlie," John said with a warning tone. "What are you doing? Come back!"

"Why did you bring me here?" Charlie asked, looking from one creature to the other. Her chest was tight and her eyes ached, like she'd been holding back tears for hours. "What do you want from me?" she shouted. They looked back at her with implacable plastic eyes. "What is this place? *What do you know about my brother?*" she screamed, her throat raw. She flung herself at the wolf, hurtling toward the gigantic beast, as if she could tear it apart with her bare hands. Someone caught her by the waist. Human hands lifted her up and pulled her back, and Clay spoke quietly into her ear.

"Charlie, we need to go, *now.*" She pulled herself out of his grasp, but remained where she was. Her breath was unsteady. She wanted to scream until her lungs gave out. She wanted to close her eyes and sit very still, and never emerge from the darkness.

Instead she looked again from Bonnie to the nameless wolf and asked, her voice so calm it chilled her to hear it, "Why do you want me?"

"They don't care about you. I'm the one that brought you here." A voice spoke from the same shadowed corner the wolf had emerged from. The rabbit and the wolf straightened their posture, as if responding to the speaker's command.

"I know that voice," Jessica whispered. A figure began to limp forward, obscured by darkness. No one moved. Charlie realized she was holding her breath, but she didn't hear anyone else breathing in the silence, either, just the uneven shuffle of whatever was coming. Whatever it was, it was the size of a man. Its body was contorted, sloping to one side as it lurched toward the group.

"You have something that belongs to me," said the voice, and then the figure stepped into the light.

Charlie gasped and heard John's sharp intake of breath. "Impossible," Charlie whispered. She felt John move up to stand beside her, but she didn't dare take her eyes off the man who stood before them.

His face was dark, the color mottled, and it was swollen with fluid; cheeks that had been hollow were now distended with the bloat of decay. His eyes were bloodshot, the burst capillaries threading through eyeballs that looked just a little too translucent. Something inside them had gone bad, jelly-like. At the base of his neck, Charlie could see two pieces of metal gleaming. They extended from within his neck, rectangular lumps standing out from his mottled skin. He wore what had once been a mascot suit of yellow fur, though what remained was now green with mold.

"Dave?" Jessica breathed.

"Don't call me that," he snarled. "I haven't been Dave for a long time." He held out his new hands: blood-soaked and forever sealed inside a rotting suit.

"William Afton, then? Of Afton Robotics?"

"Wrong again," he hissed. "I've accepted the new life that you gave me. You've made me one with my creation. My name is Springtrap!" The man who had once been Dave cried the name with a hoarse glee, then scrunched his gnarled face back into a glare. "I'm more than Afton ever was, and *far* more than Henry."

"Well, you smell terrible," Jessica quipped.

"Ever since Charlie remade me, set me free to my destiny, I've been master of all these creatures." He crooked his fingers and made a sharp gesture forward. Bonnie and the wolf took two steps forward, in unison. "See? All the animatronics are linked together; it was a system designed to control the choreography for the shows. Now, I control the system. I control the choreography. All of this belongs to me."

Springtrap shuffled forward, and Charlie shrank back. "I owe you both another debt of gratitude as well," he said. "I was imprisoned in that tomb beneath the stage, scarcely able to move, only able to see through the eyes of my creatures."

He gestured at the two who stood behind him. "But for all that I could see, I was trapped. Eventually *they* would have broken me out, but having you do it yourself was a delightful surprise." He met Charlie's eyes, and a muscle twitched in her cheek.

*Get away from me, don't come any closer.* As if reading her thoughts, he sidled nearer to her. She would have felt his breath on her face, if he still breathed.

Springtrap raised a bent hand. The fabric suit was ragged, revealing his human skin through the gaps. She could see the places where metal pins and rods had buried themselves alongside his bones and tendons, into a rusted shadow-skeleton. He touched the back of his hand to Charlie's face, stroking her cheek like a beloved child. From the corner of her eye, she saw John start forward.

"No, it's okay," she forced herself to say.

"I won't hurt your friends, but I need something from you."

"You have to be kidding," she said, her voice brittle.

His mouth twisted into something that grotesquely resembled a smile.

John heard a faint click, and turned just in time to see Clay loading one bullet quietly into his gun. Clay shrugged. "You never know when a corpse may wander out of the shadows wearing a rabbit suit." He raised his arm, steadied himself, and fired.

Springtrap recoiled. "Kids!" Clay shouted, "the door!" Charlie jerked her eyes away from Springtrap almost painfully, as if he had been exerting some hypnotic force on her. Bonnie had abandoned the exit, leaving it clear. Clay, John, and Jessica began to run. Charlie glanced back, reluctant to go, then joined the others.

They ran back the way they'd come from, Clay leading the way as they wound through the carnival games and looming, featureless mascots. He strode purposefully ahead, as if he knew the way. Charlie remembered her question that no one had answered. *How did you find me?*

They were chased by sounds: scraping metal and the clack

of the wolf's claws. In the open space, the noises echoed strangely, seeming to come from every side. It was as if an army pursued them. Charlie quickened her step. She glanced up at John, seeking reassurance, but his eyes were on Clay ahead of them.

They reached the room with the waterfall, and again Clay knew the path. He headed directly for the passage beneath the cliff, where the water emerged. They pressed through it one by one. Clay and John were too tall to walk through without bending over, and Charlie felt a quick pang of relief. *The monsters won't fit.* Halfway through the passage, Clay paused, standing motionless in an awkward position. He craned his neck, studying something just out of view. "Clay!" Charlie hissed.

"I have an idea," he said. Two shadows emerged from the far side of the room. Jessica glanced at the black-lit tunnel beside them, ready to run for it. But Clay shook his head. Instead, he guided the group backward, none of them taking their eyes off the monsters. All that shielded them now was the river that bisected the room. The animatronics were approaching the water hesitantly. The wolf sniffed at it and shook his fur, and Bonnie simply bent down and stared. "Don't run," Clay said sternly.

"They can't cross that thing, right?" Charlie said.

As if responding to her cue, the two mascots stepped unsteadily into the river. Jessica gasped, and Charlie took an involuntary step back. Slowly and deliberately, the animatronics continued toward them through the waist-high water. The wolf slipped on the smooth bottom and fell. It dunked completely under the water for a moment, before scrambling to the side, thrashing violently. Bonnie lost his footing as well but managed to grab the riverbank and steady himself, then continued forward.

"That's not possible," Charlie said. Behind her came a peal of laughter, and she whirled around.

It was Springtrap, his eyes scarcely visible, peering through the black-lit tunnel nearby. "Was that your plan?" he said incredulously. "Did you think *my* robots would be as poorly designed as your father's?"

"Well then, I'm sure you made them fireproof as well!" Clay called out. His voice reverberated in the cavernous, empty room. Springtrap frowned, puzzled, then looked at the water in the stream. It was glistening in the dim light, color dancing on its surface in gleaming swirls, like—

"Gasoline." Charlie turned to face Springtrap. Open gas cans lined the walls, some lying on their sides; all were empty.

Clay flicked a lighter and flung it into the water. The top of the river caught fire, a flame billowing up like a tidal wave, obscuring the animatronics in the middle. The creatures struggled to the side of the river, emitting guttural, high-pitched shrieks. They managed to crawl onto the bank, but it was too late. Their illusions deactivated. Their plastic skin was exposed, liquefying and falling from their bodies into little flaming pools on the floor. Charlie and the others watched as the dissolving creatures fell, writhing in agonized screams.

They all stood frozen, mesmerized by the gruesome spectacle. Then, from behind her, Charlie heard a quiet scraping sound. She whirled around to see Springtrap vanish into the mouth of the narrow, black-lit cave. She took off after him, running into the eerie light.

"Charlie!" Clay called. He began to chase her, but the flaming creatures had crawled across the floor—perhaps trying to reach their master, perhaps in mindless desperation—and now they blocked the mouth of the cave with their blazing remains. Charlie set her eyes on the path ahead. She couldn't afford to look back.

The passage was narrow, and it smelled damp and ancient. The floor felt like rock beneath her bare feet, but though it was uneven, it wasn't painful. The surface was worn and smooth. As soon as the dark of the cave closed over her, she felt a spark from her dreams: the tug of something so like her that it *was* her, blood calling to blood.

"Sammy?" she whispered. His name glanced off the cave walls, shrouding her in the sound of it. The absence inside her pulled her forward, drawing her toward the promise of completion. *It has to be you.* Charlie ran faster, following a call that came from deep inside her.

She could hear the distant echo of Springtrap's laughter at intervals, but she couldn't spot him ahead of her. Occasionally she thought she caught glimpses of him, but he was always gone before her eyes had time to focus in the disorienting glow of the black light. The cave twisted and turned until she had no idea which direction she was headed, but she ran on.

Charlie blinked as something moved at the corner of her eye, just out of sight. She shook her head and ran on, but then it happened again. An unnatural shape, neon-bright, slithered out of the wall and wriggled past her.

Charlie stopped, clapping a hand over her mouth so she wouldn't scream. The thing undulated up the wall, moving like an eel though it was climbing rock. When it reached the ceiling, it vanished, but she couldn't see a break in the rock where it might have gone. *Just keep going.* She started to run again, but suddenly more of them poured out of the seam at the base of the wall. Dozens of wriggling shapes swam and danced, moving along the floor of the cave like it was the floor of the sea. Three of them headed right for Charlie. They rippled over her feet and she screamed, then realized as they circled her, nibbling curiously at her toes, that she felt nothing. "You aren't real," she said. She kicked at them, and her foot passed straight through empty air: the creatures had vanished. Charlie gritted her teeth and ran onward.

Ahead of her, large glowing creatures like dancers made

of mist appeared and vanished one after another. They dashed across the passage, as if they were running along a path that just happened to intersect with this one. When Charlie was almost close enough to touch them, the one nearest sputtered and faded out. She ran on, listening for the sound of Springtrap's maniacal giggle, hoping that it was enough to guide her.

She turned a corner, then the passage angled sharply the other way. Charlie ran straight into the wall, catching herself with her hands at the last second. She spun around, looking for the way forward. The jolt had been enough to distract her. She couldn't tell which way she had come from. Charlie took a deep breath and closed her eyes. She could hear a soft voice in the air. *Left.* She started running again.

A burst of blue light nearly blinded her as a massive shape rose in the darkness. Charlie screamed, flinging herself back against the wall of the cave and throwing her arms up to shield her face. The thing before her was a gaping mouth full of teeth, all glowing blue. The enormous maw bore down over her.

"It's an illusion," Charlie whispered. She ducked and tried to roll away in the narrow space. Her shoulder struck a rock and her arm went numb. Charlie clutched it instinctively and looked up: nothing was there.

She pressed her back against the wall of the cave, taking deep breaths as feeling slowly returned to her arm. "It's another transmitter," she said quietly. "Nothing I see here is real." Her voice was thin in the rocky passage, but saying the words aloud was enough to make her stand again. She closed her eyes. The connection she had felt was growing stronger as she ran, the sense that she was running toward a missing piece of herself. It was unbearable, stronger than the urge to fight or flee from danger. It was greater than hunger, deeper than thirst, and it pulled at the core of her being. She could no more turn back than she could choose to stop breathing. She set off again, hurtling farther into the cavern.

Far in the distance, Springtrap's laughter still echoed.

"Charlie!" John called again, but it was hopeless. She was long out of sight, deep into the cave, and what remained of Bonnie and the wolf still burned in front of the opening.

"We have to go!" Clay shouted. "We can find another way!" Jessica grabbed John's arm and he gave in, following Clay toward the arcade entrance.

Just as they reached the door, the twisted Freddy lunged out of the shadows, almost falling to the ground. Jessica screamed and John froze, struck still at the sight of him. His illusion sputtered on and off in pieces. An arm flickered away, exposing the smooth plastic underneath. Then the fur returned and his torso went blank, revealing the gunshot holes, and the ugly, twisted metal beneath the plastic shell.

Worse was the face: not only was the illusion missing, but the material underneath. From his chin to his forehead, the left half of Freddy's face had been ripped away, revealing metal plates and gnarled wires. His left eye glowed red amid the exposed machinery, while his right eye was completely dark.

A noise behind them broke John from his horrified reverie. He looked back to see that Bonnie and the wolf had gotten to their feet, still smoldering. Their plastic casings had almost entirely melted away, still dribbling slowly off their bodies, but the robotic works beneath seemed intact. They approached steadily, moving into position, so that John, Clay, and Jessica were surrounded.

"Do you have any bullets left?" John asked Clay in a low voice. Clay slowly shook his head. He was turning in a cautious circle, shifting his gaze from one animatronic to the next, as if trying to gauge which would make the first strike.

Charlie ran steadily on, keeping her eyes on the path. She turned another corner and blinked. Something was glowing blue ahead of her. *It's not real*, she told herself. She paused for a moment, but the glowing shapes didn't move. She kept going, realizing as she drew closer that the passageway was widening, opening out finally into a small alcove where the blue glow became clear.

The floor was spotted with patches of mushrooms, their caps glowing an intense neon blue under the black light. She slowed her pace, went to the nearest grouping and bent to touch the mushrooms. She snapped her hand back in surprise when she felt a spongy substance. "They're real, sort of," she said.

"Yes," said a voice beside her ear, and then she was choking. Springtrap grabbed her by the neck, crushing her windpipe. Charlie only panicked for a moment before anger returned to her, giving her clarity. She reached her arm out forward as far as she could, then jammed it back, striking her elbow into his solar plexus with as much force as she could muster. His hands dropped from her throat and she leaped free, turning to face him as he clutched his injured gut.

"Things have changed since you died," Charlie said, surprised by the calm disdain in her voice. "For one thing, I've been doing sit-ups!"

"I think this is it," Jessica said quietly, spinning in place as the three monsters approached, leaving no avenue of retreat. John felt his chest clench, his body protesting the idea. But she was right. He put a hand on her shoulder.

"Maybe we can play dead," he said.

"I don't think we'll have to play," Jessica said resignedly.

"Backs together," Clay barked, and they backed up into a

tiny triangle, each facing one of the creatures. The wolf was crouched, ready to spring. John met its eyes. They were sputtering in and out: dark and malevolent, then completely blank. The thing drew back, and John steeled himself. Jessica grabbed his hand, and he clenched hers tightly. The wolf leaped—and then fell to the ground screeching as something knocked it viciously on its face. The figure, invisible in the shadows, grabbed the wolf's feet and yanked it backward, dragging it away from its human prey as it howled, scrabbling at the floor with its claws. It kicked its hind legs, freeing itself, and began its attack again. Jessica screamed, and John shouted with her, then watched, breathless, as the wolf was caught by its feet again. The thing that held it flipped it onto its back and jumped on top of it. The new predator paused for an instant, meeting their eyes with a silver glow, and Jessica gasped.

"Foxy," John breathed. As if spurred on by hearing his name, Foxy plunged his hook into the wolf's chest and began to tear at its exposed machinery. The screeches of metal ripping apart metal ground at their ears. Foxy continued to dig furiously, burrowing into the wolf as wires and parts fell from the sky. He snapped his jaws in the air, then tore at the wolf's stomach, wrenching out its insides and flinging them aside with a brutal efficiency. The wolf was overpowered, its limbs flailing helplessly before falling heavily to the ground.

Behind them came another inhuman scream. John whipped around in time to see the fire-ravaged Bonnie on its stomach, being dragged steadily into the shadows. Its eyes blinked on and off in a panicked, meaningless pattern. It screamed again as, with a horrible grinding sound, it was torn to pieces by whatever lurked in the shadows. Pieces of metal and shredded plastic scattered across the floor, skittering out in front of the prone rabbit, so that it could see the remnants of its own lower half. It screamed again, anchoring its claws into the tile in a last, futile defense, only to be pulled screeching into the dark as though through a grinder. In the shadows, four lights glowed. John blinked, realizing they were eyes. He nudged Jessica.

"I can see them," he whispered. "Chica and Bonnie! *Our* Chica and Bonnie!" Beside the river, Foxy had torn the wolf's limbs from its body. He leaped from the ravaged torso and took an attack posture toward the large, twisted Freddy, which twitched and flickered for a moment, then lowered its massive head and charged. Foxy leaped, hitting the twisted Freddy's face with full force and knocking it onto its back, then tearing into its head cavity, slashing at what was left of the twisted face with enthusiasm.

Something grabbed John and he snapped out of his trance. The twisted Bonnie grabbed him with an arm of exposed metal, but the eyes in the dark rose suddenly behind it. The original Bonnie grabbed the torso of the twisted Bonnie and threw it aside to where Chica waited; she grabbed the misshapen rabbit's head and wrenched it off in a burst of sparks.

John shielded his eyes. When the smoke settled, all that remained was the hollow, burnt corpse of an unidentifiable monster. Bonnie and Chica had vanished into the shadows.

Charlie ran for the mouth of the passage, but Springtrap leaped on her with preternatural speed. He knocked her to the ground and reached again for her neck with his swollen hands. Charlie rolled out of the way, and something jabbed her hard in the back. She snatched at it, and a mushroom cap came away in her hands. She leaped to her knees as Springtrap got to his feet, circling her, looking for an opening. She glanced down: a sturdy, metal spike had held the mushroom cap in place. She wrapped her hand around its base, blocking it from Springtrap's sight with her body.

Charlie looked up at him, meeting his gelatinous eyes, silently daring him to attack. As if on cue, he sprang at her, leaping with his arms thrust out, stretching again toward her throat. At the last moment, Charlie ducked her head and thrust the spike upward with all her might. It stopped with a jolt as it hit his chest, but she drove it in, ignoring his sputtering cries as he tried uselessly to beat her away. She stood, her hands shaking as she shoved the stake in as far as it would go. He toppled backward, and she knelt swiftly beside him, giving the metal spike another thrust.

"Tell me why," she hissed. It was the question that consumed her, the thing that kept coming back in her nightmares. Now he said nothing, and she rocked the stake back and forth in his chest. He made a gagging cry of pain. *"Tell me why you took him! Why did you choose him? Why did you take Sammy?"*



"Into the cave!" John shouted. "We have to get Charlie!"

They hurried to the opening, but from inside the cave came a strange, overwhelming clatter. They all stepped back as a horde of the balloon boys emerged from the cave, shaking back and forth on unsteady feet, their pointed teeth chattering loudly as they wobbled forward with staring eyes.

"Not again! I hate these things!" Jessica cried. Clay took up a fighting stance, but John could see they would be overwhelmed. There was something different about the children now, something coordinated. Though they shook and wobbled, it no longer seemed like a sign of weakness. Instead, John thought of warriors rattling their shields: the threat before the battle.

"We have to get away," he said. "Clay!"

Something shook the earth—pounding, even footsteps—as a shadow loomed above them. John looked up and saw a smiling Freddy Fazbear approaching, his hat at a jaunty angle and his massive limbs swinging. "Oh no! He's back!" Jessica screeched.

"No, wait! That's *our* Freddy!" John grabbed Jessica and shielded her with his arms. Freddy lumbered past them and into the crowd of balloon boys. With a single lunge he smashed both arms into the crowd, creating a deafening shatter of metal and plastic. The air was filled with arms, legs, and broken shrapnel. Freddy got to his feet and grabbed one of the balloon boys, lifting it up like it weighed nothing. He crushed its head with one hand. Freddy tossed the body to the ground and stomped on it, pursuing the others as they ran. They scattered, but Freddy was moving swiftly, and the room resounded with the noise of cracking plastic.

"Come on, into the cave!" Clay yelled over the din, and they ran for the passage. They hurried down the narrow path, Clay at the front and John taking up the rear, glancing behind to make sure they weren't being followed. Suddenly Clay halted, and Jessica and John nearly ran into him. Crowding up beside him, they saw why he'd stopped: the path split, and there was no trace of Charlie.

"There," Jessica said suddenly. "There's a light!"

John blinked. It was dim, but he saw it. Somewhere down the passage there was a blue glow, though it was impossible to tell how far away it was. "Come on," he said grimly, pressing past Clay to take the lead.

*"Why did you take Sammy?!"* Charlie cried again. Springtrap wheezed and smiled but did not speak. She grabbed his head with both hands, desperate with fury. She lifted his head and brought it crashing against the rock where it lay. He made another sharp grunt of pain, and she did it again. This time something began to ooze from the back of his head, running thickly down the rock. "What did you do to him?" Charlie demanded. "Why did you take him? Why did you choose *him*?" He looked up at her; one of his pupils had swallowed the iris of his eye. He smiled vaguely.

"I didn't choose him."

Hands grabbed Charlie's shoulders, dragging her up and away from the semiconscious Springtrap. She shouted and turned to fight back, only stopping herself when she saw that it was Clay. The others were behind him. She turned back, shaking with rage.

"I'll kill you!" she cried. She lifted Springtrap up by the shoulders and shoved him back against the rock. His head bounced and lolled to the side. "What do you mean you didn't choose him?" Charlie said, leaning in close to him, as if she might read the answers in his battered face. "You took him from me! Why did you take him?"

Springtrap's mismatched eyes seemed to focus for a moment, and even he seemed to have difficulty muttering his next words.

"I didn't take him. I took you."

Charlie stared, her fingers going lax, loosening on Springtrap's moldy suit. *What?* The rage that had filled her to the breaking point drained away all at once. She felt like she'd lost too much blood and was going into shock. Springtrap didn't try to get away; he just lay there coughing and sputtering, his eyes once more unfocused, staring into a void Charlie couldn't see.

Suddenly the floor rattled beneath them. The walls rocked inward as the whole cave shook, and something mechanical roared on the other side of the wall. The sounds of grinding metal filled the air.

"It's a battle royale out there!" Clay shouted. "This whole place is coming down!" Charlie glanced at him, and as soon as her head was turned she felt Springtrap slip from her fingers. She whipped back around, just in time to see him roll through an open trap door at the base of an enormous rock a few feet away. Charlie leaped up to follow him, but the floor quaked violently. She lost her footing, nearly falling as half the cave wall came tumbling down. She stopped, glancing around in confusion: real rock and dirt cascaded all around them. "It's not the fake cave that's collapsing!" she shouted to the rest. "It's the whole building!"

"Is everyone okay?" Clay shouted. Charlie nodded, and saw that John and Jessica were still on their feet. "We have to go!" Light shone through a crack in the wall ahead. Clay started for it, motioning the others to follow. Charlie hesitated, unable to take her eyes from the last place she'd seen Springtrap. John put a hand on her arm.

The walls of the fake cavern had almost completely fallen, and now they could see the actual interior of the complex.

"That way!" Clay shouted, pointing to a narrow maintenance hall that seemed to stretch off endlessly into the distance. "None of these things will be able to fit through there!" Clay and Jessica ran for the entrance to the corridor, but Charlie faltered.

"Charlie, we can deal with him another day," John shouted over the din. "But we need to survive this one first!" The ground shook again and John looked at Charlie. She nodded, and they ran.

Clay led them racing through the tunnel as the sound of its collapse chased them. The air was filled with dust, obscuring the path ahead. Charlie looked back once, but the ruins were lost in the haze. Eventually the rumble of falling rock was reduced to a distant thunder. The clean, narrow hallway began to feel removed from the madness behind them.

"Clay we have to stop," Jessica cried, holding her side like she was in pain.

"I see something up ahead. I think we're almost to the end

of this. There!" The hallway ended in a heavy metal door, partially cracked, and Clay beckoned John to help him open it. It squealed and protested, then gave way at last, opening into a simple room of dark stone. One wall of it had been knocked down, and the room gaped open, the cool night air pouring in.

John looked at Charlie. "We're out! We're okay!" He laughed.

"Don't you see where we are?" she whispered. Slowly, she walked the length of the room, gesturing to the four enormous pits in the floor, one of which contained a headless, half-buried robot. "John, this is my dad's house. It's the room we found."

"Come on, Jessica." Clay was helping Jessica through the gap in the collapsed wall. He paused and looked back to John.

"It's okay," John said. "We'll be right there." Clay nodded. He helped Jessica through and moved out of sight.

"What is this?" Charlie put her hand on her stomach, a sudden unease settling over her.

"What's wrong?" John asked. Something flickered all around them, a disorienting flash, too fast to even tell where it had come from. A thunderous crash echoed from the hall they'd just broken out of. "Charlie, I think we should go with Clay."

"Yeah, I'm coming." Charlie followed John to the gap in the wall as he climbed through it.

"Okay, come on," John shouted, holding out his hand to her from what had once been her own backyard. She started forward, then stopped as the lights flickered again. *What is that?*

It was the walls. The whitewashed concrete was blinking in and out of existence, shivering like a dying bulb. It was the wall Charlie had been drawn to the first time they came to this place. Now she felt its pull as she had in the cave. It was stronger here than it had ever been, even in the dreams that left her drained and aching. *I'm here.* She took a step toward the far wall and felt another pang in her stomach. *Here. Yes, here.*

"Charlie!" John cried again. "Come on!"

"I have to," she said softly. She went to the wall and put her hands on it, as she'd done before. But this time the concrete was warm, and somehow smooth despite the rough finish. *I have to get inside.* For a moment, she felt like she was in two places at once: here, inside the little room, and on the other side of the wall, desperate to get through. She drew back suddenly, taking her hands off the wall as if it burned. The illusion flickered, then died altogether.

The concrete wall was made of metal, and at the center was a door.

Charlie stared, blank with shock. *This is the door.* She'd been drawing it without knowing what it was. Approximating over and over something she had never seen. She stepped forward again and put her hands on the surface. It was still warm. She pressed her cheek against it. "Are you in there?" she called softly. "I have to get you out."

Her heart was pounding, blood rushing in her ears so loudly she could scarcely hear anything else. "Charlie! Charlie!" John and Jessica were both calling her from outside, but their voices seemed as distant as memory. She stood, not taking her hands from the metal but tracing her fingers along it. It felt like letting go for even an instant would cause her pain. She brought her hands to the crack in the wall: it had no handle, no knob, and no hinges. It was just an outline, and now she ran her thumb up and down the side of it, trying to find a trip, some trick that would make the door open and let her through.

She heard John climb back inside and slowly approach her, keeping his distance, as though he might scare her away.

"Charlie, if you don't get out of here, you'll die. Whatever's behind that door, it can't give you back your family. You still have *us*." Charlie looked at John. His eyes were wide and frightened. She took a small step toward him.

"We've lost enough. Please, don't make me lose you, too," John pleaded. Charlie stared at the ceiling as it trembled; clouds of smoke were pouring out of the corridor they'd come from. John coughed heavily; he was choking. She looked at him. He was terrified, unwilling to draw closer than he already was.

She turned again, and the world around her faded; she couldn't hear John behind her, or smell the smoke filling the air. She laid her hand flat against the wall. *A heartbeat. I feel a heartbeat.* Though she made no intentional movement, her body turned to the side. She tensed, committing to remain where she stood, without ever making the decision. Something began to hiss: the steady, gentle sound of air being released. From the base of the door came a rhythmic clicking. Charlie closed her eyes.

"Charlie!" John grabbed her and turned her forcefully toward him, shaking her out of her stupor. "Look at me. I'm not leaving you here."

"I have to stay."

"No, you have to come with us!" he cried. "You have to come with *me*."

"No, I . . ." Charlie felt her voice trail off; she was losing strength.

"I love you," John said. Charlie's eyes stopped drifting: she fixed them on him. "I'm taking you with me, right now." He grabbed her hand roughly. He was strong enough to pull her away by force, she knew, but he was waiting for her to acknowledge him.

She looked into his eyes, trying to let them bring her back. It felt like trying to awaken from a dream. John's gaze was an anchor, and she held it, letting him keep her steady, draw her back to him. "Okay," she said quietly.

"Okay," John repeated, heaving the words out in a sigh. He'd been holding his breath. He walked backward, guiding her as he went.

She climbed to the top of the broken wall and paused, bracing herself against the insistent pull of the door and what lay behind it. She took a deep breath—then was torn backward by a colossal force. She ripped back through the rocks, her arms pinned to her sides. Charlie screamed, struggling to get away. Dimly she heard John shouting close by.

As she whipped her body back and forth against its grip, Charlie glimpsed the immense thing that had caught her. The twisted Freddy stared blankly forward, or at least what remained of it. It held her with one arm; the other was gone, and wires hung from its shoulder like extra bits of sinew. Its plastic casing had melted away, and what remained were metal plates and stays, a skeleton with unnatural bulges and gaps in its frame where the collapse had mangled it. Its face was a gaping hole, spilling teeth and wire that hung in shapeless masses. Charlie couldn't see it legs, and after a second she realized they were gone. It had dragged itself, one-armed, through the rubble. Wires spilled out of its body like guts, and when she saw its stomach, Charlie went cold with terror.

Its chest had parted at the middle. Sharp, uneven teeth lined both sides. Charlie kicked at the animatronic, but it did no good: it forced her instantly into the chasm. The thing embraced her, pushing her deeper inside its chest as they toppled backward together. The metal rib cage snapped shut: she was caught.

"Charlie!" John was kneeling beside her, and she reached out through the metal stays. He grabbed her hand. "Clay!" he shouted, "Jessica!" Jessica was there in seconds; Charlie could see Clay struggling back through the narrow opening.

"Wait!" Charlie cried as Jessica tried to pry the chest open. "The spring locks, they'll kill me if you touch the wrong thing!"

"But if we don't get you out, you'll die anyway!" Jessica shouted. Charlie saw for the first time that the mouth wasn't finished closing. It was layered somehow, and metal plates began folding over her like petals of a horrid flower. John started to stand, but Charlie tightened her hand around his.

"Don't let go of me!" she cried, panicked. He dropped back to his knees and pulled her hand to his chest. She stared at him, even as the metal plates closed over her, threatening to seal her off. Jessica tried to jam them delicately, without setting off the spring locks. "John—" Charlie gasped.

"Don't," he said roughly. "I've got you!"

The plates continued to slide down and meet in the center. Charlie's arm was trapped in the corner of the strange mouth, protruding from the only gap where the plates didn't meet. She looked around wildly: another layer was closing. She was wedged into the suit haphazardly, her whole body crammed into Freddy's torso, and she could see nothing but dimming figures as more layers of metal and plastic closed over her. Above her, Jessica was trying to stop the next layer from emerging, and she felt Freddy's mutilated body lurch.

"Jessica! Look out!" she screamed at the top of her lungs. Jessica leaped back just in time to avoid Freddy's violently swinging arm. The animatronic was on its back, but it struck out randomly, beating Jessica and Clay away. Its body rocked back and forth, and Charlie eyed the springs and robotic parts all around her: she drew her knees up to her chest, trying to make herself smaller.

John let go of her hand, and she grabbed at his absence. She could no longer see outside. "John!"

Freddy's body shook, struck by a massive blow.


"Let go of her!" John screamed. Clay hefted a metal beam from the ground and struck at Freddy's head. The twisted bear tried to strike with its remaining arm. Clay ducked out of the way and hit it again from the other side, out of reach. Jessica was still at the creature's chest, trying to find an opening to pry at, but each layer melded seamlessly together. There was nothing to catch at. John moved in next to her, trying to help. Clay struck at the head over and over, making Freddy's whole body jolt with every blow.

"I can't get to her!" Jessica yelled. "She's going to suffocate!" She tried to steady Charlie's trembling hand. Clay hit

Freddy's head once more with a resounding crash, and they heard metal cracking as the head was knocked off the creature's body.

"Can we get her out through the neck?" John asked urgently. Freddy's arm continued to flail, but it had weakened, and was just rising and falling, seeming to swing without purpose.

"Clay, help!" Jessica cried. He ran to take over, digging his fingers between the plates to pry them open. Jessica continued holding Charlie's hand, which had gone limp. "Charlie!" Jessica cried. Charlie's hand closed over hers again, and Jessica gasped with relief. "John, Clay, she's okay! Hurry! Charlie, can you hear me? It's Jessica." There was no sound from inside Freddy's sealed chest, but Charlie held on tightly to Jessica's hand as the others grimly worked to free her.

Suddenly a single high-pitched click reverberated through the air. John and Clay froze, their hands still hovering above Freddy's chest. For a moment, the air stood still, then the metal body convulsed violently. It launched itself off the ground, and a ghastly crunch of metal pierced the air. All three pulled back instinctively. Clay and John jumped away from the thing, and Jessica scrambled backward, dropping Charlie's hand.

The suit fell again and was still. The arm was splayed on the ground at an awkward angle. The room was silent. "Charlie?" John said softly, then his face went white. He ran to the place where her arm was exposed, falling hard on his knees, and grabbed her hand in both his own. It was limp. John turned it over and tapped her palm with his fingers. "Charlie? Charlie!"

"John," Jessica said very quietly. "The blood." He looked up at her, confused, still holding on to Charlie. Then something wet dripped onto his hand. There was blood running out of the suit and down Charlie's arm. Her skin was slick and red, except the hand he held. He watched, unable to look away, as it dripped steadily from the suit, pooling on the ground and beginning to seep into his jeans. It covered his hand and hers, until his skin was slippery and he began to lose his grip. She was sliding away from him.

Sirens were suddenly nearby, and John realized vaguely that he'd been hearing them in the distance. He looked dazedly up at Clay.

"I radioed them," he said. "We aren't safe in here." Clay took his eyes off the suit and looked up to study the ceiling. It was bowed and cracking, on the verge of collapse. John didn't move. People were shouting outside, and flashlights bobbed up and down as they ran toward the crumbling building. Jessica touched his shoulder. Breaks and cracks resounded through the space.

"John, we have to." As if to mark her point, the floor shook again beneath them and something crashed loudly not far away. Charlie's hand didn't move.

A uniformed officer pressed through the crack in the wall. "Chief Burke?"

"Thomson. We have to get the kids out, now." Thomson nodded and motioned to Jessica.

"Come on, miss."

"John, come on," Jessica managed to say, and a thunderous clatter sounded from behind them. Clay looked to the officer again.

"Get them out of here." Thomson took hold of Jessica's arm and she tried to shove him away.

"Don't touch me!" she shouted, but the officer firmly pulled her up and over the rubble, half dragging her outside. John only half heard the commotion, then someone's hands were on his shoulders as well. He batted them away, not looking around.

"We're leaving," Clay said in a low voice.

"Not without Charlie," John responded. Clay took a deep breath.

John saw him signal someone from the corner of his eye, then he was grabbed forcefully by two large men and dragged toward the opening.

"No!" he shouted. "Let me go!" They shoved him roughly over the broken wall, then Clay struggled out behind them.

"Is everyone out?" a female officer called.

"Yes," Clay said hesitantly, but with the ring of authority.

"NO!" John shouted. He broke free of the officers holding him back and ran for the opening again. He had one foot through the gap, then stopped dead as a sweeping flashlight briefly illuminated the room in front of him.

A dark-haired woman knelt in the pool of blood, holding Charlie's limp hand. She looked up sharply and met his eyes with a piercing black gaze. Before John could move or speak, hands grabbed his shoulders again and drew him back, and then the whole house collapsed before them.

# CHAPTER FOURTEEN

e don't know for sure," Jessica said, firmly setting down the fork she'd been playing with on the diner table. It made a disappointing click.

"Don't do this," John warned. He didn't look up from the menu, though he hadn't read a word since he picked it up.

"It's just, all that we saw was, you know, blood. People can survive a lot of things. Dave—Springtrap, whatever he wants to call himself—he survived one of those suits, *twice*. For all we know she might be trapped in the rubble. We should go back. We could—"

"Jessica, *stop*." John closed the menu and put it down on the table. "Please. I can't listen to this. We both saw it happen. We both know she couldn't have . . ." Jessica opened her mouth again, about to interrupt. "I said, *stop*. Don't you think that I *want* to believe that she's okay? I cared about her, too. I cared about her a lot. There is nothing I want more than for her to somehow have escaped. For her to drive up in that ancient car and get out all furious and say, 'Hey, why'd you leave me behind?' But we saw the blood: there was too much. I held her hand, and it didn't feel like anything. As soon as I touched her, I just—Jessica, I *knew*. And you know it, too."

Jessica picked up her fork again and twirled it between her fingers, not meeting his eyes. "I feel like we're waiting for something to happen," she said quietly.

John picked up the menu again. "I know. But I think that's just how this feels." From behind him, he heard the waitress approach for the third time. "We don't know yet," he said without looking up. "Why am I even looking at this?" John set the menu back down and covered his face with his hands.

"Can I join you?" John looked up. An unfamiliar, brown-haired young man slid into the booth next to Jessica and across from John.

"Hey, Arty," Jessica said with a weak smile.

"Hey," he said, glancing from her to John and back again. John said nothing. "Everyone okay?" Arty asked finally. "I heard there was some kind of accident. Where's Charlie?"

Jessica looked down, tapping the fork on the table. John met the newcomer's eyes, then shook his head. Arty blanched, and John looked out the window. The parking lot outside blurred as he fixed his gaze on the smudged and streaky glass.

"The last thing she said to me was . . ." John lightly touched his fist to the table. "'Don't let go of me.'" He turned back to the window.

"John," Jessica whispered.

"And I did. I let go of her. And she died alone." There was silence for a few moments.

"I can't believe it," Arty said, his brow furrowed. "We had just started dating, you know?"

Jessica kept her face smooth, and John turned his thousand-yard stare on Arty. The boy faltered. "I mean, we were going to. I think. She really liked me, anyway." He looked to Jessica, who nodded.

"She liked you, Arty," she said. John turned back to the window.

"I'm sure she did," he said evenly.

Random thoughts swirled through his mind. The mess of her room. The pang of concern when he saw her childhood toy, Theodore the stuffed rabbit, torn apart. *Charlie, what was wrong?* There was so much more he wanted to ask her. Those blind faces with their smooth, nearly featureless faces and their couplet word games. Something—everything—about them had disturbed him, and now that he pictured them again, he was bothered for another reason. *They looked like William Afton's designs—the blank faces with no eyes. Charlie, what made you think of that?*

Jessica made an indistinct cry, and John startled back to the present to see her racing to the door, where Marla had appeared. He got up more slowly and followed her, with a sense of déjà vu. He was waiting his turn as Marla hugged Jessica close, stroking her hair and whispering something John couldn't hear.

Marla released Jessica and turned to him. "John," she said, taking both his hands. The sorrow in her eyes was what broke him. He leaned in and hugged her close, hiding his face in her hair until he could compose himself. When his breathing had steadied, she pushed him gently back and took his arm. They all went back to the table where Arty waited, peering uncertainly over the side of the booth. They sat down again. Marla slid in next to John and looked from him to Jessica. "You have to tell me what happened," she said quietly. Jessica nodded, letting her hair fall over her face for a minute in a shiny brown curtain.

"Yeah, I want to know, too," Arty piped up, and Marla glanced at him as if only just registering his presence.

"Hi," she said, sounding slightly puzzled. "I'm Marla."

"Arty. Charlie and I were—" He glanced at John. "We were good friends."

Marla nodded. "Well, I wish we were meeting under different circumstances. Jessica? John? Please, tell me."

They glanced at each other. John looked to the window again. He was content to let Jessica do the talking but felt an obligation—not to talk to Marla, but to talk *about* Charlie. "Charlie was chasing something from her past," John said, his voice calm. "She found it, and it didn't let her leave."

"There was a building collapse," Jessica added. "Her father's house."

"Charlie didn't make it out," John said roughly. He cleared his throat and reached for the glass of water in front of him.

John vaguely heard Marla and Jessica exchanging words of comfort, but his mind was elsewhere. *The woman, kneeling in the pool of Charlie's blood, holding her hand.* He had only glimpsed her for a moment; she had looked almost as surprised to see him as he was to see her. But there was something familiar about her.

He turned away from the others again and closed his eyes, trying to picture it. *Dark hair, dark eyes. She looked severe and unafraid, even with the ground shaking and the building tumbling down over her head. I know her.* The woman he remembered looked different, younger, but her face was the same . . . Suddenly he had it. *The last day I saw you, Charlie, back when we were kids. She came to pick you up from school, and the next day you weren't there, and the next day, and the day after that. Then even us kids began to hear the rumors, that your father had done what he did. And that's when I realized I would never see you again.* John shivered.

"John, what's wrong?" Marla said sharply, then blushed. "I mean, what are you thinking?"

"Her aunt was there," he said slowly. "Her aunt Jen."

"What?" Marla said. "Where?"

"They hadn't spoken in months," Jessica said doubtfully.

"I know," John said. "But she was there. When I ran back, just before they pulled me away, I *saw* her. With Charlie."

The thought struck him like a blow across the chest, and he looked out the window again so that he wouldn't have to meet anyone's eyes. "Charlie's aunt Jen was there," he repeated to the dirty pane of glass.

"Maybe Clay called her," Jessica offered. John didn't respond. No one spoke for a long moment.

"I think it's best not to look for more mysteries," Marla said slowly. "Charlie was—"

"Are you all ready to order?" The waitress asked brightly. John turned to look at her with impatience in his eyes, but Marla cut him off.

"Four coffees," she said firmly. "Four eggs and toast, scrambled."

"Thanks, Marla," John whispered. "I'm not sure if I can eat, though."

She glanced at the rest of them. Arty looked briefly as if he wanted to say something, then he cast his eyes down at the table. The woman departed, and Marla looked around. "We all have to eat. And you can't sit around in a diner all day without ordering anything."

"I'm glad you're here, Marla," John said. She nodded.

"We all love Charlie," she said, looking at each of them in turn. "There's never a right thing to say, is there? Nothing ever makes it okay, because it's not."

"All those crazy experiments," Jessica said suddenly. "I didn't understand, but she was so excited about them, and now she'll never get to finish."

"It's not fair," Marla said softly.

"So what do we do?" Jessica said with a plaintive note in her voice. She looked at Marla like she must have the answer.

"Jessica, sweetie," Marla said. "All anyone can do is hold on to the Charlie that we all loved."

"It's over," John said hoarsely, turning away from the window abruptly. "That . . . that psychopath murdered her, just like he did Michael and all those other kids. She was the most fascinating, the most amazing person I have ever known, and she died for *nothing*."

"She did *not* die for nothing!" Marla snapped, leaning in

toward him. Rage flashed in her eyes. "No one dies for nothing, John. Everyone's life has a meaning. Everyone has a death, and I hate it that this was hers. Do you hear me? I *hate* it! But we can't change it. All we can do is remember Charlie, and honor Charlie's life, from the beginning to the very end."

John held her stormy gaze for a long moment, then broke away and looked down at his folded hands on the table. She mirrored the movement and placed one hand over his.

Jessica gasped, and he turned back to the table wearily. "What, Jessica?" John asked. Her nervous energy was beginning to exhaust him. She didn't answer, but gave him an incredulous look, and turned back to the window. Marla leaned past John, craning her neck to see. Reluctantly he looked, too, letting his eyes focus for the first time on the parking lot outside the window, and not the pane of glass itself.

It was a car. The woman driving killed the engine and got out. She was slim and tall, with long, straight brown hair that glistened in the sun. She was wearing a bright red, knee-length dress with black combat boots, and she strode purposefully toward the diner. They all watched motionless, as if the slightest sound might rupture the illusion and send her away. The woman was almost at the door. Arty said it first:

"Charlie?"

Marla shook her head. She leaped up and turned, calling from the seat, "Charlie!"

She ran for the door, and Jessica was quick on her heels, crying out after her. They rushed to the doorway to meet her just as she walked in.

John stayed where he was, craning his neck to see the door. Arty seemed confused, his mouth open slightly and his brow furrowed. John watched for a steady moment, then turned away decisively, facing across the table with a grave expression. He didn't speak until Arty met his gaze.

"That's not Charlie."

## About Scott Cawthon

Scott Cawthon is the author of the best-selling video game series Five Nights at Freddy's, and while he is a game designer by trade, he is first and foremost a storyteller at heart. He is a graduate of The Art Institute of Houston and lives in Texas with his wife and four sons.

## About Kira Breed-Wrisley

Kira Breed-Wrisley has been writing stories since she could first pick up a pen and has no intention of stopping. She is the author of seven plays for Central New York teen theater company The Media Unit, and has developed several books with Kevin Anderson & Associates. She is a graduate of Cornell University, and lives in Brooklyn, NY.

# A DEADLY SECRET IS LURKING AT THE HEART OF FREDDY FAZBEAR'S PIZZA . . .

#1 *New York Times* Bestseller

**FIVE NIGHTS at Freddy's**
**THE SILVER EYES**
SCOTT CAWTHON
KIRA BREED-WRISLEY

The sequel to the #1 *New York Times* bestseller

**Five Nights at Freddy's**
**THE TWISTED ONES**
SCOTT CAWTHON
KIRA BREED-WRISLEY

**Five Nights at Freddy's**
The Freddy Files

Unravel the twisted mysteries behind the bestselling horror video games and the *New York Times* bestselling